CLIQUE BAIT

CLIQUE BAIT

ANN VALETT

wattpad

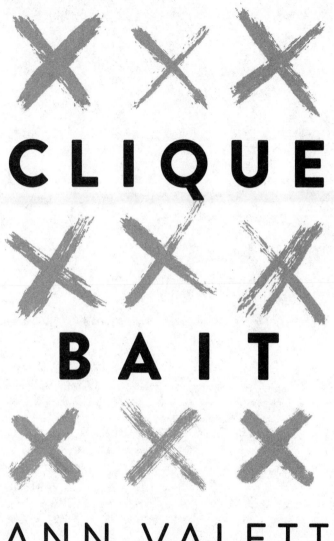

HarperTeen is an imprint of HarperCollins Publishers.

Clique Bait

www.epicreads.com

wattpad

Library of Congress Control Number: 2019948022
ISBN 978-0-06-291808-6

Typography by Corina Lupp
20 21 22 23 24 PC/LSCH 10 9 8 7 6 5 4 3 2 1

First HarperTeen edition
Originally published by Wattpad as *High School Hit List* in 2016

To my grandma, for nurturing my love for stories

THE LIST

1. *Lola Davenport*
2. *Sophie Rutherford*
3. *Francis Rutherford*
4. *Madeline Danton*
5. *Zachary Plympton*
6. *William Bishop*

STAGE ONE
OBSERVATION

ONE

Dear Monica,

Summer wasn't the same without you. Instead of us bingeing on gelato at Scoops'n'Treets or you finally making a move on that cute lifeguard, I was inside my house wishing you were here. I'm still so angry you aren't. But I know that anger shouldn't be aimed at you. I know that now.

That's why I've devised a plan. One that might make things right.

Hope you're happier than I am.

Love, Chloe

THE FIRST TIME I wore this shade of lipstick, I was eleven. Monica had pulled at my chin to pop open my mouth, painting my lips with the brightest cherry red, her amber eyes following her movements carefully—an artist examining her work.

"Done," she'd announced, flipping her auburn hair over a shoulder and tilting her head to the side, her blue-shadowed gaze taking in my appearance with satisfaction.

I'd swiveled in my chair to see my reflection in her mirror, contorting my face. "I look like a clown."

Monica paused, looking serious before snorting with laughter. "A beautiful clown."

Since then, my freckled face had lost the baby fat and my lips didn't look so corny lined with red. Now they were almost menacing, especially when I pulled them into the confident smirk I'd been perfecting over the summer. Exactly the look I was going for. I gave one final glance at my reflection in the rearview mirror before putting my Audi into reverse and pulling out of the driveway.

Today was the first day of senior year, the first school morning that I wouldn't see my best friend in the parking lot. It was usually routine that we met before class, ever since we'd started at Arlington Preparatory, the glamorous private school reserved for the children of Wandemore Valley's elite, from company heirs to celebrity love children. Nestled in the canyon just north of Beverly Hills, the suburb was a haven for the most influential families of Los Angeles.

This semester I had a lot of work to do. Not academically. No, grades had always come easy for me. This work came in the form of a list. A list of people who were going to pay.

Arlington had a system. It wasn't exactly a monarchy or a pyramid. No, it was much more complex than that. Monica and I had figured out that everyone could be sorted into one of five different groups, or levels as we called them.

Level Five was freshmen and social pariahs. It wasn't somewhere anyone wanted to be. It was open hunting grounds, and those who resided at Level Five suffered everything from disgusted looks to being shoved around in the hallways.

Level Four was for anyone "uncool." The harmless who didn't quite fit in. In sophomore year, Monica and I had upgraded from five to four, where we sat at a table of outcasts in the lunch hall.

And then there was three. My safe zone. The level where you were too high to be targeted by bullies and low enough to be safe from a fall. Level Three was invisible. I was invisible, safe with only a handful of friends and far away from the drama. The only problem was that Monica wanted to be higher.

Level Two, the loudest level, was for the people who wanted to be Level One. They were the people who worshipped the ground people like Lola Davenport walked on, and they were willing to do whatever it took to impress the people on top. Halfway through junior year, Monica decided she wanted to upgrade.

Level One was as high as it got. The popular clique. If the whole school was a television series, the people on Level One were the main characters. The stars. They were the beautiful, the rich, and the mean.

The thing that made the Level Ones so powerful extended much deeper than their fortunes. They were charming, with dazzling smiles that made your heart stop. They looked like their clothes came right off the runways in Paris, holidayed in tropical paradises, and always seemed to be having more fun than everyone else.

It was practically impossible to break into their group, perhaps because each member of their clique served a purpose. Sophie was law enforcement, with a sneer that would bring anyone to their knees. Francis, her brother, had a much more deceptive evil—all charisma and clever remarks. William was his best friend, good looks and talent. As the captain of the lacrosse team, he gave them the power of the jocks. I hypothesized that he was the rational one, the one who noticed things Francis overlooked. That's what Monica said, anyway.

Maddy was the daughter of a pop star, granting Level One the privileges that came with fame: limousines, and red carpets. Zach monitored all the gossip in Arlington, keeping Level One ahead of the game. And Lola oversaw them all. The six of them were, until now, unbreakable.

But I was determined to break them.

I wasn't like Monica. Monica always wanted to *be* them. She wanted the spotlight, and she wanted the adoration that came with being on top. But to them, Monica was like a newborn foal trying to stand. She was cute, but she could be easily knocked over. And when they knew of someone's vulnerabilities, the games began.

No, I didn't want to *be* them. I wanted to destroy them. To expose them for what they were, to make them feel as humiliated as their victims, to make them pay for what they did to Monica. I wanted to show everyone what they did, no matter how hard they tried to cover it up.

Observe, blackmail, initiate, infiltrate, intelligence, collect, and expose. I had it all planned out. An undercover exposé, one Monica would be proud of. One that would make things right.

"Chloe Whittaker. That is *not* you."

I couldn't prevent myself from jumping as a figure slid into my peripheral vision. I'd chosen a table upon the mezzanine overlooking the cafeteria, hoping it'd be the best place to observe the Level One clique eating lunch without being noticed. But clearly I hadn't hidden myself well enough.

"Jack," I said through gritted teeth, my shoulders relaxing slightly and the corners of my lips raising in a small smile at the familiar face.

Jack Thomas's dark eyes zigzagged as he assessed my appearance. "Makeup? Since when?"

I let my mouth curl further into a smile. "Do you like it?"

He snorted. "It's quite an improvement."

"Thanks," I responded with a tight smile as he greeted me with a hug.

Jack was sweet and unbearably awkward. He'd somehow managed to remain acquainted with me throughout high school, despite how little effort I'd put into hanging out with anyone but Monica.

"So, what are you doing up here? Spying on *Level One*?"

"Don't say that," I grumbled. The Level designations belonged to Monica and me. "I'm just enjoying the quiet."

"Right . . ." he said, his voice trailing off a little. "It must be really hard coming back without her here."

I didn't respond, avoiding his gaze and letting my attention drift back toward the cafeteria.

It was enormous, with a high ceiling and large tables spread neatly around the hall. Today it was filled with conversation of adventurous summers and laughter as groups of friends reunited. As if by some unspoken law, Level Ones sat at the table in the center.

The table was occupied by Arlington's six elite, each member's name printed onto my list. *Almost* fully occupied. The seventh seat, which had housed their past experiments, was empty today. At one point in time, it had belonged to Monica.

My eyes found William Bishop, a tall boy with a sharp jaw and dark brown hair. At the moment, William was the most important member of the group.

Because William was my in.

Over the last few months, I'd been carefully mapping out what made each member of Level One tick. Sophie wore secrets like armor, teasing the outside world with a plethora of possible scandals, plenty of potential dirt to be dug up beneath her designer heels. Maddy was the opposite. She was an open book, almost to the point of being an exhibitionist, and I hoped her recklessness would become a powerful tool.

Something I could use to catch clues. Lola and Francis ruled the kingdom, but I knew there was more to their relationship than met the eye. And with those two at the peak of Arlington's hierarchy, there was far to fall when it came to unraveling their games. Zach was ego-driven, and that trait alone meant he'd be easy to knock down. Large egos meant easy self-destruction. And William?

I narrowed my eyes, taking him in. Of all Level One, his reputation appeared the most pristine. That was, until I investigated his family.

My father had showered me with countless gifts throughout my lifetime, but none was as important as the one I'd stolen from his emails two weeks ago. His news corporation had plenty of unpublished stories, thanks to his company accepting some hefty bribes. Dad's business was dirty, sure, but not quite as scandalous as what I'd found. Charles Bishop, the long-term mayor of Los Angeles, sabotaged his opposition's campaign by paying off his rival's assistant, quite possibly the sole reason he wound up in power to begin with. William's dad was a fraud. My leverage.

"Hey, Jack?" I asked, tearing my gaze from Bishop. "Is there anything on this weekend?"

The most valuable thing about Jack was that he was Level Two through and through. His life revolved around Level One and their social calendar.

"The twins are having a party on Friday since everyone's finally back in town," he said.

"Oh, really?" I raised a brow nonchalantly.

"Are you going to come?" Jack asked, surprised.

"Maybe."

"You totally should. It's senior year. You have to start being a part of these things, you know?"

There was no way I could miss an opportunity. I needed to confront William Bishop on his own, and everyone knew it wasn't difficult to get a Level One boy alone at parties.

William was last on my list. In fact, I'd debated for a while whether to add him at all. Even though he was just another spoiled rich boy who ruled the school, he was probably the only one of them who was kind to Monica.

But even then, his kindness wasn't enough to stop what they did. I'd never tried blackmail before, but there was a first time for everything.

"You're right," I said to Jack. "I'll definitely make an appearance."

STAGE TWO
BLACKMAIL

TWO

Dear Monica,

You'd think Arlington would be a little darker without its brightest star.

Okay, that was lame. I know. But point is, it isn't. Nothing's really changed since you left.

It's like the start of sophomore year, when you dyed the bottom of your hair neon pink, expecting everyone to be in awe. I've always envied your fearless style. But nobody seemed to care. It's like nobody here notices you unless you're in with Lola Davenport.

Anyway, there's nothing wrong with being invisible sometimes. It makes it easier to spy.

Love, Chloe

I FOLDED UP the patterned paper, my fingernails gliding against its edges. I promised her I'd write every day I could.

All these letters would drive her crazy, but she should have been here anyway.

My eyes felt like they weighed a ton beneath the charcoal that coated them. It had cost me more than I was willing to admit to stock up my makeup collection, and now, wearing more makeup than I had in my entire life, I started to question whether it was worth it. But if I wanted to take down the Level Ones, I was going to have to blend in with them first.

After a week of eating my lunch with Jack and playing Level Two with his table of friends, it was finally Friday, the night of the Rutherfords' start-of-semester party. Finally time to go past simply observing the Level Ones and make my first move.

It had taken hours just to shower and primp. My mother, ecstatic that I had the so-called *privilege* of attending a high school party, had stuck her head into my room at every opportunity, offering me tips and motherly reminders like *Don't take drinks from strangers!*

I loved her deeply, really, but my mother could be too enthusiastic for her own good. And I meant enthusiastic about *everything*. I guess it would take an optimist to stay with my dad.

"Are you sure you don't want to try the golden dress we picked out at the start of summer?" she asked, her chestnut locks bouncing against her shoulders as she darted into my room again.

"Yes, Mom," I replied in a clipped tone. I knew the more

reasons I offered for why I didn't want to wear the dress, the more reasons she'd provide for wearing it. It was gorgeous, I'd give her that, with full sleeves and a skirt that fluttered around my knees, but it'd be social blasphemy to wear something last season. The Level Ones would pick it up in an instant.

Instead I was wearing an off-the-shoulder shirt with a patterned skirt and strappy heels, something that felt so unfamiliar it made me uneasy. My wardrobe before this summer was filled with denim jackets and simple silhouettes. I was never attracted to feminine florals or frills like the Level Ones. Though I was only showing a portion of my torso, combined with the amount of my legs visible, I felt exposed.

"Really, this is a pretty casual party. Just trust me," I reasoned. Mom's weak spot was the words *just trust me*. My dad used them on her all the time.

"Well, make sure you're not out too late. And text me. Really, I don't mind waking up in the middle of the night to pick you up."

I gave her a weak smile. She wouldn't have to worry. I doubted I'd be gone long. "Yes, Mom."

I'd said yes when Jack offered to Uber with me to the party. The car pulled up outside my house at exactly half past nine, and he let out a low whistle when I slid inside.

"You look great, Chloe."

"Thanks," I said, shooting a welcoming smile at Jack as I climbed in next to Claire Waters. I'd known Claire since freshman year, and we occasionally helped each other with homework and exchanged small talk. We hadn't spoken much since Monica's rise to Level One. After that it had felt like my connection to our small friend group was fractured. Without my best friend, I'd been lost.

"Seriously, where did you get your top?"

My answer was forgotten when the stereo was turned up too loud for my voice to carry. No longer forced to make conversation, I tried to order my mind. I needed to get William alone.

Arlington's elite attended parties regularly. The pictures flooded my Instagram feed every weekend, varying from small gatherings to huge events, catering for hundreds of drunk teenagers from Arlington and other private schools in the area.

The Rutherford house was enormous, to no surprise. It was only fitting that they lived in a mansion. After being dropped off, passing through the ten-foot-high gate guarding the perimeter, and making our way up a large, winding driveway, I saw the party was already well underway. People milled on the balcony above us and the front door was spread open to reveal a busy foyer.

Furniture had been pushed back to leave room for dancing, and I was sure the most fragile of the Rutherfords' valuables had been moved to another floor. The kitchen had turned into a full-fledged bar, different spirits lining the table and large containers spilling with ice holding what looked like bottles of champagne.

"Come on, Chlo, let's get you a drink," Jack said, grabbing my shoulders excitedly.

"A drink sounds great," I said, injecting my voice with equal enthusiasm.

"A shot," he persisted as he led me to the large bottle of vodka.

The others had already been absorbed into the crowd. There must have been hundreds of people on the ground floor, and I recognized only a few of them. My task was becoming daunting.

Jack pressed the shot glass into my fingers and before I knew it he was counting down from three and the burning liquid was making its way down my throat.

"One for the road?" he asked as he turned away again to grab two paper cups.

"I'll just have a soda," I said quickly, my tongue desperate for something to remove the alcoholic tang from my lips. I shouldn't be drinking anyway, not if I was here for Monica.

"Are you serious?" he asked, laughing in amusement. "Come on, it's your first party, right? You have to let loose a little."

I shrugged and filled my cup, sipping it tentatively as I surveyed my surroundings. I'd have to break away from Jack soon if I wanted to find my targets. If he was with me, he could easily get suspicious. Not to mention, a Level One would never be seen with a scholarship kid like Jack.

"You know, I always saw you as the quiet one," Jack mused. "Something tells me things have changed."

I didn't know whether to feel insulted. "What makes you think that?"

"I don't know. The way you're dressing, and the fact that you're even here to begin with. It's like you're finally done blending into the background." He leaned back against the wall and observed me.

Over the course of the summer I'd gone from the awkward girl with bony legs and mousy hair to someone who dived into her allowance for designer clothes and makeup. It wasn't that I didn't care about my appearance before, I just never really tried. I could tell it was working in my favor too. I hadn't missed the lingering glances and double takes when I stood by my locker. My physics teacher since junior year had even questioned who I was when I went to sit down in class.

But even so, I knew that alone wouldn't be enough to crawl onto the radar of Level One.

Which is why I was going to use someone else.

"Maybe I never belonged in the background," I murmured, playing the role I'd cast for myself: the ruthless girl ready for her turn in the spotlight.

"Maybe you didn't," Jack agreed. His dark eyes lingered on mine.

I gave him a confident smile. "I'm going to find a bathroom. I'll catch up with you later?"

I sensed Jack's surprise, but his expression didn't falter. "Sure thing."

Before I could find an excuse to chicken out, I dived into the crowd, finding enough space to maneuver to the staircase. It was dotted with people sitting, some on others' laps and some looking as if they were already close to passing out. I ascended, knowing that the crowd I was looking for wouldn't be lingering with the commoners down here.

I found twenty or thirty people on the large balcony overlooking the well-tended backyard. I recognized them instantly: Sophie clad in a sparkly dress and draped on a banana lounge and Lola and Francis making out on a nearby love seat. William and Zach were standing against the railing, consumed by laughter.

Others who seemed vaguely familiar from lacrosse games and interschool events had also made the cut. Everyone was beautiful and poised compared to the drunken teenagers downstairs. Confidence seemed to seep through the open sliding door.

How do I get in there? How can I break into their circle after seeing the damage they can do?

I took a step back, stumbling on my heels. I knew that behind the veil they cast they were ordinary, nothing truly worthy of being admired or worshipped. But I also knew they were dangerous, and one wrong step would leave me vulnerable.

If I wanted to get near enough to find my evidence, I couldn't waste time floating on the sidelines. I needed to confront William Bishop and I needed to do it now.

I let my gaze linger on William, taking in his carefree posture as he spoke with his friend, an easy smile playing on his lips. Zach slapped him on the back, motioning to his cup and indicating he needed a refill, leaving William alone. My in. I let one final wave of fear pass over me before straightening. I needed to play the part.

I pushed my shoulders back and plastered a smirk upon my lips. *One foot in front of the other*, I told myself. *Act like you're supposed to be here.*

"William Bishop?" I asked once I was in earshot.

Everyone knew that people like William belonged in fashion campaigns, not in high school. An assortment of optimized genetics and a knack for every sport the school had to offer gave him a frame to be pined over and a smile that stopped hearts.

He turned around, looking bored as his eyes traced me up and down. "And who are you?"

"My name's Chloe Whittaker," I said, trying to make sure to breathe normally. "And you're about to know me very well."

William straightened, intrigued. "And why is that, Chloe Whittaker?"

My lips curled as I tried to sound confident. "Would you like to find out?"

"I would."

"Well, maybe it's a private matter." I let my eyes dart to the crowd of people surrounding us. "Here's a little too . . . public."

William raised his eyebrows. "You think you can seduce me that easily, huh?"

His jaw pulsed, and I realized he was observing me with curiosity rather than lust, which hadn't been my initial goal. I'd expected to capture his romantic interest and lead him away from the throng of the party, but maybe that wasn't as easy as I'd imagined. I'd have to lure him away in a more forward manner.

I narrowed my eyes, placing a hand to my hip. "Who says I want to seduce you?"

His lips found a half smile. "And now you're playing games with me. Drop it, pretty. You won't like it when I win."

"Funny. Because, I don't know that it's *possible* for you to win."

He moved his head to the side curiously and took a step closer. "And why is that?"

I took a step forward so I could lean up and meet his ear. To everyone else, we undoubtedly looked like we were flirting.

"I came across some fascinating business undertaken by our trusted mayor. Planting weaknesses in his opposition's campaign. Bribery upon bribery. Pity if it landed with law enforcement."

"Huh," he said after a moment. If he was surprised, he didn't show it. "I doubt you even know what you're talking about."

I pulled out my phone. I'd anticipated this. Locked behind a passcode in my camera roll was a screenshot of one of the highly confidential emails. Charles Bishop and the assistant of his opposition ensuring Charles would have an easy win when he ran for mayor last election. And those were just a few of his crimes.

William's gaze didn't falter. "A girl who comes with blackmail. Just my type."

I didn't say anything as he sighed, his hands diving into his pockets. His voice lowered. "Come on, privacy it is."

I followed Bishop off the balcony and into the sitting room. He didn't even hesitate to check that I was still following him when he split off down a hallway and into a guest bedroom.

"How did you get it?"

I cocked a brow, deciding that pacing around the expensively decorated room would be the best way to maintain my cool.

"Hey, I'm the one calling the shots here."

"What are you, a cop or something?" he scoffed. "Chances are your parents' business is as dirty as mine, Whittaker."

"I never said it wasn't dirty." I smiled.

He muttered something under his breath, revealing how pissed he was growing. "How much?"

"Pardon?"

"How much for you to forget about whatever you know."

"It's not money I'm after."

"Then what is it?"

I had to say, pissed off was a good look for William. In any other circumstance my legs would be jelly and my hormones going haywire. Instead, all I felt was the rage I'd been feeling since last year,

"I want a favor," I said. "A big one."

We circled each other, William's arms folded defensively over his chest.

"I need you to get me into the in-crowd. Arlington's elite."

He gave a dry laugh. "You want *popularity*? How shallow."

I tilted my head. Maybe it'd be best if he believed that my intentions were shallow. It'd be too late for him when he realized they were anything but.

"That's none of your concern," I said smoothly. "But if you want your father's sneaky politics out of the news, you'll find a way to get me in."

William practically crackled with anger as he swiveled to face me, taking my wrist. I scowled, keeping my confident demeanor as I pulled my arm from his grip.

"Do you have any idea what you're messing with?" he asked, the volume of his voice inching toward a flat-out yell. "How did you even get it?"

"I have my way—"

"Any more of this mysterious bullshit and I promise I won't do *anything* for you," he said in a cool, menacing voice.

"My father is CEO of a major news corporation," I said, meeting his gaze with venom and omitting as many details as possible. "He stumbled upon some information, and while your family bribed him to keep it safe, you can't bribe me. Not with money."

"You're using multimillion-dollar scandals to fuel your petty high school delusions?" The way William's stare pierced me made my blood run cold. "There's more."

"And that's *my* business, not yours," I reminded him. "It's your corrupt politics you should be worrying about."

"My *father's* corrupt politics," he said. "Would you rather talk to him about this?"

I froze. The last thing I wanted was the mayor himself getting involved. Also, as much as he was a lousy father, I couldn't have my dad getting in trouble for his security slip. "It wouldn't be difficult, you know. What I'm asking. I'm sure *you'd* prefer leaving Daddy Bishop out of this."

At least, I hoped so. I might not be able to fight his dad's corrupt leadership, but I could overthrow his son's high school reign.

He paused, his emerald eyes simmering in calculation. "So . . . you don't want money. You want popularity."

My chest rose. Was this progress? I'd never predicted it to be easy, but this was draining me. "Yes."

Silence stretched for what felt like an eternity as William continued to assess me. He tilted his head to the side before finally speaking. "I'll do it. But if you so much as slip up with that information . . ."

He didn't need to continue his threat for its severity to

register. The Bishop name alone had enough power to tear down anyone his family desired. My shield of blackmail was all I had to protect myself, and I had to hope it'd be enough.

William turned and left the room, and I struggled to match his stride. He was leading us toward the stairs.

"I need time to think this over," he said. "If you're serious, then I need to be serious too."

"I don't need you to think it over," I said with frustration. "I want in. Now. Tonight. I'm the one in charge, remember?"

William shook his head before running a hand through his hair. "You don't understand. It's a complicated system."

Trust me, I know.

"You're going to make sure we do this properly?" I clarified. I needed him to be clear on this. I was depending on him.

"Yeah." He shrugged, already moving toward the staircase.

"What am I supposed to do, then?" I gritted my teeth. I couldn't keep waiting for this. I couldn't depend on him keeping quiet when he had every chance to run.

"Wait. Stay out of their view." He pointed toward the balcony. "We're going to need to be careful."

"How long will this take?" I asked.

William sighed and retrieved his phone. "Give me the weekend. I'll make sure we talk before school. Put your number in."

"I want yours," I said defiantly. We exchanged phones. It felt strange, holding William Bishop's cell. I thought of all the secrets it could hold.

"Stay out of trouble. You're already causing enough."

Oh, just you wait.

William left to return to the others before I could come up with anything else to add. I wasn't happy that he needed time, and I was especially unhappy that I'd have to waste the rest of the party avoiding the other Level Ones.

If I wasn't here to do my job, then I had no desire to be here at all. Not when I kept expecting to spot Monica in the crowd—I kept thinking I saw a swish of her red hair among the designer outfits or heard her gleeful laughter as a champagne bottle was popped. Every time I blinked and cleared my vision I realized that she'd never want to come to one of these parties again.

As I grazed my hand along the polished railing of the stairs, I looked curiously over the throng of people, wondering if they even missed her. With my eyes focused below, I failed to notice the figure in front of me until I had almost tripped over her.

"Shit!" her voice slurred drunkenly before she let out a giggle. "You scared me!"

Maddy Danton was a beautiful mess, her curls bouncing around her face. Something had caused her eyeliner to smudge and her lipstick had found its way onto the silk of her white dress. Even though Level Ones were known for their partying, it was unusual to find one looking anything less than perfectly pulled together.

"Sorry!" I said after only a brief hesitation, my voice dripping with the same drunk-girl friendliness. "God, I hope I didn't hurt you!"

Her eyes darted over me as she did a once-over. "Just watch it next time, bitch! Love your top by the way."

And with a breathless laugh she trotted away from me like we'd never interacted to begin with. Girls in the Level One clique spoke in only insults and compliments, both often laced with sinister intentions. For now, I'd consider her noticing me as a move in the right direction.

I used my vantage point to spot Jack. It wasn't difficult. He stood out with his lanky frame. When he saw me worming my way toward him, he shot out an arm and hung it around my shoulder. Leaning in close, he yelled in my ear over the heavy music. "Chlo! You disappeared!"

"I bumped into some friends!" I yelled back. "But I really have to head home now."

He frowned, as if disappointed, and maneuvered us toward a quieter corner of the dance floor. "Where were you?"

"I just caught up with some friends," I said nonchalantly. If William cooperated, Jack would know what I meant by that on Monday. For now, vague answers were all I could give.

"From Arlington?" he pushed. "I saw you just came from upstairs."

I shrugged and yawned, feigning fatigue as I pulled out my

phone to punch out a quick text to Mom. "Yeah, I just used the bathroom up there."

Jack seemed to accept my explanation and launched into a play-by-play of how a guy from Richmond Prep had used one of the Rutherford's rare antique vases to chug his beer. I apparently hadn't missed much by going off on my little mission. Nothing that would have helped me, anyway.

Mom picked me up on the street, casting me excited glances from the driver's seat the entire ride home. I figured she'd be excited by the prospect of taking me home, giving her some involvement in my night. The heavy pop music was still echoing in my ears as we finally pulled onto our street, my mind faraway, analyzing the events of the party.

I climbed to the second floor before shedding my heels, rubbing the soles of my feet in the hopes the pain wouldn't carry through to the morning.

I'd really done it. I'd confronted William Bishop. And God, it'd been harder than I thought. I could only hope he'd come up with something that worked for both of us. I hated relying on other people.

I breathed a sigh of relief when I slipped into my silky pajamas, but my night wasn't over yet.

I pulled my laptop from my desk and climbed into bed before flipping it open and typing in the multiple passwords I'd secured it with. While I waited for it to unlock, my eyes wandered toward the list's hiding place. One step at a time.

I smiled at the desktop background of me and Monica on

the Ferris wheel at Santa Monica Pier last summer, but I didn't let the memories distract me for now. I logged on to social media and began noting tonight's interactions on the digital flowchart I'd created. It was important to track the Level Ones online. It was almost as significant as their real-life activity.

For example, after noting Sophie's sudden lack of flirtatious likes and comments, I suspected she was sneaking around with someone. Sophie didn't usually keep her own romantic encounters hidden within her treasure trove of secrets, so her hiding it was a big deal. If I could work it out, I would have the first weapon to bring her down.

I sighed, scrolling through their feeds. It was like they were obsessed with making people covet their lives. Once, Monica had even told me that they'd hired their own photographer to follow them around at parties, but all the research I'd done into it had led to dead ends. It was just another rumor.

"Soon I'll make things right, Mon," I whispered. "I haven't forgotten what they did."

THREE

Mon,

Do you remember your first Level One party? I do. I helped you try on a gazillion outfits just for you to choose the first, the bright blue jumpsuit. You always loved bright colors, while I was all for textures. You invited me along, but of course I refused. I loved you, but I didn't love high school parties. At least not back then.

Now I wish I'd gone anyway. Just so it didn't come to this.

Love, Chloe

IT WAS ONE of the first weeks of freshman year, our shirts freshly ironed and our summer tans fading, when Francis Rutherford set his eyes on Lola Davenport.

The Rutherford siblings—a pair in which both twins were the evil one—with their ice-blond hair, chilling stares, and insane trust funds, were destined to be popular.

But even they couldn't compete with Lola Davenport, her daddy heir to an American cosmetics brand and her mom, a Vietnamese industrial conglomerate. The Davenport name alone was worth more than Level One's wealth combined. And most important, they were one of the most crucial investors to the Rutherfords' international real estate company.

Whether it was that or Lola's beauty that caught Francis's attention, I don't know. I just remember him taking her hand in his and asking her to be his girlfriend in front of the whole freshman class. It was cheesy, awkward, and it drew the whole school's interest. Francis was charming. A heartthrob.

She said no.

After that, flowers started showing up everywhere, scattered around the campus, sitting on Arlington's statues, poked into the vents of lockers, all labeled with her name.

And then, on the last day of the week, Francis arrived with the biggest bouquet I'd ever seen.

She said yes after that.

Their friends converged and others joined, the power couple the founders of a new clique. That was the beginning of Level One.

I was thinking of this—of how a group so popular and powerful grew out of such a cheesy gesture—as I killed time. Saturday was passing at a sluggish pace that left my skin crawling. I hated waiting for William to text. I wasn't used to depending on people, especially people I didn't trust.

What could he be doing? Maybe finding a way out of my leverage.

With nothing to do but wait, I spent the afternoon finishing homework and scrolling through photos from the night before. It didn't feel productive, though. My mind was busy running around in paranoid circles. If William knew how much keeping me in the dark was making me squirm, he'd leave me hanging forever.

I'd just rechecked all of William's social media accounts for the hundredth time when my mom came knocking on the door to announce we were going for dinner. She was already dolled up, cooing in excitement and completely oblivious to my lack of enthusiasm.

"Your father sounded really excited on the phone. He's made reservations at La Lanterne. Did you know that's where he took me for our first anniversary?"

"That's great, Mom," I said, trying to inject some happiness into my tone for her sake. My mother was great at deluding herself, pretending everything was fine when our family was completely dysfunctional. But even so, I wasn't about to burst her bubble. Besides, if Dad really had gone to this effort, then maybe tonight would almost be nice.

"That computer will ruin your vision, you know."

I rolled my eyes, glad I was facing away from her so I didn't have to paint on a smile.

The golden dress Mom had tried to convince me to wear to the party was still hanging on the back of my door, and I pulled it on just for her. Part of me was stupidly clinging to the flimsy possibility of tonight turning into a pleasant family dinner. Her enthusiasm was contagious, even if I knew deep down it was misplaced.

I hadn't seen Dad all week. He usually slept until I went to school and then spent his evenings at the office. Some nights, I was convinced he didn't return home at all.

I watched Mom from the corner of my eye as she drove us in the Mercedes Dad had bought her only months before. She had aged gracefully, partly thanks to a few surgeries and miracle creams. People said I was a mirror image of her in her youth, with warm brown eyes and chestnut hair. I thought she was beautiful, the corners of her mouth worn with smile lines from her wide grin. But her confidence had taken a nosedive when Dad had decided he preferred women under thirty.

"He did say he'd be a bit late," Mom said when we entered the extravagantly decorated restaurant. It screamed expensive meals, ones that probably consisted of a few ornamental leaves arranged decoratively on a plate. Dad often thought spending money on us was the same as spending time.

Of course he'll be late, I thought silently. *He probably has to say goodbye to the secretary he's been holed up with all week.*

We sat at the table for three he'd booked by the window. Mom went into overdrive pretty quickly, filling the silence with yet another interrogation about the party.

"Were there any cute boys?" she asked with wide eyes, flattening her manicured fingers over the leather-bound menu.

"Hardly," I said. I scrunched up my nose. "High school boys."

"Oh, the horror," Mom said sarcastically.

Really, it wasn't high school boys that were the problem. It was just the ones at Arlington who had turned me off dating. This meant that I was one of the few senior girls who'd never had a first kiss, let alone a boyfriend.

"I was just like you at your age," she went on. "Very cynical, always giving my parents attitude."

"I don't give you *attitude*," I said pointedly.

Her amused smile let me know she wasn't offended. Though Mom and I bickered, we were in some ways all we had.

Half an hour had passed, and the empty seat remained unoccupied.

"It's probably traffic," Mom insisted.

After another half hour I was beginning to grow tired of Mom's excuses. I sighed, giving her the most sympathetic look I could muster. "We should just order dinner."

I expected her to scold me for interrupting her rambling about repaving the driveway, but instead her smile wavered. "Yes . . . maybe we should."

We were halfway through our tiny servings of French food when Mom's phone chimed. I raised an eyebrow, waiting to hear whatever excuse Richard Whittaker had come up with this time.

"He can't get away from work. He's . . . He has to leave for an urgent trip to Seattle."

Of course.

I wanted to question his excuse, but I knew Mom knew the answer as well as I did: he just didn't care.

To him, affairs came before family. As long as he showered us with materialistic affection, all was right in the Whittaker household. I mean, his job running an international online news outlet was demanding, of course, but it still hurt that he chose it—and the lifestyle being a rich CEO came with—over his family.

"Come on, Mom," I said after a few moments of silence. Her face had fallen, and she'd resorted to moving her champagne flute around in circles. "Let's get some ice cream, go home, and watch TV."

She nodded, and I took her hand in mine as we left the restaurant, the bill paid on Dad's credit card.

I was peeling the top off a tub of coconut yogurt when my phone chimed Sunday evening.

Give me your address, I'll pick you up in an hour to talk.

I wasn't the least bit surprised when he pulled up in a BMW, but the contrast it gave to my scruffy attire was off-putting. Even though I had plenty of time to change, I decided to stay in my favorite ripped jeans, loved for their comfort rather than how they looked. They hardly screamed beautiful and popular, but then again William already knew I was an impostor.

Casting a look over my shoulder at my neighbors' houses, hoping none of them would say anything to my mother, who was busy out at a girls' night, I discreetly slid into the passenger seat. I briefly admired the luxurious interior before taking in the beautiful face of William Bishop.

"Evening, Whittaker," he said stiffly as he drove off from the curb.

"Where are we going?" I asked, dumping the pleasantries.

"Nowhere anyone will see us," he replied, his eyes a hauntingly dark shade as they flicked to his rearview mirror.

Something had changed. When I'd confronted him, he'd been angry. Tonight, he was calmer. Almost *smug*.

We drove for a few miles before he pulled into an unfamiliar, empty parking lot, killing the engine. The lights of Wandemore Valley were long gone, and all I could see out the window was darkness.

"Is this where you dump your dead bodies?" I asked as I followed him out of the car into the darkness.

He chuckled. "Not quite. If I was going to murder someone, I'd take them farther than here."

"Reassuring," I muttered. I wrapped my hands around my elbows to fight off the chill that was scattering goose bumps across my skin.

William strode toward the trees that bordered the parking lot, and I quickened my pace to keep up with him. After a few rows of tall oaks, I saw the glittering of lights below us. We were at a lookout, high enough for Wandemore Valley to look like a sea of stars.

"Nice," I said, an understatement. I pried my attention from the skyline, reminding myself I didn't come along so he could show me a pretty view. "So, have you come up with a plan?"

"I've done a lot of research this weekend," he said, leaning against a tree trunk. His coat looked much more weather-appropriate than my thin shirt.

"Like?" I pressed.

"Like working out why a girl like you would blackmail me for high school popularity. It seems a little simple of a bargain for someone carrying this much leverage." His voice was deep and slow, as if he was enjoying watching me squirm.

"Are you saying I should ask for more?"

"I'm saying that there's more to it than you're letting on."

"There always is, isn't there?" I tried to sound unconcerned, but my mind was racing almost as fast as my heart. *Does he know?*

"That's right."

I pressed my lips together, trying to keep my face blank.

His eyes twinkled in the light of the half-moon above us, and I swear I saw the smallest smirk etched into the side of his lips. "It all made sense when I found out you were best friends with Monica Pennington."

Obviously, it'd come out that I'd once known the infamous Monica Pennington, but it was never supposed to be traced back to my motives. That was what William Bishop was supposed to protect me from. He was supposed to give me an in—an excuse. By the time they dug beneath the surface, they'd know me as the girl they met through William. Not Monica's best friend. The connection wouldn't be so obvious.

But I hadn't expected William to make the connection so fast. Not before he was in too deep, at least.

"I have to say, it surprised me," William continued. "But it makes sense. You want revenge for her."

"You don't need to bother yourself with what I want."

He took a step closer. His eyes were menacing, locking with mine in a way that made my knees tremble.

"Let me get this straight. You want to destroy us," he said, "because of Monica."

I lifted my chin. He may have worked out more than he should have been able to, but that didn't mean I could give up. "You don't know what you're talking about, Bishop."

He shrugged, his eyes following me darkly. "I can put the pieces together."

I tightened my jaw. "Think what you please. If you don't want the world to know that your family's power is built on bribery, then you'll keep your mouth shut."

William raised a brow cockily. "You think I'd just let this go?"

"You have no choice."

His eyes narrowed, a smile suddenly breaking onto his lips,

causing a heavy pound through my chest. He was adoringly handsome, and I could tell he thought it might give him some kind of leverage. But not with me.

"Who said I wasn't going to cooperate?"

"What?"

I quickly shut my gaping mouth and reprimanded myself internally. I couldn't be caught off guard. If he knew my aim was to bring down him and his friends for what they did, then why would he play along?

"Maybe I'd still be willing to help you," he said.

"Why?" Until now, I'd expected William to be predictable. He was turning out to be anything but.

His eyes twinkled as he shoved his hands in his pockets. "Because maybe Monica deserves it."

My eyes widened. "If you . . . if you knew, then why did you let it happen?" My voice broke, my throat thick with emotion.

He was silent for a moment. "Like I said, our world's more complicated than you think."

My expression hardened. I didn't know whether to be pissed off that he knew the truth about what his friends did to Monica or relieved that he seemed willing to help.

"Which is why you need me if you want to get in." He began to pace, the glimmering city a backdrop to his silhouette.

"How?" I asked, hating how long he was taking to get to the point.

"I'll need time," he explained. "If we rush, it will seem

temporary. They'll need to know you're a permanent fixture if you want any power."

My mind fumbled over his words. *Permanent fixture.* My plan was to have this over with as soon as possible.

"I know you're impatient," he said, reading my thoughts. "But you'll just have to trust me."

We were at a stalemate.

My attention returned to him, sizing him up as I channeled strength into my tone. "Then tell me your plan and stop being vague, William."

He sighed. "Nobody calls me William. It's Will. And it's vague because it won't be fixed until we know how they'll react."

I didn't want to exactly jump to nickname basis with William Bishop. We weren't here to be pals. I nodded. Initiation into their group wouldn't be straightforward.

"So, where do we start?"

He moved closer to me, as if invisible figures in the dark might overhear our plan. "Tomorrow afternoon. At Jermaine's."

"A coffee shop?" I narrowed my eyes.

"Yep. It's a popular place. I know Lola, Sophie, and Maddy usually go there after school." He exhaled quickly, and I could feel his cool breath on my cheeks. "If we show up, it will catch their attention."

"Why?"

"Because we're going to go on a date," he said.

My breath hitched in my throat. "I am *not* dating you!"

He chuckled. "Of course not. That's the beauty of our deal. It's not real, but they'll think it is."

"Why do we need to *date*? Why can't we just, I don't know, be friends? Introduce me as your long-lost cousin or something?"

He shook his head. "It won't work."

"Why not?"

"If you want them to really notice you, then you need to make them jealous."

It was clever, really. It wasn't a secret that William Bishop rarely dated. I didn't even remember the last time he'd had a girlfriend, and so a new one would spark all kinds of gossip. And jealousy.

He'd clearly put a lot of thought into this. That, or he was setting me up and risking his family's reputation.

"I do have one request, though," William said when I didn't reply. "If I help you, I need to be exempt from your plans. You can't take me down."

I raised a brow. "Scared?"

He gave me a stern look. "I'm serious."

"Fine," I said. But I didn't mean it for a second. He was on my list, after all.

A silence fell between us, and I found myself thinking of Monica again. "How did you find out?"

"About you and Monica?" he asked. I nodded in response. "The yearbook from when we were freshmen."

"Wow, you *did* do your research." I sighed bitterly. Since the beginning of the year, I'd erased what I could of my friendship with Monica from the public eye, deleting my social media accounts and making sure what pictures were left were private, something I knew she'd be pissed about. I needed to make sure it wasn't easily accessible. But of course, it was impossible to get everything.

"Let's just hope none of the others do the same," he said carefully. "You can't look suspicious. I hope you're a damn good actor."

I shrugged. "I guess we're going to find out."

"This isn't a joke. I'm putting a lot on the line here."

"What, your cozy little spot with the popular kids?" I asked. The look he sent me in return gave me the chills. "You're rich and good-looking. You were born into that spot. They won't take it from you."

I tried to hide the flush that washed over me from my words. *Did I seriously just tell him he was good-looking?* Like he even needed the ego boost.

"Here's a question, then," he said. "If all it takes is to be pretty and rich, why aren't you already up there? Your family is ridiculously wealthy."

"Because I didn't want to be up there."

"You choose to be invisible," he clarified. "You know how much damage they can do. I don't want to be on their bad side because you screw me over."

I pressed my lips together tightly. "I'll do my best."

William gave me a guarded look. "I'll take you home."

The drive home was silent, giving me time to mull over the plan. As much as I hated to admit it, it seemed ideal. An easy way in, and an easy way out. I could only hope it'd give me the access I needed to truly expose them.

As I unclipped my seat belt and opened the door of William's idling car, I gave him one last glance.

"So we have a deal?"

He gave a small nod. "This starts tomorrow."

STAGE THREE
INITIATION

FOUR

Dear Monica,

How stupid that we once thought that having it all meant a Level One boyfriend and a car. Life seemed so simple back then. Anyway, fast-forward a few years and I have both.

Ha, got you. I'm just kidding. Half kidding. I have a car. You know that already, though. The Level One boyfriend is just a ruse. I'm telling you first before it's all over Instagram. William Bishop isn't my boyfriend. If he was, you'd be the first to know.

After all, we had a pact, right? No secrets.

Or at least, that's what I thought.

Love, Chloe

IF YOU'D TOLD me last year that I'd be spending my Monday-morning free period balancing on the toilet seat in an out-of-order stall, I would have snorted in laughter.

But a lot had changed since last year.

After class this morning, I'd heard Sophie Rutherford behind me in the hallway by her locker. Her voice seemed to be on its own unique frequency, making it easy to overhear. Of course, I was all ears. She'd asked Lola to meet her in the girls' toilets after the next period. She needed to tell her something.

Lola Davenport was the sun to Arlington's solar system, Sophie orbiting as a close second-in-command. With raven hair and sweet wide eyes that drew adoration with their gaze, Lola had the school wrapped around her little finger. She was easily likable.

But her best friend, Sophie, with ice-cold Rutherford genes and a default resting bitch face, was one indicator that Lola wasn't as nice as she seemed.

I decided to duck out of class early by faking a headache so I could stake out the girls' bathroom in the main building. I made a scrappy *out of order* sign on the back of one of the many anti-drinking posters that plastered the corridor so I wouldn't be busted spying, before locking myself in the stall. Now all I had to do was wait.

And God, they were taking forever.

My knees were beginning to hurt. Let me tell you, balancing on a toilet was *not* something you want to do in heeled boots. If they didn't hurry, I'd have to give up. And if they turned up to talk about lipsticks for twenty minutes, I was going to kill someone.

I was contemplating whether my legs would go numb

after a while, or whether I'd be better off amputating them altogether, when the door swung open.

"Jesus, I am sick of having biology this early on a *Monday*." Lola sighed dramatically. I heard the thud of her leather bag being plonked on the sink.

"Hey, at least it's Mr. Hammond," Sophie's voice responded. I heard the pop of a lip-gloss bottle opening. "There are worse ways to start your week."

The door opened again, and the intruder's footsteps clicked across the tile toward the stalls, making me panic for a second before they entered the stall beside me. Lola and Sophie fell into silence, no doubt waiting to continue their session when the intruder was gone.

When she left after an excruciating three and a half minutes, I heard a musical laugh.

"Oh, that is *so* gross! Who took that?" Lola's voice asked.

"Someone on the lacrosse team. They sent it to Zach, who sent it to me," Sophie boasted. "She needs to control her alcohol."

"Right? Such an embarrassment. And to think her daddy was just nominated for another Grammy."

At this, I realized exactly who they were talking about. There was only one girl at our school with a pop star father. *Maddy Danton*. When I'd seen her at the party on Friday night, she had been stumbling everywhere. A complete mess.

"Should we mail it to him anonymously?" Sophie asked lazily. I could almost picture her leaning carelessly against the basin, amused by what must have been a scandalous snap. "Post it on Instagram for the media?"

"I don't know. Who'd want to see their daughter like *that*?" Lola snickered.

"True," Sophie said.

"No, just keep it up your sleeve. She's our friend, remember? Tell the boys not to spread it anymore."

"Maybe she should stop spreading it for your boyfriend." Sophie snorted.

I had to hold a hand over my mouth to stop from gasping. Now *that* was juicy. Maddy Danton getting it on—or at least trying to—with Francis Rutherford. Maybe Arlington's favorite couple wasn't as golden as they led us to believe. And maybe the girls' friendship wasn't as tight as it appeared to the public.

Lola was quiet, and I found myself holding my breath in anticipation of her reaction.

"You'd think your brother would have higher standards," Lola finally said in a small voice. Even before everything with Monica, I'd never confused Francis for a nice guy. While his twin sister was subtler in her cruelty, using gossip as her weapon, Francis could regularly be found hazing freshmen and making sleazy comments about the girls at school. Still, I was surprised that he would not only dare to cheat on his girlfriend of three years, but that Lola knew about it. I heard her sigh and a zipper close. "But still. Bitch needs to pay."

"And this photo isn't enough?" Sophie asked. "God, she definitely has it coming."

“She certainly does.” I heard the clatter of products being spilled onto the counter. It was strange that Lola didn’t direct her anger toward her boyfriend. But the girl he was cheating with? I was sure Maddy would be as good as a Level Five when Lola was done with her. Maybe worse.

“Did you catch up with your side guy?”

“He wasn’t there.”

“What, he didn’t go to the party?”

“He doesn’t go to parties,” Sophie said defensively. “Not his scene.”

“I never thought you were into that type,” Lola noted. “Whatever, it’s so weird that you aren’t telling me who he is. Is he, like, older or something?”

“No! I’m just having fun with him. If we go public, I’ll have to have him hang around all the time,” Sophie said, but her voice quieted at the end.

There was a stretch of silence before Sophie spoke again.

“Come on, I said I’d give Zach my Spanish answers,” Sophie said.

Lola sighed. “Okay. I’ll see you at Jermaine’s.”

“Bye, bitch!”

There was a muffled sound that I assumed was them collecting their belongings, and then I heard two pair of heels click their way out of the room.

After the door closed I waited a few moments longer before stepping off the toilet seat and unlocking the stall. I cursed as I regained full feeling in my legs, shaking my ankles out. I made sure to rip the Out of Order sign from the door, relieved that I hadn't been busted.

The cramped toilet stall I'd spent my morning in was upgraded to a deserted aisle of the library for lunch. Obeying William's instructions, I'd avoided the cafeteria altogether, waiting for our meeting after school to reveal whatever we were supposed to be. My classes stretched out almost unbearably long, my body riddled with a nervous excitement for what was to come.

William found me after the final bell. It was becoming routine that by three o'clock my feet had enough of being confined in designer heels, and pain shot through my every step, making me crabby.

"Don't look so miserable to see me, Whittaker," he said. "This is the part you've been waiting for."

He was right. If I wanted this to work, I had to paint on my game face.

"So what makes it so special?"

"Oh, you'll see," he said casually. "Do you want to drop your car at home first?"

I noticed a few students milling around turn their attention to us. They were no doubt watching William, either swooning or desperately trying to squeeze out some gossip. Probably both.

"Sure."

I didn't miss the eyes that followed us as we navigated the crowd, or the way our peers parted as we walked down the hallway side by side. I kept hearing snippets of conversation around us.

"Who's that? Besides Will with the—"

"—I wonder where they're going? Did she arrive with him this morning?"

"Where did she get those *boots*?"

"I heard she hooked up with him at the party. Do you think they're an—"

"What did you do at lunchtime?" I asked William once we cut through the bottleneck of students and strode across campus, still the focus of several curious glances.

"I disappeared," he replied.

"You didn't mention me?" I asked. Wasn't the whole point of this to get my name into the mouths of Level One?

"No," William said, frustration bordering the edge of his tone. "That would make them suspicious in the wrong way. Like I've said before, *permanent fixture*. I need to bring you in slow. It would be weird if I automatically started dating someone and pulled them in straightaway."

"Right."

"You still don't trust me?"

"This isn't about trust. It's about you keeping up your end of the deal," I reminded him.

"I forgot it's all about pulling puppet strings for you. Do you even have feelings?"

I clamped my lips against each other in a bid to stop myself from telling him to back off. We were just entering the parking lot, and I was thankful our cars were a fair distance away from one another. "I'll see you at my house."

As soon as I fell back into the leather of my car seat, I let out a huff. Partly because I was pissed at William for making this more difficult than it needed to be, and partly because I *really* needed to take my shoes off.

William must have been going way over the speed limit because he beat me to my house. I pulled into the family garage and stepped inside quickly to grab a smaller purse.

"Let's get this over with," I muttered to myself. As much as this would be a huge stride forward in my plan, it was also going to take a lot of energy.

"Okay, we need to sort out details," William said after I slid into his car. "So to them, we're dating. And I have the right to publicly dump you if you do *anything* to embarrass me or play any games. I'm safe, remember?"

"Fine," I said. By the time I got to William, I wouldn't need the protection of his status anyway. "But it has to be serious for you to resort to that."

"And if you really want to feed them this dating line, we need some PDA," he said next. His confidence was admirable. "What are your limits?"

I snorted. "If I didn't know any better I'd say you were *trying* to get with me, Bishop."

His knuckles whitened over the steering wheel. "You're really not my type."

"Whatever," I said. I knew I shouldn't be offended that I wasn't the type for the guy I was blackmailing, but it was hard not to feel stung. "Hand-holding is fine. I guess we could hug. But that's it. Nothing more."

"That should be fine for a few weeks. As long as we keep up the act and people don't ask questions. How long *is* this going to last?"

I thought about it. I needed the infiltration and collection phases to be relatively quick, but who knows how long it'd take to earn their trust. "A few months, tops."

His eyes flickered from the road to me. "You're saying I might have to pretend to date you for months?"

"Well, yeah." He was the one who suggested me being a permanent fixture, after all.

He sighed heavily as he hit the brake pedal for a red light.

"Is there a problem?"

"*Loose ends* more like."

"Oh, right." Suddenly it made sense. "I'll be stopping you from getting some."

William didn't say anything, his jawbone pulsing.

"Well, as long as people don't know you're cheating on me, it's fine." That was how relationships worked for Level One, wasn't it?

"I think you'll discover it's more difficult than that," he said.

"How so?"

He took a left, swinging into the parking lot beside a hidden building, decorated with overgrown potted plants in golden baskets. Across its front door was a wooden sign painted to spell Jermaine's.

William inhaled deeply before killing the ignition. "You're probably about to find out."

FIVE

Monica,

Remember when bathroom stalls were our headquarters? I feel like we spent a million hours in them. You let me sit on the counter and vent about my dad until we were both late for class.

Of course, you had your fair share of bad mornings too. It's still crazy to me how upset your mom got any time you had a graze or even a cough. You're right. She is the most protective parent in our grade. I've never seen the other parents act like that, or even really care what their kids are doing.

I miss venting to you. These letters feel silly.

Love, Chloe

WILLIAM HELD THE door for me as I stepped into the snug little coffee shop. The inside was as dainty as the outside, adorned with flowers and ribboned decorations. It reminded me of those alternative joints that hipsters flock to for "candid" Instagram shots. It was the opposite of where I'd have pinned Level One to hang out. For them, I expected sophistication and glamour.

I regretted not changing from my school uniform when I spotted the girls at the table in the corner. Lola and Sophie sat on a light pink leather couch that lined the wall. Opposite them was Maddy with a cup held in her fingers. Unlike me, all of them had made a wardrobe change between school and here.

Sophie's eyes were the first to flit up to mine. They were ever so slightly creased in the corners, as if she knew a brilliant secret that you'd never catch on to. Her gaze traveled between me and William, and then she lazily turned her head to Lola.

"What do you want to drink?" William asked.

"Um, coffee?" I glanced away from the group, not wanting to draw the wrong type of suspicion.

"No, I mean, *what do you want to drink*?" he asked.

I looked at him in confusion.

"This isn't just a coffee shop. Not for us," he clarified.

The appeal of the isolated coffee shop suddenly became apparent. "They serve alcohol?"

William nodded. "The owner's a family friend of the Rutherfords."

My eyes returned to the group, who was surveying us subtly over the rims of their cups. It made sense they were here for alcohol—only flaunting their status as above the rules—especially if it was via a connection to the evil twins.

I felt the gentle push of William's hand against my waist and immediately stiffened. I'd forgotten we were supposed to look like a new couple. "Come on, go sit down and I'll order us drinks."

There was an empty table for two by the window, and I moved to take a seat where I could see the Level One girls, and they could see me. Being scrutinized by them was an unavoidable by-product of my plan, but it was also intimidating. I leveled my chin and crossed my legs, hoping a flush wasn't developing on my cheeks.

If only I could hear their conversation . . .

William returned, pulling out the chair opposite me before glancing over his shoulder. As if on cue, Sophie raised herself from her seated position and clicked her way over the tiled floor. Her red painted fingers landed on William's shoulder.

"Hey, Will, fancy seeing you here," she said, her sky-blue eyes assessing his.

"Hi, Soph," he said.

"It's quite the coincidence," she continued. "We were just talking about you, actually."

"Really?" His gaze flickered to mine before returning to Sophie's. "What were you talking about?"

"The party, of course," she said. "You disappeared pretty early. Come to think of it, Zach *did* say you were busy with someone . . ."

Sophie's gaze fell on me as she said her last words. William let out a breathy laugh before turning his chin in my direction. "Sophie, this is Chloe. Chlo, Soph."

My surprise at his casual use of my nickname wore off quickly when Sophie's eyes locked on mine again, this time in a chilling stare. Her smile didn't falter, though, her demeanor remaining as pleasant as it had been with William. "I recognize her. AP Chem, right? Are you two . . . a thing?"

I looked to William, figuring that my blush was now probably good for our act. I was surprised Sophie paid attention to anyone below Level Two, but I was confident she wouldn't connect me to Monica. Monica hadn't exactly flaunted our friendship, especially after she'd made it onto Level One's radar.

"We are actually," William said, his expression not faltering. "We started seeing each other this summer."

Sophie's eyes narrowed slightly. "Weird. I didn't think you were seeing anyone, Will. Especially after Lola's end-of-summer pool party . . ."

William brushed off her comment with a nonchalant wave of his hand. "Oh, that was Chloe. You were pretty wasted, Soph. You probably don't remember."

Sophie narrowed her eyes. "Very funny, Will."

A waitress appeared with two mugs, interrupting us. With a wink, she set each down on the table. "Two double-shot cappuccinos."

"Thank you," William and I said in sync.

"Anyway, I'll let you two enjoy your *coffee*," Sophie said.

"You should come around and properly introduce Chloe to the rest of us, Will. We're all very . . . excited."

"Of course you are," he said blankly.

"We're just happy for you. It's great that you're moving on . . ."

Moving on? From who?

The muscle in William's jaw twitched as he plastered on a bright smile. It seemed to satisfy Sophie, and she grinned, pulling her full lips into a charismatic smile once more before retreating with a flick of her ash-blond hair. I didn't miss the stares from each member of their table as she returned to her seat.

"Moving on from who?" I searched my memory again. I didn't recall William dating anyone all junior year. Was this what he meant by loose ends?

His expression gave nothing away.

"I'll find out anyway," I reminded him.

"That might be true, but I don't care. I don't want to talk about it."

I brought my cup to my lips, the biting taste of gin and tonic from the mug surprising my taste buds.

"So, Chloe. What interests you? Apart from revenge, that is," William asked. His body language had done a 180, no doubt for our audience. I was thankful that he was as committed to our image as I was.

I shrugged. "Shoes, shopping . . ."

He scoffed, apparently not believing me. "You're not like them."

That was true. What had I even done all summer except for plan out my vendetta? "Well, I guess I'm not much like you guys. Maybe even the opposite. I like indie music, thrifting clothes . . . math and stuff, I guess."

"Interesting," he said, as if he genuinely cared. If he *was* interested, he could be looking for cracks. It's not like he'd actually want to hear about my long-term aspirations for a Nobel Prize or my short-term goal of finding the best places for undiscovered vintage pieces in LA. He might have said he was with me on my revenge against Level One, but that didn't mean he wasn't looking for a way out of my blackmail. "What kind of music?"

It seemed like a harmless question, but revealing any more of myself than I needed to made me feel uneasy. For similar reasons to keeping his full name, I wanted to keep our agreement formal. I'd keep my love of British indie rock to myself. "Lots of stuff. What about you? Any hobbies?"

William raised an eyebrow, and I realized how stupid the question was. William was one of those people who was involved in *everything*. "Well, there's obviously the lacrosse team. I swim, sometimes I do polo . . ."

"You even have horses?"

He nodded.

"Right."

I looked over his shoulder at the girls again. They were having what looked like an intense conversation, and it made me squirm in curiosity. Were they talking about William's last girlfriend? Who *was* she?

"What about your parents?" he asked. "Your dad's a CEO. What about your mom?"

"She used to model," I said. "She retired before I was born."

"Oh?"

I could see him putting pieces of me together. God, this was turning into first-date conversation for real. "So . . . are we able to function as a happy couple now?"

He shrugged. "I guess. You know, I never would have picked Monica to be best friends with someone like you."

I stiffened, and I hastily looked behind his shoulder to check that his words hadn't carried. "Why do you think that?"

William stirred his near-empty mug, his face smug. "She was so carefree and crazy. You're different. All business."

If he knew that my insides felt like they were constantly being twisted as I battled to stay composed every day, he wouldn't say that. I needed to be all business. How could I keep going as my old self after everything that happened last year?

"I guess I've changed without her here," I said, avoiding his gaze. Though my mouth softened, the rest of my muscles remained stiff, like any second I could buckle.

"So have a lot of things. I mean, even the girls have—"

"Stop," I said, cutting him off. I didn't want to hear excuses. I wanted my best friend back.

We sat silently. The only noise in the little shop was the upbeat music drowning out the conversation occurring across the café.

It was fascinating to see their body language, to see the dynamics in action. Maddy sat opposite Lola and Sophie, completely oblivious to their scheming. As much as I wanted to stare openly at them, I tried to remain inconspicuous. I was supposed to be Will's latest love interest, not a not-so-secret agent.

"They won't stop looking at us," I said to William. "They want your attention."

"They can wait," he said simply. "Like I said, this needs to take time. We should leave."

"Already?" I asked, looking from our table to theirs.

"We've planted the seed, now we have to let them water it," he explained. He then looked to his watch. "I also have practice in twenty-five minutes."

I rolled my eyes. "What is it? Lacrosse or swimming?"

"Neither, actually. Tennis."

"Are you serious?" I asked. Did he sleep?

He shrugged, scooping his keys from the table and standing up. I followed suit, grabbing my purse and smoothing my skirt over my tights.

He nodded goodbye to the girls, and my heart thudded heavily as they gave me a final once-over. Little smiles remained on their lips as their hungry eyes searched for flaws. The scrutiny made my insides squirm.

The car ride back to my house was silent. For one day, I had a whole lot of information to digest. I was finally activating my plan, and tomorrow would be my first official day as William Bishop's girlfriend.

"I'll see you tomorrow, Whittaker," he said as he pulled up outside the front of my house.

"You too, Bishop," I murmured, my thoughts far away. His comment about the contrast between Monica and me was still a heavy weight on my mind. I'd thought of us as sisters. Yes, we were different, but we balanced each other. Didn't we?

"Join us for lunch tomorrow," he said. "I'll save you a seat."

SIX

Mon,

Earlier today I was thinking about how we used to think we were sisters. Separated at birth, remember? I don't know if it is sad or funny that we thought our parents had an affair together. After all, in retrospect, considering how much they get around, it wasn't outside the realms of possibility.

Anyway, as we grew up, I guess we've sort of become opposites, haven't we? You like fashion and pop music and hanging out at the mall, while I prefer my few edgy thrift finds and buying vinyls at street sales. I'd rather eat my lunch while doodling in a notebook on the lawn, and you'd rather gossip about the most recent party or watch the jocks play sports. I didn't mind that so much, as long as we were still best friends.

We balanced one another.

Hope you're doing okay.

Love, Chloe

MY PEN DREW spirals down the margin of my binder as I waited for first period to start. The sooner lunch came the sooner I could make progress. I was detailing flourishes in the corner of the paper when a hand tapped my shoulder, pulling me from my focus.

"Chloe, good morning!" Jack said with unnecessary enthusiasm.

"Hi, Jack," I said warily. Nobody ever spoke to me in physics. I was renowned for keeping to myself, preferring the company of my own mind when it came to understanding Newton's law of universal gravitation.

His smile crept into a curious look. "I heard some interesting news this morning."

"Did you?" I asked, raising a brow. My eyes darted to the desk he sat at with his friends on the other side of the laboratory.

"I did. Why didn't you tell me you were dating *Will Bishop*?"

I was surprised. Though Arlington's rumor mill worked fast, I didn't realize it worked *that* fast. But then again, if anyone was the first to know gossip, it was Jack. "Who told you that?"

He rolled his eyes, like it was a stupid question. "Everyone. So, are you confirming it?"

Instead of replying I gave him a bashful smile, looking back down to my notebook and adding today's date in the corner of the page.

"No way." His eyes widened, and he rested his palms on the table. "When did it happen? Why didn't you tell me?"

I shrugged. "Summer. I didn't think it was a big deal."

"Are you serious? He's *William freaking Bishop*!"

"Please be quiet," I said under my breath. Though the attention was important, I was starting to feel uncomfortable.

"Why wouldn't you have mentioned it . . ." he pressed. "Monica would be—"

"Why are you so interested?" I snapped, regretting it instantly when I saw his face fall. "I'm sorry, it's just—it's still a relatively new thing, and it's weird to have it analyzed."

"You're right, I'm sorry," he said with a slow sigh. He straightened. "I just can't believe you'd date a Level One after what they did last year, after how upset you were after everything. . . . But good for you for having an open mind. Will's a good guy."

"The Level system is something stupid Monica and I came up with. It's not real," I said.

"Sorry, it's always been hard to keep up with you two," he said. His face turned somber as he gave me an apologetic smile. "Anyway, I'll see you around, Chloe."

He gave a slow wave and stepped back toward his desk just as our professor walked through the door. *I can't focus on what he thinks of me*, I thought. *He'll understand when I make things right.*

When lunch period came, I felt my palms grow sweaty at the thought of sitting with Level One.

I was hesitant when I crossed the threshold of the cafeteria, my hands clenched around my lunch tray. As usual, I had on a full face of makeup, but it didn't bring the sense of security I'd hoped for. I felt exposed.

I slowly navigated my way to their table. Around it were swarms of Level Twos, all with a nice view of whatever drama was going down at the Level One table at any given time.

Please let William be here already.

The hairs on my arms rose when I heard a scream from behind me.

I spun on the heels of my pumps to see the source of the commotion. The cafeteria was loud but not loud enough to drown out the sound of despair that had erupted from a nearby junior.

Her hair was a faded version of Monica's orangey-red color, and she stood almost six feet tall. Her face was contorted in terror at the sight in front of her, her soda splashed all over the skirt of Lola Davenport herself.

"I'm *so* s-sorry, Lola."

Sophie stepped forward from her position beside Lola, her scowl fixed on her delicate features. "Did you seriously just do that?"

"I'm sorry!" she repeated, her horror-struck gaze moving from the stain on Lola's dress-code-violating skirt to Sophie's electric eyes.

"How am I supposed to spend the rest of the day in a soaking skirt?" Lola hissed. The cafeteria had quieted, and her voice now carried easily to where I stood frozen between tables.

"Sorry isn't going to fix this, *honey*," Sophie said mockingly, taking another step toward the junior. She may have been tall, but the way her knees trembled made her seem small. "Give her your skirt."

"Wh-what?"

"Your skirt," Sophie said. Her lips pulled into a condescending smirk. "Give it to her."

"Oh, of course," the redhead stammered. "We could go and swap in the bathrooms—it's no big deal."

Sophie's amusement grew, her hand lifting to her hip. "I don't think she can wait."

Sophie and Lola exchanged a look before Sophie spoke again. "Give her your skirt. *Now*."

There was a dramatically long pause as the entire school held their breath.

"Um . . . here?" the girl asked.

"What do you think I mean? I'd hurry up if I were you. You don't want to be on our bad side for too long."

The girl's hands trembled as they moved to the waistband of her skirt. I wasn't surprised that she was cooperating. Level One's wishes were law around here, and Sophie was right. It could get much worse than a little public stripping.

She popped off the buttons and then stepped out of the plaid skirt, her face flaming red. Sophie held her hands out expectantly and she handed it over, standing there in only her underwear. The few teachers who were there to supervise lunch notably turned away from the commotion. Even they were at the mercy of Level One and their influential families.

"Nice granny panties," Sophie commented. "Next time don't wear polka dots, though. They stand out."

I heard a few giggles from my peers, and I didn't miss the sparkle of tears developing in the girl's eyes.

"Someone will drop off Lola's skirt to you later," Sophie continued. "Until then . . . I guess you just have to cover up."

A girl stepped out to join the redhead, grabbing her hand and whispering rapidly before taking off her blazer and handing it to her.

Sophie and Lola let out one last chuckle before moving through the parted crowd and toward the restrooms. I let out the breath I didn't realize I had been holding.

I *hated* them.

I was about to dart to my usual lunch spot on the mezzanine when a pair of boys caught my eye. William was flanked by Zachary Plympton, who might have been the only boy at Arlington taller than William, with dark skin and kiss-worthy lips that framed an irresistible smile. It was too bad for all the girls who swooned over him that Zach liked boys.

"That's her," I heard William say as they got closer.

"With the brown hair?" Zach asked.

When they were only a few steps from me, I forced my legs to move forward to meet them. My throat felt like it was caked with glue as I moved my lips. "Hey."

"Hey, Chlo," William said. I knew we were in full-blown acting mode from his easy use of *Chlo*. "This is Zach."

"Hi," I said timidly. My heart began to beat so hard I was frightened it would rip free from my chest. I waited in terror for them to recognize me, to immediately link me with Monica. It didn't come.

William's arm moved to hover awkwardly over my upper back, catching me off guard and instinctively causing me to recoil. Luckily, my avoidance of William's touch went unnoticed. They had already dived into mindless banter.

The guys moved toward the Level One table, where a seat was waiting for me. The seventh seat. Monica's seat.

I couldn't stop fidgeting with my fingers as I sat down beside William, my tray of salad on the table. *Compose yourself.* It wasn't so much nerves that gripped me, it was anger. The girl with the soda reminded me too much of the way they'd treated Monica.

The guys picked hungrily at their trays of food, while I tried to calm my stomach enough to swallow my own lunch. I'd halved my serving size to fit in with the Level One girl requirements (thin and fragile), but my nerves had put me off even that.

Francis soon emerged from the crowd, his angelic features disturbed by what I could only describe as a menacing smile. He greeted each boy with his customary high five. Soon after, Maddy, swatting thick extensions over her shoulder and regarding me with a curious stare, joined too. I watched as she began moving her salad around her plate. It looked even smaller than my own.

Lola and Sophie returned almost immediately after, Lola now wearing a skirt that was a little bulkier than before.

I counted my breaths to make sure they were evenly paced as they took the seats in front of me, Lola directly opposite my place.

"Oh, so you weren't kidding," Sophie said loudly when she noticed my presence. "I didn't realize how serious you two were. Bringing your girlfriend to lunch is a big deal, Will."

"Well, we *are* a big deal," he said after finishing his mouthful of food. I cringed at his broad grin and tried to mask my discomfort with one of my own.

"Don't hide her, then," Lola said from in front of me, her honey-laced eyes locking smugly with mine. "Introduce her properly."

William scanned his friends, who'd fallen silent at Lola's words. "This is Chloe. But I'm sure Soph's told you all about her already."

"She has," Maddy said, following his words. "You're our mystery girl."

"Mystery girl?" I questioned.

"The one who's popped up out of nowhere," she said, as if it were obvious. "It's not often Will dates. Especially someone so . . ."

"Off the radar," Lola finished with a definitive click of her fingernails against the tabletop.

"Right."

Lola leaned in closer, the cold red smile painted on her lips sparking goose bumps to erupt down my back. I let a smirk creep onto my mouth, my armor forming the shield I needed to keep her out. Her tone was low so only I could hear her.

"Trust me, you did really well. He's *great* in bed."

SEVEN

Monica,

We've been back less than two weeks and the Level Ones are already torturing juniors. I guess you came to love them like everyone else in the end, but I never quite understood. We used to see right through it, making the Level system to mock them. I don't know what happened. You weren't just entertained, you were entranced.

But beauty only runs skin deep. Beneath they are pure evil. I guess you know that now.

Anyway, I found that hairpin you left in my car, the one with the little golden flower at the end that you used to clip behind your ear. Hope you didn't want it back—it's mine now.

Love, Chloe

MY MIND REELED as I tried to make sense of what Lola had just said. William *slept* with her? What about Francis?

Or, perhaps it was a lie and Lola was just trying to defend her territory. Trying to scare me away from them.

I smiled, mimicking her warm expression, as if she'd just shared a heartwarming compliment.

"That's good to know" was all I said in return.

Lola cocked her head, her loose curls grazing her cashmere-covered shoulders. I had the sense that my response caught her a little off guard. "This girl's skirt sucks," she said, dismissing me and turning back to the rest of the group, pulling at the waistline of the pleated skirt. "She hasn't even had it tailored."

"What's her name?" Sophie asked, barely looking up as she scrolled through her phone.

"Stephanie Griffith," Maddy said. "She's a junior."

"Let me guess, you girls are going to make her life hell?" Francis asked. "You're so predictable."

Lola laughed. "What would you do, France? You're the creative one here."

I looked between them. Considering the easy way she smiled at him, it was hard to believe that Lola knew Francis had been cheating on her with one of her supposed best friends. Clearly she was willing to go to great lengths to keep up the appearance that their golden romance was perfect.

"You need to give her something to lose if you want something to take," he said nonchalantly.

"What does that even mean?" Sophie snorted.

"Doesn't she already have plenty to lose?" Maddy said from the end of the table.

"Let's see," Zach interjected. "She's clearly desperate to impress you. She's basically a nobody. I say there are ways to bring her down."

"As always, I love the way you think, Zach. What do you think, Chloe?" Lola asked, prompting everyone at the table to turn their attention toward me.

I gulped. I hadn't considered that I'd have to step on people to bring myself up the ranks. But if my list worked, it would save girls like Stephanie Griffith in the future. And it would avenge those they'd already hurt.

"I think maybe . . ." I hesitated. "Maybe invite her to a party."

Lola's eyes sparkled, telling me I'd hit the mark. Meanwhile, William's dark eyebrows were drawn together in a frown.

"Huh, I like it," Lola said, clasping her hands together. "Maddy, darling. Have that skirt dry-cleaned and hemmed for Stephanie Griffith. Maybe we should invite her to the party next weekend."

"Perfect," Sophie said. She looked across to me. "I love it when we have a newbie."

"You coming to training, Will?" Zach asked from William's other side as the bell rang.

"Yeah, man. I'll meet you there. I just need to talk to Chloe first."

"So now that you have a girlfriend you're *that* kind of guy?" He laughed, slapping William around the shoulders. "I get it."

"Hey, it's not like I'm skipping training to help pick party dresses."

"That was one time," Francis chimed in. Beside him Lola poked her tongue in his direction.

"True. You're not Francis-level whipped just yet."

"And I hope to never be. See you guys later."

Helping me up from my chair, William led me into the hallway. Sun streamed through the arched windows cut into the stone.

"You blended in pretty good," he mused, leaning against a bulletin board. It was plastered with futile posters reminding students that bullying was wrong.

I shrugged, feeling devoid of energy, as if Level One had drained the life out of me. "Told you I was good."

"You scare me," he said. Then he sighed and scratched the back of his neck. "And look, I really do hate to ask this, but about my dad . . . I'm worried, okay? I know things have been hard for him lately, starting his reelection campaign and all. I just want to see exactly what's been leaked. I can't exactly just ask. If Dad knows I'm being blackmailed by some high school girl . . ." He visibly cringed.

I sighed reluctantly. I needed to keep William on my side, and after toying with the idea for a long moment, I figured there would be no harm in showing him exactly how bad things were for his father. "I guess I could show you what I have."

"You guess?"

I shrugged.

"Chloe."

"Fine." I narrowed my eyes. "But not in public. And you're not having your own copy. This isn't a chance to get out of our deal."

He didn't look thrilled, but he wasn't exactly in a position to ask for much more. "Okay."

"How's after school tomorrow?" I offered.

He nodded. "I'll pick you up in the morning?"

"Okay." I could already picture what everyone would say as they saw me exit William's shiny BMW.

The thought was exhilarating.

I couldn't sit still in math class. The integrals on the board blended together into an intricate pattern that I didn't understand, or even *care* to understand. I was consumed by my plans and the scraps of information I'd uncovered.

Sophie's mystery guy.

Maddy's affair with Francis.

Lola's claim that she'd slept with William.

I mean, the idea didn't seem that far-fetched. William was no Francis when it came to power, but he was good-looking and available. Was she his mysterious ex-girlfriend? The one Sophie had mentioned at Jermaine's?

I shook my head, hoping to clear my mind at least a little. For now, I needed to know how to integrate by parts, not how I was going to infiltrate their group.

After class, I was surprised to be greeted by Claire's chirpy voice.

"Hi, Chloe!"

"Hey, Claire," I said kindly as I gathered my pens from the table.

"I, um, I heard about you and William. I just wanted to say you make a great couple," she said.

"Oh, thanks," I said, feeling a weird creeping sensation across my skin.

"You guys seem super into each other. I was wondering how it started? Come on, we have class together. We can walk."

I was startled when Claire's arm linked with mine, pulling me from my seat, her fair skin flushed with excitement. Taking a breath, I struggled to answer her question. "Um, I guess we just started talking and it went from there."

"How sweet!" Claire said, letting out a sigh. "I saw you sitting with him at lunch today. You two are so cute! And I know I've already said it—but you look *so* good this year. I mean, you were never ugly or anything, but you look gorgeous! Did you lose weight?"

I'd never understand why girls put so much energy into

scrutinizing one another. I'd known image would be a huge factor in my quest for Level One, but it just seemed so . . . unnecessary.

"Uh, thanks," I said, increasing my pace in an attempt to end the conversation as quickly as possible. Lunch with Level One had turned me into a person of interest. My plan was working.

"Anyway, do you want to sit together?"

I gave her a smile. "Sure."

My feet were still damp from my shower as I propped them gingerly onto the scales the following morning.

I sighed in frustration. I couldn't afford to slip back up a clothing size. My stomach looked bloated, bringing a wave of insecurity. The last thing I wanted was to stand out beside the girls at the lunch table by contrasting with their Victoria's Secret–model standard of beauty.

A murmur from the hallway distracted me from my train of thought, and I took a step closer to the bathroom door, wrapping a towel around my body in the process.

"Friday?" I heard Mom say. Her voice was barely audible over the whirring of the bathroom fan. "Richard, you *know* we have dinner with the Thompsons on Thursday night."

There was a pause, and I heard Mom pacing the hall.

"Can't you attend the meeting online and come home after tomorrow? I swear you spend less time on our family than you do the company, and don't even get me started on the example it sets for Chloe—"

Her footsteps accelerated as she walked past the bathroom door again.

"I'm *not* using her to manipulate you, Richard. It's just . . ." There was a sigh and a light thud as she closed a door, cutting off the rest of the conversation.

My breath hitched as a hollowness opened deep within my chest. Sometimes I really hated this house.

I pulled on the clothes I had laid out for the day, pinning my hair back with the golden pin Monica had left with me. Working on my appearance helped to distract from the twisting frustration I felt when I thought about my parents.

William was idling on my street as I stepped out into the unseasonal LA rain, pulling the hood of my coat over my head and letting out a half-hearted yell to my mom that I would see her tonight.

"Morning," he said, with a tone much more perky than the one he usually greeted me with. His knitted sweater looked much more comfortable than the drenched coat I was wearing. I'd only walked twenty or so yards, but it was enough to soak me.

"Hi," I said, taking a deep breath as I tried to slip into my Level One character for the day as opposed to the Chloe I became at home. It was growing harder and harder to separate the two.

He switched the radio on, allowing my thoughts to drift. I

wondered how things would be today. Would I be welcome at the table again? Would Claire insist I join her in physics class?

My questions were quickly answered. I gave a feigned flirty farewell to William and headed to class to be enthusiastically greeted by Claire again. She babbled to me about her invitation to a party held by a student from Richmond Prep this weekend.

"Anyway, you should totally try and make it," she concluded, her voice low so the teacher wouldn't overhear. "It will be so much fun."

"I'll check my plans and let you know," I assured her. By *check my plans*, I meant check if Level One would be attending. But with Claire's enthusiasm, I was already suspecting they would be.

"See you later," she said once class ended, giving me a wave before disappearing into the throng of students.

The rest of the morning flew by, and before I knew it, it was time to face the Level Ones in the cafeteria. I went to my locker, dropped my textbooks onto the shelf, and swapped them for a purse so I could buy a cappuccino. As I closed it, I saw Sophie making her way over to me.

"Hey, Whittaker," she said. Her pale eyes studied my face intently.

"Hi, Sophie," I said, injecting an extra dose of friendly into my voice. "How are you?"

"Just peachy," she said. Her fingers reached to touch my hair, and I had to force myself not to duck from her hand. "Cute pin."

My cheeks warmed at her noticing it. Did she know it was Monica's, or was that supposed to be one of her intimidating not-quite-compliments? "Thanks."

"Coming to lunch?" she asked. "I hear Will's saving you a seat again."

"Yeah," I breathed. "That sounds great."

She gave me a smirk before spinning on her heel. I followed her hesitantly, paranoid that she had some kind of sinister motive.

"Chloe!" A hand tapped my back before I could process the voice. It was Jack, his black hair mussed from the rain. "I was trying to find you."

A sharp dread filled me as I looked from him to Sophie. I hadn't considered a situation in which he would be close enough to cause trouble with my plan. He knew too much about me and Monica—it would be so easy to slip . . .

"Coming, Chloe?" Sophie asked, her eyes flitting to assess Jack in the way someone might look when testing whether food had gone spoiled.

"Yeah—I just, um, why were you looking for me?" I asked Jack, internally swearing at myself for displaying my inner conflict.

"I was wondering if you wanted to eat together . . . but—"

"Don't you know she has a *boyfriend*?" Sophie asked patronizingly.

Jack looked at her as if she had just brought a knife to his throat. "Of course."

"Then stop being so obsessed," she said bluntly. Then she turned to me as if I was her best friend. "Come on, Chlo, I have to talk to Maddy about an assignment."

I tried to give Jack an apologetic look as I followed Sophie to the cafeteria, guilt creeping over me. He was hurt. It was obvious.

William was already waiting for me with two coffees in his hands. The aroma of the one he held out brought a grateful smile to my lips. "Thank you."

"You're welcome."

I couldn't tell if it was part of the act, or a genuine gesture, but it helped calm my nerves a little. It was a small—and probably delusional—reminder that at least someone was there to stop me from being plunged into the depths of Level One alone. Even so, a feeling of dread slowly settled in my abdomen.

Having William Bishop by my side was growing much too comfortable.

Luckily, my presence was largely ignored at the table today. Sophie was busy giving homework answers to Maddy, while William and Zach did a play-by-play of yesterday's lacrosse practice. I picked at the salad I'd packed and tried unsuccessfully to tune in to Lola and Francis's murmured conversation.

"Still on for tonight?" William asked, pulling me from my attempted eavesdropping.

"Yep," I said. "I've got it all with me."

"Great." He looked a little relieved but quickly turned back to Zach to resume their conversation.

"So who was that guy, Chloe?" Sophie asked, propping her chin on her knuckles and raising a brow.

"Oh, Jack?" I asked, trying my best to keep a poker face as she scrutinized me.

"Yeah. He seemed really into you."

I hesitated. I wasn't expecting that conclusion from our encounter in the hall, but I guess to someone grappling for drama it'd be a viable interpretation.

"So you're breaking some hearts, Chloe?" Maddy asked, winking at me from Sophie's side.

"He's just my friend," I said, finally finding the ability to mirror their confidence.

"Should I be jealous?" William asked. I hadn't noticed our conversation attracting the rest of the table's attention.

"No," I said, placing a reassuring hand on his arm. In my head, the action had seemed appropriate, but with his forearm beneath my fingertips making my heart tremor I wasn't quite sure.

"He's a loser," Sophie said snarkily. "Right, Chloe? He seems obsessed with you."

I cast a glance between the Level Ones as they watched

me expectantly. Of course this would just be more juicy gossip to add to their lunchtime entertainment.

"Kinda," I said, thinking quickly. "He won't leave me alone."

"Oh, seriously?" Maddy asked, leaning in closer.

"Yeah." I racked my brain for something to say. Something to feed their sudden interest in me. "He follows me everywhere. Sometimes he leaves notes in my locker. I tried telling him to lay off, but he's got no idea he's way below my standards. You're right, he is a loser."

I shot a side glance at William for good measure. Outside, I was playing the bitchy Level One girl perfectly. Inside, I felt a heavy ball growing in my stomach, making my muscles so tight I thought they'd burst in guilt. I wondered what Monica would think of me sitting here and saying that.

I wondered if she'd be proud.

EIGHT

Monica,

I was sorting through my nail polish last night when I found the shimmery gold enamel, the one speckled with flakes of glitter. Do you remember that night like I do?

It was last Christmas, and of course my dad had spoiled the whole holiday. You invited me and Mom to your house that night, and we exchanged those little gifts. You gave me the nail polish, and I got you the key ring, remember? I hope you didn't lose it.

When we painted our nails that night, I remember closing my eyes and praying we'd always have each other.

That's why I'm doing this, Mon. Because Level One ruined your life. They took you away from me, so I need to take something from them.

Love, Chloe

I MET WILLIAM after school, drawing the same attention we had these last couple of afternoons. I wondered how long we could keep up the illusion of our relationship by just hanging out together. At the moment, it seemed to satisfy Arlington's gossipmongers, but I could hear the questioning whispers. Couples here generally moved fast, and the closest we'd come to PDA was a hand on the back.

William held the door open for me to get into the car and then turned down the volume to the radio. "Is everything okay?"

I nodded immediately, not sure how to pinpoint what precisely was bringing my mood down. Maybe my mother's pleas to my father on the phone, or more likely the trash talk I'd made up about Jack at the table. The memories of Monica didn't help; I wished she'd come back to Arlington more and more with every slash of the windshield wipers.

"How well did you know Monica?" I asked, my voice hesitant in the space between us.

William paused. "I think I knew her relatively well. For the short time I actually did."

I was quiet, hoping he'd elaborate. It was a delicate subject for so many reasons. Pushing it too much could break the fragile bond William and I had developed.

"She was too good to be falling over Lola's feet," he said after a few long moments, carefully navigating after-school traffic. "I tried to look out for her when I could . . . but she liked trouble."

She sure did.

"She can be impulsive," I said in agreement. "Reckless."

He gave me a funny look as I sat there waiting for him to say more. But all that stretched on was silence as bad weather forecasts murmured from the radio speakers.

"The lookout?" William offered as a destination. Obviously neither of our houses was an option, not with prying parents, and especially not with the information I carried on my laptop.

"Sure."

William navigated toward the foothills, and I watched the rain dampen the busy streets out the window. I played with the hem of my skirt, wondering what Monica would be doing right now, wondering what she'd think of my plan if I was crazy enough to divulge it to her.

"Was it true? What you said about that guy?"

"About Jack?" I shook my head. "I was sort of in the moment, I was trying to tell Sophie what she wanted to hear."

"Well, it looked like it worked."

It had. Sophie and Maddy had spent the rest of lunch telling me about all the persistent boys they'd dealt with over the years and how I could shake Jack for good.

"I don't really know what I was saying," I admitted. "Once I started I couldn't stop. It was all lies. Apart from Mon, Jack's really been the only friend I've had at school. I just . . . I feel bad."

William said nothing, and it only made me feel worse.

For some reason, I sensed he disapproved. Even someone bad enough to be on my list was judging me.

I pulled the laptop from my bag once William cut the engine. In daylight, the lookout was unremarkable, a gravel parking lot isolated from the busy road, framed by oak trees, the view hidden by a few yards of foliage. It felt comfortable, a small nook away from the world.

"This is it."

I turned the laptop in his direction and watched his face carefully. Even if this was an ambush to steal my evidence, I had copies backed up on my hard drive at home.

"You know, I still don't know why you had to resort to blackmail."

"What, I could have just asked you?" I raised a brow, my eyes scanning over his shoulders at the thread of Charles Bishop's email correspondence, one from his opposition's assistant describing the weak spots in his opposition's campaign. Weak spots she'd planted under Charles's command. It was well known that the revelations discussed in these emails contributed to his opponent's drop in the polls after they were leaked to the media. The cherry on top was a darkened CCTV image of him and his opposition's assistant shaking hands outside a hotel in town.

I saw him purse his lips. I was suddenly reminded of what Lola told me about him. "Did you know that Lola said she slept with you?"

"I didn't realize she'd say that." As if the stress of the blackmail was raising his temperature, he shrugged off his blazer, tossing it into the back seat. His gaze was fixed on the screen as he began to scroll. By now the rain had clouded the windows, trapping us in the luxury interior of the BMW.

"I didn't think it was true," I mused. Half of me was pissed off that I didn't already know about it, and the other half was disappointed, though I wasn't entirely sure why.

"I didn't think it was really your business, but I guess it is." He sighed, running a hand through his hair.

My cheeks flamed, my heart beating heavily in surprise. "Was it serious between you?"

"No. Considering the situation and all, I mean."

"You mean, considering she has a *boyfriend*?"

"You don't know the dynamics between Lola and Francis," he explained.

I didn't know why I was so worked up, but the subject had me feeling hot all over. "When did this happen?"

He shrugged.

"Oh no," I groaned. "Lola was who Sophie was talking about at Jermaine's."

"It was last year, and it isn't something that's even worth talking about now," he said, his voice stiff. "Can I just focus on this, please?"

He was right, I told myself. The sooner he'd seen what he wanted, the sooner I could go home. I wasn't about to give him his own copy. It could land me in trouble. I clenched my teeth.

If Lola and William were a thing, that put a pretty huge target on my back. Did William realize that? Was he oblivious to the position he'd put me in, or was this just as much his game too?

"Did you come up with the dating idea to make her jealous?" I blurted.

He hesitated before answering, "Let's just say you're not the only one who has a problem with Lola Davenport."

"You're going to have to give me a better reason than that," I said, shaking the image of Lola and William from my mind. Something about *William* sleeping with her. Even though he was Level One, he was supposed to be the best of them.

He exhaled quickly, his frustration evident as he turned back to the laptop screen.

Instead of giving up, I pushed. "I need to know, William. We can't both have hidden agendas here."

"It's *Will*," he reminded me. "And I don't know if it's something I want to talk about."

Using his full name was one more boundary I could put in place as a reminder I was the one in control. At first it was a formality; now it was out of spite.

"Did you love her?"

I bit my bottom lip as silence filled the car. *Too far, Chloe, you idiot.*

"I don't know. It's not important," he said quietly, like he wouldn't mind at all if I didn't hear his answer. "What's important is that she and Francis are together. And that's never going to change."

"She wouldn't leave him for you?" I pressed, wanting desperately to form a clear picture. Or maybe I was just being nosy.

In one sudden movement, William slammed my laptop shut. "I think I'm done. I'll drop you home."

"There's still time to look. You've hardly even seen the worst of it—"

"Just drop it, Chloe," he said. "I'll look again another day."

Now I was just pissed off. "You didn't want me to find out, did you?"

"It'd be easier if you hadn't."

"What, because you could use me too?" I asked. When it was time to take down Lola—number one on the list—would he stop me?

How could he *love* her?

"No, because you wouldn't understand. *Especially* someone like you," he said. Now he was angry too. His brows were furrowed, his lips pulled into a scowl.

"Someone like *me*?" I questioned, grabbing my laptop from his hands and shoving it back into my schoolbag.

"Yes. You're crazy, you know that? Doing all of this—nobody sane would make that decision. Nobody would give up their life to get revenge for someone else."

"So that's what you think," I muttered. It had been a long time since I'd been this angry. "I thought you understood."

"I understand your motivation. I understand why," he said, clutching the steering wheel even though the car wasn't running. "But I don't understand why you're choosing it over a normal high school life. You could have had it easy, coasting through and acing all your classes. But instead you're playing another bitchy popular girl and throwing your life away to get revenge for her."

My hands were shaking now, and my eyes burned with unshed angry tears. He'd obviously done more research on me than I'd thought. I wasn't familiar with arguing. In my family, conflict was resolved with passive aggression and emotional manipulation. It was never confrontational. "Are you saying Monica isn't worth it?"

"No, I'm not saying that. This isn't about her, Chloe. It's about you. I'm not sure you even know who you are without her."

"I know exactly who I am," I said harshly, my voice low. But he'd hit the mark, as if he could read my damn mind. "And it's not someone who'd sleep around with someone as horrible as Lola."

Without saying another word, he turned on the ignition and the radio drowned out whatever might've remained of our conversation.

The ride home was confusing. My cheeks were pink from the car's heating, or maybe just from the rage circling my mind. I was so angry and bewildered with this revelation. *I could use it*, I reminded myself. In fact, using it could be a huge advantage. Francis and William were close friends, and I was sure that Francis couldn't know about William and Lola. He wouldn't let him live if he did.

"Look," William said coolly when we arrived outside my house. He pulled over and shut off the engine again. "I'm sorry for what I said before, okay? You just confuse the hell out of me."

I took a deep breath. His apology helped a little, but the anger still simmered in my chest. Was I sorry? Not at all. He should have told me about Lola from the start.

"Will your feelings for Lola impact my plans?" I asked bluntly.

"Your revenge?" he clarified.

I nodded.

He shook his head.

"So, you have no feelings for her anymore?"

He hesitated, sun-bronzed strands of hair falling across his forehead. "Nothing that will get in the way."

"Do you promise?" I asked. I might be a liar, but I sensed he had a little more honor than that, at least from what I'd observed junior year, and from the snippets Monica had told me. I was such a hypocrite, deceiving everyone but expecting their honesty.

"Yes," he said in one short breath. He looked conflicted,

maybe even a little remorseful, but his tone was clear. Enough for me to believe him, at least. "I'm all in."

In for destroying his own friends.

"Okay," I said. I knew there had to be much more to Lola and William's relationship, but for now I wouldn't press the topic. Our relationship was fragile.

"I'll see you tomorrow."

"See you at lunch," I said, stepping out of the car and shutting the door behind me. He drove away almost instantly. Like me, he was probably still fuming and masking it for the sake of our deal.

I had a feeling he wasn't quite aware of what he was getting himself into when it came to me taking down everyone on my list.

Including him.

NINE

Dear Monica,

I don't think I ever said this to you, but I knew you were serious about being popular when you pierced your ears. God, a simple thing, right? Even I had my ears pierced. But you were never allowed.

You know, when your mom found your studs in your drawer and she drove to the school and walked you out of campus I told everyone your dog was sick, which was why you needed to leave so suddenly. I knew you were so embarrassed. I wanted to make sure nobody started talking about you.

See, we protected each other from the start. I'm not going to stop now.

Love, Chloe

CLAIRE'S PRESENCE WAS becoming routine. I seemed to always have someone wanting to sit with me or walk with me between classes. It made me uneasy after being so comfortable with silence.

"Sitting with them again?" Jack asked as we reached the entrance of the cafeteria at lunch on Thursday. My stomach turned in guilt.

I gave a meek smile. "Yeah, I haven't seen Will all day."

"Right," Jack said. His smile was friendly, but I could tell he was disappointed.

"I'm sorry." I *was* sorry. For using him. For talking about him behind his back. But it was all for the greater good. "I'll see you in chem?"

"Of course." He hesitated, and I wondered if he was expecting some kind of apology for how Sophie treated him, but I couldn't. I had to look united with Level One, I couldn't let them think there were cracks in my relationship with William by disagreeing with Sophie.

William and I had settled into a familiar pattern, as if we were performing from a script. In front of his friends we continued to act like we were in the honeymoon stage of dating, and when we were on our own we were learning to keep a sensible distance, tiptoeing around conversations that barely scraped past the surface.

His secret past with Lola was constantly nagging at the corner of my mind. I noticed subtle things now, things I'd never registered before. Across the table, Lola and William never seemed to meet eyes, and they avoided responding to anything the other said. I wondered how it had started, and just how many others knew about their affair. It could help me determine just how beneficial it would be to expose it when the time came.

I was becoming a fixture at the Level One table, never directly invited into conversation, but still present enough to gain more and more information about the internal dynamics of the group.

"What are you wearing tomorrow night?" Maddy asked Sophie, not raising her eyes from her salad.

Sophie screwed up her face in thought. "Hmm, the two-piece I bought in Paris this summer."

"Ugh, I need to go shopping," Maddy said dramatically. "Would you come?"

Sophie barely hesitated before responding, "I have a family dinner."

Maddy looked hopefully to Lola beside her, who was busy playing with Francis's hair, her legs resting over his lap. She looked toward Maddy in disinterest. I watched her carefully, the disdain in her eyes evident. "Why don't you ask Chloe?"

Maddy looked at me questioningly. Her eyes were kind, almost innocent. I recalled the moment she'd seen me at the party last weekend and complimented my top. I also recalled the fact that she was sleeping with Francis, who was two seats down from her and currently kissing Lola.

This was the opportunity I'd been searching for, a chance to get to know the other Level Ones better so I could dig deeper.

"I could help," I said.

"Great!" Maddy said, her posture visibly slackening with relief. "How about we meet at the mall at four?"

"Sounds great."

"Hope you don't mind me stealing your girlfriend, Will," she added.

William stopped prodding the plate in front of him to peer up at her. He hesitated too long, and his tone was just a little off what would classify as casual. "As long as you look after her."

I rolled my eyes, hoping I was coming across as playful rather than annoyed. Our feigned relationship was starting to take its toll. Maybe it was the secrets, or maybe it was the weight of what we were doing. We couldn't get attached, after all. I was here for a reason. Maybe it was better if we remained distant. "Like I *need* to be looked after."

He gave me a tired look before cracking a shallow smile for the benefit of our audience. "Of course not."

After last period, I returned to my locker to grab my bag. William was already waiting, his backpack slung over his broad shoulders.

"Hey," he said. His features had somewhat relaxed since lunchtime.

"Hi," I greeted. I gave him a smile, mostly out of courtesy.

"Chlo?" he asked. I froze, his shortening of my name

catching me off guard. Nobody was close enough to hear it. When I didn't respond, he dropped his bag to his feet so he could lean against the locker beside mine. "I'm sick of this weird formality between us. It's not making it easy."

I narrowed my shoulders, unsure of what that meant. When I didn't reply straightaway, he continued.

"You know I've been thinking of what I said the other day."

"You have?" I asked.

"Yeah, and I don't think what you're doing is completely irrational," he said. "What I said was out of line—I know you're only doing what you think is best. She was your friend, after all."

I shut my locker, a little relief seeping through me. "I'm glad you came to that conclusion."

"I just figured it's been bothering you. You've been quiet lately."

I was quiet because I wanted to keep my distance from him, especially with the image of him and Lola still fresh in my mind. This wasn't about trust, not when he had no choice with my blackmail, but still, I'd developed some kind of irrational idea that he was different from the others. That he was better. It was a reminder to keep my distance.

"Are you going to be okay with Maddy?" he asked.

I frowned. "Yeah. I mean, should I be worried?"

He laughed. I couldn't help but study his features, in awe of how he could look so charming, even with the bags beneath his eyes. "I doubt it. Maddy's pretty innocent, I guess."

"What do you mean?" Was he unaware of her affair with Francis? I wondered how that fit in with Level One's complicated love triangle.

"Her intentions aren't terrible. . . . She can just be impulsive," he explained, pausing to give me a thoughtful look.

"Okay," I said, adding that to my mental Maddy file. "Thanks."

He cast a look to the students around him as a particularly loud group of juniors walked past. "Did you know there's a rumor going around that we're not even touching until marriage?"

I snorted, aware of why this would bother him. "Are you worried you'll look bad to your buddies?"

"No," he said. "More worried that people will find out we're hiding something."

Right. And that would be bad for both of us.

"What are you suggesting?" I asked.

He took a step forward, the distance between us halving, and halving again as he took another. My heart stuttered, partly because I had no idea what he was doing, and partly because I wasn't used to being so close to a guy—especially not in front of as many people as there were around us now.

"We just need to play our part a little better," he murmured.

He was right, but I still wanted to protest. Being so close to him was having a strange effect on my breathing. He closed the distance and embraced me. His hands fell around my waist and my hands rested against his shoulders in a careful act to look normal.

The warmth of his arms wrapped securely around my waist had me fumbling for coherent thoughts. I reminded myself that it was just due to my usual lack of human interaction.

"Is this better?" I asked, as if filling the silence between us would help kill the butterflies in my stomach. I was sure that if I stared into his eyes any longer I'd go dizzy. How could they be such a brilliant shade of green? Mine were a muddy brown, nowhere near as alluring.

"Well, it probably makes us look a little more like a normal couple," he said, and I noticed that he was studying my face too, bringing a wave of insecurity. "I hope you have fun shopping. I'll see you tomorrow morning."

I nodded, holding my breath as his head ducked closer, carefully grazing his lips against my cheek.

And then I was released, and he shot me one more annoyingly charming smile before picking up his bag and becoming lost in the crowd.

STAGE FOUR
INFILTRATION

TEN

Dear Monica,

How do I even start to dress for a party? Closed-toe or straps? Legs or boobs? Magazines are only so helpful. I wish you were here.

We never really went shopping together, did we? Our styles clashed too much and we could never decide which stores to stop in—you thought vintage smelled too much like old people, and I got bored with the repetition of the mall. But when we did I got to see another side of you. Lost in glamorous labels, playing dress-up in front of a mirror. You were always made for more, weren't you?

Maybe Level One knew it too, and that's why you scared them.

Love, Chloe

THE MALL WAS a fifteen-minute drive from school, twenty minutes in the heavy traffic. I arrived early, killing time by strolling past the shop windows. My eyes skimmed over a magazine rack and found today's paper.

Curious, I strolled inside and picked it up. William's dad was on the front page, standing behind a lectern with a wide smile. One email and I could ruin his career, ruin William's family. The magnitude of that possibility made my fingers tingle, and I carefully placed the paper back onto the stand.

I met Maddy outside a Victoria's Secret store. She was leaning against the wall in thigh-high boots and her plaid school skirt, her black hair raised in a high ponytail and her face dimpling as she smiled in greeting.

"Hey, Chloe. Thanks for meeting me!" she said. Unexpectedly, she wrapped her arms around me in an extravagant hug.

"Thanks for asking me to come along," I said. Even though I knew I was a last resort.

"So, do you have something to wear?" she asked, strutting down the mall with me in tow, her eyes skimming the selection of designer stores.

"No," I said, struggling to match her long stride. "Not yet, at least."

"That's perfect," she said, flashing me her teeth in a glamorous grin. "We can find something together!"

We ducked into a small boutique, one hidden away in a

corner. Despite its unimposing entrance, its interior was large and inviting, the walls lined with a row of expensive-looking clothing.

"Camo or chic? Glamour or simple?" Maddy asked, fingering the luxurious fabric.

"Uh . . ." I glanced around the store for inspiration. "I think glamour."

"Good call. You know, I bet lace would be awesome on you. You seem like a lacy person. Maybe a plunging neckline with a flowy hem?"

"Sure," I said quickly, barely able to picture what she meant. I was *anything* but a lacy person.

An assistant emerged from behind a clothing rack and began collecting the items Maddy clicked her red-painted nails toward.

I fidgeted with my fingers nervously as I stood at her side, nodding or shaking my head arbitrarily when she looked to me for an opinion. While I was fumbling to pass her fashion pop quiz, beneath the surface I was confident. Being alone with Maddy was a golden opportunity for executing my plan.

"So, are you into anyone at the moment?" I asked, running my fingers over the sleeves of a jumpsuit.

Maddy's smile grew a little. "Here's the tea: I've yet to find anyone in high school good enough to fall for, guys *or* girls. And if they're not perfect, there's no point in being locked down. I'm a free spirit."

Well, she must have an extreme sense of freedom if that extended to sleeping with Francis Rutherford.

"But don't let that put you off Will," she continued. "He's a really good guy. You're lucky to have him."

"Lucky?" I pushed, now letting my hands find a tulle dress in front of me, the fabric rough between my fingers.

"Yeah, I mean, he's the most eligible bachelor of Arlington, isn't he? Oh, Chloe, not that one, it would make you look . . . you could look much better. You need something figure-hugging."

My hand fell from the dress I'd been observing. "Yeah, I mean he is really great. Only . . ."

I let my sentence trail off.

"Only?" she asked after a few small seconds. I could practically sense her gossip radar pulsing.

"You can't tell anyone," I said, my words accompanying a reluctant sigh. "It's just—Lola said something . . ."

"Lola?" Maddy asked. She looked confused, but I could see the spark of interest in her eyes. "What did she say?"

I hesitated. "She, um, just mentioned that she *may* have slept with Will. I don't know, I don't want to cause any bad blood. It just had me—"

Maddy's laugh drowned out the rest of my words, her body language sympathetic as her arms fell around my shoulders. "Oh, babe, Lola and Will? Nuh-uh. She's probably just saying that to mess with you. She has Francis, after all . . ."

I ducked my head, feigning embarrassment. So Maddy

didn't know about Lola and William. "I knew it was stupid. Never mind."

"Lola can mess with you sometimes," Maddy continued, picking out a black piece hidden deep in the rack she was scanning. "Oh my God, try this on."

I carefully handed the dress to our mute shop assistant, who was already disappearing behind a mountain of dresses.

"She's probably just trying to be funny. To test you. I mean, we don't know you very well." She let out a frustrated sigh, reaching the end of the rack and letting her hands fall to her sides. "Can you help me find something?"

As much as I'd worked to perfect my Level One transformation, their taste in clothing didn't come easily to me. As a general rule, I stuck to the brands with the highest price tags in order to blend in with Arlington's high fashion.

I used that as my guide as I glanced over the dresses in a nearby display. The higher the price, the more likely she'd like it.

"How about this?" I suggested, pulling out a burgundy dress with a triple-figure price tag.

Her eyes swept over it. "I'll try it on."

Maddy led us to the fitting room, which was decked out with plush couches and bouquets of white roses. As soon as I was safely in the confines of a dressing room, I tried to let go of the tension that had been building in my shoulders. I missed the security of having William by my side. I didn't realize how much easier it was to have him to fall back on if I said the wrong thing.

I fumbled with the zipper of the dress. It was beautiful, the delicate black lace somehow creating curves on my rectangular body shape. Even though my chest was exposed, it covered enough skin elsewhere to make me feel somewhat modest. The dark fabric and sexy neckline had me feeling . . . powerful.

I heard the door beside me open and so I ventured out too, slightly in awe of what I was wearing. I felt like I was in costume, pretending to be someone much more sophisticated than I was on the inside. But that's what I'd been so used to doing lately; disguising myself as someone else. Chloe 2.0.

"You're *so* buying that," Maddy said, her eyes wide as she took me in. But then she quickly brought the attention to herself. "Can you help me with the strap? Ugh, this dress is so tight."

She was wearing the dress I'd chosen, and I was suddenly anxious that she'd hate it. I mean, it represented my taste. If I got this wrong it'd definitely hinder my chances at breaking into the girls' group. I knew how superficial they could be.

I helped her loop the strap at the back, and then she stepped in front of the huge mirror. I mean, I thought it looked good, its texture complementing her dark skin and its cut making her body look toned. I held my breath as she twirled.

"Okay. I look hot."

I smiled in relief as she gave a dramatic squeal of glee and pulled my waist toward her so we could both pose for a shot in the mirror for her Instagram story. My reflection didn't betray any of my anxiety, my smile was wide and my cheeks rosy with adrenaline.

We paid for each item and I exited the store beside her, chatting about a newly discovered mutual obsession with *Black Mirror*. When I noticed that my smile wasn't held up by pure will for the first time in a while, I felt a pang of guilt. It was almost like the old days. Like being with Monica.

"I'll see you tomorrow, then?" Maddy asked, oblivious to my newfound turmoil.

"Of course," I said, trying to match her excitement.

"I can't wait!" She leaned in and air-kissed my cheek.

I couldn't stop the crawling sensation over my skin as I made my way back to my car.

ELEVEN

Monica,

Do you remember last winter? How after a day of rain, we headed to our swimming hole, diving and somersaulting into the water? Don't you wonder if it's still the same? Now that we aren't, I mean. I wished our parents hadn't forbidden us from returning. Maybe it would have been something else keeping us close.

I really mean it when I say this—I should have been a better friend. If I was enough for you, then maybe you wouldn't have wanted to join them. Maybe you'd still be here, and we'd still be able to visit our secret swimming hole.

Love, Chloe

FRIDAY MORNING I sifted through my textbooks, watching Lola Davenport over the door of my locker. Francis towered over her, one hand against the wall as the other played with a strand of her hair. Her lips were glossed with fuchsia today, and she was wearing her most intimidating smirk as she murmured something for only him to hear.

And then Francis Rutherford turned to look at me, his glance piercing. I looked away quickly, shutting my locker and turning to see William already approaching.

"Classes are canceled. We have another school meeting today," he said, giving a long sigh and stepping in to hug me. My cheeks flamed, but this time I was able to manage my composure as my hands flattened on his back. Behind him, I saw Lola and Francis saunter away.

"Really?" I asked.

He nodded. The school had warned us that teachers were checking in on students' social media, and now any time they suspected we were underage drinking or bullying one another they gave us another lecture on safety. I wished they could just talk to the people who were guilty instead of forcing us all to listen.

"Wanna skip it?" William offered. "I need to talk to you about something."

This piqued my interest. Sit and listen to the "Do Better" spiel or possibly obtain more information? The idea of sitting through another futile round of teachers addressing binge drinking and playing reckless games to impress each other made me nauseated.

"Sure."

William led me out of the school building, but instead

of turning to the parking lot we wandered down the pathway and across the lawns, the sun brightening the well-tended garden. We headed down a grassy slope, where we were just out of view of the rest of campus, and William tossed his jacket down, offering it for me to sit on.

"Thanks," I said, making myself comfortable. The last thing I wanted was grass stains on my skirt.

"Lola is suspicious," he said, skipping any lead-up and getting straight to the point.

I had to do a double take. "What?"

"She was asking about you."

That wasn't good. Not at all. "Should I be worried?"

"About her digging or my loyalty?"

"Both."

"You should probably be more worried about her digging."

I let out a tangled breath. *Shit.* "Tell me everything."

"She just knows me too well," he said. "She knows it's weird for me to just come out and date someone, especially someone like you. Especially when there's all the . . . stuff between her and me."

"Right," I said, running my fingers through the grass in frustration. "So, she knows we're not real."

"Not that we're not real. Just that there's more to our relationship than we're letting on. We just have to act extra cozy. I tried to convince her that you just swept me off my feet. And, well, I think she's going to make your life hard."

"Because she thinks you moved on and is jealous?" I shook

my head, the whole situation not making much sense. "I need to know more. To protect myself."

"What do you want to know?" he asked.

"Well, how long were you two a *thing*? Does Lola have many, you know, extra boyfriends?"

He visibly cringed. "Maybe three months, tops? And no. As far as I know, I'm the only one. Other than Francis, obviously." He paused. "Man, this sounds so messed up."

"That's because it is," I couldn't help but say.

"Not helpful."

I shrugged. "So . . . if it wasn't an intentional thing, what happened?"

I felt a wave of annoyance as I took in the small smile across his full lips. He had to fall for *her*, of all people. Even if he was the only one to really help Monica last year, to try to guide her out of parties and make sure she got home okay, he was still screwing with the enemy. Literally.

But if I wanted to stay on his good side, and to get the most information possible, I needed to keep my cool. I needed to act as if I was on his side.

"Well, it wasn't something either of us saw coming."

I didn't know how to respond to that without betraying my anger. I watched a butterfly dance around a hedge, wondering if it too was appalled by this conversation.

"We were drunk when it first happened," he said. "It was my birthday party last year. I was stupid, very stupid, trying to impress everyone with how much I could drink. And she was fighting with Francis." He let out a breath. "I don't think either of us knew what we were doing, but we talked for hours, just the two of us. We never had a sexual relationship like she said, if that's what you're getting at."

I bit my lip, holding back any commentary. I wasn't oblivious to his body language or his tone. He didn't expect a response. He just wanted to talk.

"Francis and I have been friends since we were old enough to hold a lacrosse stick. His dad literally based how much he'd sponsor the club on what position Francis played and how much game time he got. Even though Francis loved it, he always seemed like a lonely kid. It's why we became such good friends. I think I was one of the only ones to see that side of him. But he always got what he wanted, never really caring who he stepped on to get it. It's just who he is, especially now."

He sighed, pushing his hair away from his face, the sunlight catching its highlights.

"The point is, Francis always wants more. The people who care about him are never enough. He won't be satisfied—she's just an accessory to him."

"She seems pretty happy to be there," I noted, careful to assess his reaction. He gave a half smile.

"Oh, she is. I think she really fell hard for him, at first at least. And she loves impressing people. She always puts on this act of how wonderful her life is, but that night I'd never seen her so vulnerable."

Of course vulnerability would be something William found attractive. He seemed like just the type who wanted someone to save.

"I know you're judging me right now. You obviously hate her. I just want you to understand that she's human too. Her whole bad-bitch persona only runs so deep. It's no excuse. It's just that there's something behind all of that that isn't completely screwed up."

"Are you seriously giving me a reason to *like* her?" I asked, failing to keep up my supportive demeanor. "After everything she did to Monica?"

William slowly shook his head, his eyes meeting mine before darting away, looking back to the garden in front of us. "No. I'm not. I guess I'm just trying to help you understand. We were just two people drunk out of our minds at a party. Our understanding of Francis was really the only connection we had. I've been his best friend for so long and she's his girlfriend. We know him almost better than anyone, for better or worse. We almost got excitement out of deceiving him. It was toxic."

"And what stopped it?"

"Francis, of course," he said. "He thought she was cheating, and he must have done something to stop it. She didn't want to blur boundaries anymore. It was a wake-up call. For both of us. It was so wrong, and ever since then Francis has had it out for me. But he knows I'm the only friend he has who really understands him. It's . . . complicated."

"Sounds like you still have some loose ends to me."

He shrugged. It occurred to me that out of all the targets I could have chosen to connect me to Level One, I'd picked the worst. If Lola had feelings for William, then I was 100 percent going down for this.

"I mean, it wasn't like I struggled to move on. Especially after . . ."

"After Monica?"

"After Monica." He cleared his throat. "When Monica started hanging with us, things got messy. She was something else back then, that was for sure."

I was unable to look him in the eye.

"Monica seemed to have this sense of people's weaknesses, and when she—"

"Stop," I said, bringing my fingers to my temples. I closed my eyes.

"I'm sorry."

Why was he trusting me with this to begin with? It made no sense for him to confide in me about Lola, especially when he knew the truth about my plan.

"William, I—"

"Will," he corrected, a small smile playing on his mouth, like he'd gone from finding it annoying to amusing. But it wasn't the full kind, it wasn't traveling farther than his lips. His eyes were still hardened.

"I just . . ." My voice trailed off, and I decided against questioning his trust. It might make him question it too, and he'd stop sharing these details with me. "I'm glad you can talk to me about it."

His brows softened, and he hesitated, as if deciding what exactly to say. After a moment, he rolled to his side, making himself comfortable on the lawn. "Anyway, I just wanted to warn you. Be careful tomorrow night."

"I'll do my best," I said, though my tone made it clear that I didn't believe it would be enough.

"*We'll* do our best. My head's on the line as much as yours, and you're not exposing us, Whittaker."

"Right."

"And, Chloe?"

I looked to him, his tone bringing goose bumps to the nape of my neck.

"At the party tomorrow . . . don't play the girls' games."

Games. It was their favorite pastime. I released a long exhale. I had already prepared myself to do what I needed to get in. And playing their games was just another challenge to gain my place.

"If only Monica had your guidance," I said, an edge of bitterness tainting my words.

William paled, his expression now grim, and I knew I'd crossed a line. He felt guilty for what had happened to Monica Pennington.

I watched as he ran his fingertips over the grass in front of him, his thoughts far away. Why did I feel the urge to comfort him when I should only feel angry? It felt foreign to be with someone who was close to her too. Sometimes I felt like I was the only one who even remembered what Arlington was like with her here.

"Come on," I said, standing and brushing grass from my legs.

"Where are we going?" he asked, his brows furrowing as he hastily picked up his jacket to follow me through the hedge.

"Away," I said. I wanted to visit the place Monica and I went to when things still felt like they were normal. "Away from Arlington. At least for a few hours."

I shook off the feeling that this was a stupid idea. I wanted to hug my best friend, to stop missing her and to just hang with her for a day. But things weren't that simple anymore. Instead, I'd settle for anything that would bring me even a tiny bit closer to her.

But as much as I wanted to reconnect with her, I didn't want to face another harsh reminder that Monica had left me alone to fend for myself through the hell that was Arlington. For now, William was the only person at this school I didn't have to pretend around. And even if it was just through blackmail—even if it was just temporary—I could use that. I could use his company.

Besides, part of me wanted him to see it too. I wanted to somehow show him what things were like before everyone knew Monica as just another girl in the Level One clique.

After a dry summer, I wasn't confident that our swimming

hole was anything more than cracked mud at the bottom of the secret valley, but the rain from the other day gave me some hope. I hadn't really thought of the place much since Monica sprained her ankle and her mom said we weren't allowed to go anymore, but now that I'd remembered, all I wanted to do was to see it again, to be reminded it was real. That she was real.

I led William back to the parking lot, and when we were in the car I gave directions that he followed with some reluctance. Even though he didn't even know where we were going, he humored me anyway. Though I was already breaking our pact by showing him, it felt like actually mentioning it aloud would be a betrayal to Monica.

When we finally arrived, I realized that heeled boots were not going to be ideal for hiking from the road to the water hole. I kicked them off in William's car. Walking in only my socks over the dirt, I started clearing trees from our path, leading him into the edge of the forest.

"You're still not telling me where we're going?" he asked in disbelief after we'd been walking for at least ten minutes. It was muscle memory, which branches to duck beneath and which rocks to avoid. I felt twigs dig into the soles of my feet and winced.

"I don't need to tell you. You're about to see."

Just as I pushed aside branches from a blooming wild milkweed, I saw the familiar landscape, the hard rock falling to a crystal pond.

I smiled. Though it wasn't even half as full as it used to be when Monica and I had practiced diving—fracturing the glass-like surface and emerging at the shore—it was still stirring memories. The happier ones.

"Wow," William said. "How did I not know about this?"

"That's the best part about it," I said. "Even in this huge city nobody ever comes up here. We always kept it a secret."

"We?"

"Me and Monica," I said. "Her parents used to take us as kids, and then we started coming here alone when we were old enough."

William was walking along the rock, kicking his shoes off. He knelt down next to the water, dipping a hand in. "It's freezing."

I followed him, taking off my socks and sitting on the smooth rock, letting my toes dip in. He was right. It was like ice.

"We never used to care about the cold." Monica didn't care about a few goose bumps when it came to having fun.

I wiggled my toes in the water, feeling the cold travel up my body, cooling me. Though the pool was shaded by tree branches, I was still hot from the walk.

"You guys spent a lot of time together, huh?"

"All our time," I said with a small smile. "Until last year, at least."

"You know, I never had a friend like that," he said, perching on the rock beside me. "Francis isn't exactly someone I can just hang with for fun. He's too competitive."

I looked at him curiously. "What was it like? Growing up, with your dad and everything, I mean?"

After all, if his oldest friend was Francis and his dad was a corrupt political figure, then I was curious as to how he ended up as he was today. Monica was right. He wasn't quite like the others.

"He wasn't always like this, you know." He kicked his feet, stirring ripples. "He still isn't, not outside his job, I mean. He's my dad. Mom warned me things were getting bad when he started running for mayor. He was so stressed, it put a strain on our whole house. He was just doing what he thought was best for us. I never exactly agreed with his decisions, but I didn't want to get on his bad side by speaking up."

Just like my dad. I couldn't exactly call him out when it'd only make him frustrated—ruining whatever rare family time we got. We were the kids. We weren't supposed to have opinions against our parents.

"I'm not saying I regret it but . . . I'm sorry I have to use your father's mistakes against you."

My heart thudded, waiting for his response. Was that too far? Was it going against everything I'd worked toward with my revenge plan?

"I'll make it right, someday," he said. "I'm not going to be like him."

And I wasn't going to be like my father either. Our flawed parents would teach us what not to do.

"Here," I said, finding a smooth pebble at my side. I handed it to him, his fingers enclosing a little too soon, the warmth of his skin making my chest pound. I pulled my hand away quickly.

Finding my own pebble, I tossed with all my might, the rock hitting the water at the perfect angle, bouncing off the surface one, two, three, four times. A lousy throw. I used to manage over ten before the rock would hit the other end of the pool. It felt good, dissipating the heaviness growing between us.

"How do you—" William cut off his sentence with a grunt as he hurled his pebble. It fell in the water with a messy splash, spraying our faces.

I laughed at him.

"Like this." I tried to show him, slowly releasing a new pebble and watching it skim lightly, as if it weighed nothing.

It was strange to be here with someone else, someone new. I wondered what Monica would say. I peeked at William from the corner of my eye, watching him as he narrowed his eyes in utmost concentration, again failing to bounce his rock.

"Goddammit."

I felt strangely satisfied knowing I was better at it than him. After all, he was a prodigy in everything he tried. I was just a nerd who had a pass from phys ed so I could take extra math units.

"Are you laughing?"

I shrugged, picking up another rock to throw. If we threw for long enough, maybe we'd forget about the rest of

Wandemore Valley and it would forget about us. It sounded so simple.

"Whittaker, you better show me how to skim these rocks properly. My ego can't handle it."

I pursed my lips. I always imagined Level One only cared about titles and money and appearances, not about throwing pebbles across a pond.

STAGE FIVE

INTELLIGENCE

TWELVE

Monica,

You said so much about William Bishop last year. I mean, you wouldn't shut up about Level One, but I remember what you said about him the most. The others blurred together into superhuman beings, beautiful and bad. But you always made him sound like the nice guy. The hero who drove you home from parties, who stopped Francis and Zach from getting in fights with people from Richmond Prep when they were drunk.

You know, I believed you until that night.

Love, Chloe

FALSE EYELASHES WERE never my thing.

I'd been battling with them for at least ten minutes when my mother walked through the door, tittering dramatically as she came to my aid.

"Now why would my daughter be putting on false eyelashes at eight p.m. on a Saturday night? Another party?"

I couldn't roll my eyes with her thumb strategically moving my eyelid in place. Instead, I let out a little sigh, to let her know that I totally didn't need her prying. "Yes, a party."

"Two parties in two weekends. What a social butterfly you're becoming," she said with a smile.

"What can I say, it's senior year," I said with sarcasm.

"Are you still missing Mon?" Mom asked. "You know, if you're not coping well we can go and talk to someone. I was on the phone with Melanie Pennington the other night—"

"I'm fine, Mom," I insisted. Though my tone was rude, I really was appreciative of her concern. I just didn't want to talk about Monica. Or her mom.

"Good, honey," she said. She fanned my face for a few seconds. "There. All done. Now, what are you wearing?"

I cast a glance to the black lace dress on my bed, and she stepped over to ogle it while I started framing my lips with a red liner.

"Is Mayor Bishop's son picking you up?" she asked knowingly.

I groaned. Gossip spread through the parents of Arlington Prep almost as fast as it did through its students.

"No, we're all riding in a limo." Apparently it was Maddy's dad's private limousine. She'd called me an hour ago to announce she'd be swinging by my place.

"Well, I'll leave you be. But be home at a reasonable hour," she said, raising her overgroomed eyebrows in my direction and leaving the room.

Because I lived the closest to the party, I was the last to be picked up, squished into the back seat of a limo designed for six, our legs pressed against one another and glasses of champagne dispersed as we settled in for the journey. There were whoops of joy and animated laughter. The group was lightly tipsy, with just enough alcohol to warm them up for the night ahead.

I churned over my game plan for the party. I needed to eavesdrop, especially as the night went on. I needed to know who spent one-on-one time with who, who people were getting in bed with, and where everyone would return to sleep for the night. I'd infiltrated the group, and now it was time for the next stage. Getting intelligence.

I was deep in thought, unaware how much my body language was conveying until William's hand landed on my knee and gave it a gentle squeeze. The touch was light—and dangerously careful—but enough to remind me that I needed to put my mask back on. I gave him a thankful smile. I was wasting valuable time.

"Hold still," Zach said over the beat of party music playing through the limo, holding a champagne flute above Maddy's lips. Her hair was smoothed back out of her face, and her cheekbones were contoured so sharply they could be weaponized. The car took a turn and the bubbly liquid spilled onto her chest.

"Zach!" she said between laughter.

"Sophie, your turn."

"Hey," Lola said, interrupting their games. Her hand rested over Francis's knee, and while it seemed like an affectionate gesture, under careful scrutiny it might have been a possessive one, like she was protecting him from Maddy beside her. "If any of you see that Stephanie girl, you know what to do, right?"

"We haven't forgotten, *Delores*," Francis said flirtatiously as he poked her ribs. She brushed him off.

"Nobody is going to mess with you once we remind them what happens," Maddy reassured. "We'll make sure of it, babe."

"What about you, Will? Are you in on this?" Francis asked, his eyes sparkling beneath the limo's disco ball.

"In on what?" He'd been preoccupied refilling our glasses with champagne.

"I don't know. Be creative. Remind her why someone like her should be more careful around someone like us," Francis said.

William rolled his eyes. "What are you going to do, throw your drink at her?"

"I want worse," Lola said. "Worse than she did to me."

"Is this going to be a competition?" Zach asked. "The prize, your adoration?"

Zach leaned across and made kissing noises, causing her to brush him away with a smirk.

"That's not something easy to win, is it?" Francis said,

snaking his arm around Lola. I watched Maddy, who quickly downed her drink. Level One was starting to feel like a dysfunctional family. While I could see their close relationships, the underlying tension was obviously a problem. Why were they even friends still? Maybe it was to keep their image. Or maybe it was because they were in too deep.

"Almost there!" Sophie said, finally putting her phone in her purse and grinning. "Did someone suggest a competition?"

I couldn't even recall the name of the private school kid who owned the mansion we arrived at. All I knew was that he was from Richmond Prep, and—judging by the noise emanating from the house and the colorful lights leading a path to the back of the house—that it was exactly the kind of party I was expecting.

We made our way past the Japanese garden and straight to the huge front door, avoiding the side fence gate where most party guests seemed to be flooding into. We were VIP.

A hand clenched around mine, and for a moment my heart did a little somersault, my mind instantly jumping to William. But it was Maddy, her bright lips pulled in a broad smile.

"The dress looks great, by the way," she said. "I love that clutch!"

I laughed nervously, feeling my cheeks heat. "Oh, thanks! You look amazing."

Her grin grew as she swung our arms between us like children.

We went up a set of winding ivory stairs and into a bustling room, one side lined with plush sofas and the other containing gaming tables for foosball and pool. It was crowded with people, all seeming a little misplaced in their glamorous cocktail wear as they leaned over tables and balanced their cues. Unlike regular house parties, teenagers in Wandemore Valley liked to show off with high-end designer suits and dresses, as if we were adult enough to be attending sophisticated galas.

Level One was already scattering, a few of the girls sauntering toward a drink table, which held a hefty crystalline centerpiece. The guys, who seemed to know a large group of boys by the foosball table, gravitated toward the games, blending into a sea of crisply ironed shirts and well-fitted trousers. William stayed by my side with Maddy. Of all Level One, I was strangely comforted by these two the most.

"You can let your girlfriend roam free, Will," Maddy said, snaking an arm possessively around mine. "It's her first proper party with us, after all."

William looked hesitant, but he gave Maddy a tight-lipped smile. He nodded in the direction of a group of unfamiliar boys. "I guess I'll go and say hello, then."

He rested his hand across my waist, his eyes connecting with mine for just a second. His touch lingered long enough to let me know he would return to my side within a second if I needed him.

"Now that he's not lurking, do you want to do some shots?" Maddy offered as soon as William was out of earshot.

"Sure," I said. I planted a sheepish smile on my lips, recalling

William's warning from yesterday. "You know, I'm really not used to drinking very much."

"Well, tonight is a special occasion," Maddy said perkily. I was wondering what exactly she meant by *special occasion*, but before I could process what she said a shot was pressed to my palm. "Drink up."

I did as told, adding a silent promise to myself that I'd be careful about my consumption. I needed to be tipsy enough to blend in, but letting my guard down around Level One could be my downfall.

"Maddy . . . Chloe, there you are," Sophie said as she emerged from the throng of people, her nose upturned in my direction. "Come down the hall. We're going to play a *real* game."

I looked to Maddy, who looked back at me with an unwavering smile. This was it. My first real Level One test.

Lola was in the exquisitely decorated study, perched on the corner of the mahogany desk.

"We should kick the night off with some fun," she said innocently. I noticed an object in her hands, what looked like a sparkling pouch she'd pulled from her bag.

"Chloe's new," Sophie said wickedly, her gaze raking over my skin like cat claws. "She should go first."

"Oh please," Maddy said dismissively, but she seemed interested in whatever was inside the sparkling pouch. "This again?"

Lola's glare could have shattered iron, but her glossed grin didn't falter. "The cards have changed, Madeline. Fresh tasks for fresh meat."

My stomach turned.

Lola giggled delicately before emptying the contents into her palm. It was a deck of cards. She gestured for me to move closer. "Go on, Chloe."

I wasn't familiar with this game.

I took one of the cards, moving to turn it over when Sophie's hand around my wrist stopped me.

"Uh-uh, we turn them over to look once we've all chosen." Her smile was unsettling. "Then we compare at midnight."

I watched as each of the three girls took one for themselves. Lola put the rest back into the little bag. "And let's begin!"

Hesitantly, I flipped over the card.

Steal the phone of a junior

"And . . . go," Lola said, sliding from her perched seat and leading us out of the room. I looked to Maddy, who was smirking with Sophie beside her.

The first thing I did upon returning to the throng of the party was seek out William. The comfort of his presence around the Level Ones might help me collect my thoughts and decide how to handle this secret mission.

"Hey," he said. He was midway through pouring a new drink, and when he saw me coming his way, he offered it to me, grabbing another cup for himself.

I shook my head, cursing under my breath as I looked around, observing the crowd. One thing was for sure, and that was that if I wanted to gain Lola and the other girls' trust, I'd need to complete this task. Impressing them was my in. And I *needed* to impress Lola. I needed her approval desperately if I wanted to gain anything from my status as undercover agent.

Then it struck me. Their joking about competing for her adoration in the limo.

There was a crowd of girls nearby I recognized to be Arlington juniors. I'd never spoken to any of them, but I remembered a few faces from my Instagram stalking. I assessed each as they laughed, trying to work out the easiest target, trying to ignore whatever sinister plan Lola had for their phone.

Then I saw her, Stephanie Griffith, clutching a drink in her hand and scowling at a boy making a crude gesture to suggest she should flash him her underwear.

"Christ," I muttered, shaking the severity of what I was about to do from my conscience and downing William's drink. I motioned to him I'd be right back.

I tried to pretend I was making a beeline for the hallway the girls were standing beside, but doubled back once I passed them, enough to eavesdrop on their conversation. If I stole Stephanie's phone for the Level One girls, it'd be a golden ticket into their good graces. It'd ultimately help me bring them down once and for all. They wouldn't do this to anyone ever again. The guilt was horrific, but right now it was me—the greater good of Arlington—or Stephanie. It was a sacrifice I needed to make.

I could see their purses lying on the shelf behind them.

Three designer purses, and three girls. I narrowed my eyes, trying to decide which belonged to who. This was where all of Monica's babble about accessorizing an outfit came in handy.

Neutral tones with bolder dresses. Stephanie's friends had dresses much bolder than hers, as if she was trying to blend in with the background, avoiding attention. That meant it was likely the jeweled diamante clutch was a better fit than the beige and white leather purses beside it. It was worth a gamble.

Now I just needed a distraction.

I looked around the room, colored lamps illuminating the space of drunken teenagers. I needed invisibility.

I needed darkness.

I stepped back into the hallway, finding what I was looking for. Learning about electrical circuits in physics class was suddenly very valuable. A power outlet half-hidden by a cabinet. I was still holding my drink in my hand, and with a careful glance over my shoulder I splashed the liquid into the socket, just enough to shut off the circuit but hopefully not enough to damage it permanently.

Almost instantly, the house plunged into darkness.

With the darkened sky outside, it was now pitch-black. I probably had seconds before people reached for their phones and turned on their flashlights. Quickly, I headed back into the main room, everyone already in a frenzy. I'd memorized the position of the purse, and I didn't hesitate to grab it, feeling its crystals beneath my fingers as I opened the flap and slid out Stephanie's iPhone, diving away before anybody could see.

A sick feeling bubbled in my stomach. As I hid from view again, hearing people announcing they must've tripped the power with the size of the stereo system, I unlocked the phone. Relief flooded me when I saw it had a password.

At least Stephanie's privacy might be safe.

Just as they managed to restart the power, I found my way to William, who was still in the same corner as before.

"You guys are all crazy," I said when I caught my breath.

"I thought you already knew that," William said, his tone amused. "Can you believe they tripped the power?"

"Crazy," I repeated. In my own purse, Stephanie's phone felt like it weighed a ton. I looked toward the trio of girls, who were currently oblivious as they chatted loudly about the blackout.

"Do you want some air?"

"I'd love some." I'd spoken too soon. Just as I looked wistfully toward the staircase, I spotted Francis and Lola walking briskly across the room, his hand locked possessively around hers. "Where do you think they're going?"

"No idea," William said, taking a drink. "But I'd really rather not know."

Still high on a dirty adrenaline, I bit my lip, debating whether it'd be a good idea to go after them. "I would."

"What are you doing?"

Before I could explain, I was already deep into the crowd of partygoers. Channeling all the stealth I could muster, I scanned for Lola and Francis. I spotted them as they rounded a corner and disappeared down the hall.

I didn't follow immediately. Instead, I paused in the threshold, trying carefully to hear over the music. After a moment, I heard it. The closing of a door.

My gut told me Lola had probably taken Francis back to the study, so I quickly made my way to the room next to it. Thankfully, there was no drunken couple making out in the dark room. It appeared to be a sitting room of some kind, family photographs spanning its walls. I turned to see if the door locked. It did.

I turned to the wall that separated me from Lola and Francis. It probably wasn't thin, but I could only hope to make out at least something. I pressed my ear to the wallpaper.

"How could you, Lola?" The volume of Francis's voice surprised me as it carried through the walls.

"You're pretending you don't do the same thing all the time," Lola said coldly. Her voice was quieter, a little less easy to understand.

"What, brag to people that I'm sleeping around?" he asked.

So, he knew. Maddy must have told him about what I said at the mall. He knew that Lola told me. That was what this was about.

"It was a *joke*, Francis!"

"And you expected Chloe to think it was a joke?"

"Yes! Please, she wasn't going to believe me anyway. It's not even true. I've told you that. We never *actually* slept together."

Lola Davenport was not someone to beg. Maybe Francis Rutherford was enough to make her weak.

"So, word got back to me because she *didn't believe it*, huh? I don't think so."

There was a pause, and I pressed my ear even harder to the wall.

"Are you *trying* to humiliate me?" Francis asked. "Trying to make me look like an idiot?"

"No!" Lola almost shrieked. As someone who always seemed in control, I'd never heard so much emotion from her before.

"You swore to me what happened with Bishop wouldn't get out," he said. "Yet, you still let it."

Then there was the sound of shattering glass. Then silence, broken by what sounded like a frantic sob.

A sudden, unfamiliar feeling ripped through my chest, and I pulled away. I was *worried* for Lola Davenport and what was happening in that room. She was in trouble. I debated whether I should barge in there and break them up. But that would mean I'd be caught spying, and the implications of that would mean an end to my position on Level One. Reluctantly, I resumed my position against the wall.

"How much have you had to drink?" Lola asked, her voice thick with what I assumed to be tears.

"What does that have to do with anything? What matters right now is the fact that my girlfriend's going around talking like a whore."

"I'm sorry, France, you know we never slept together. I wouldn't go that far—I wouldn't do that to you. I *love* you. Why won't you believe me?"

"Because you're clearly full of shit," he spat. "I don't want to see you for the rest of the night."

"You're such a hypocrite!" I heard her scream. I was sure that even those a couple of rooms away would have heard it.

There was the slam of a door, and then footsteps down the hall. My bet was that Francis had left.

Arlington's power couple was certainly much more complicated than I'd thought.

Straightening and shaking out the cramps in my toes, I took a deep breath. The argument next door had sobered me a little. My head didn't sway. But my heart still pounded hard with anxiety, both from the stolen phone in my bag and the fear of getting caught eavesdropping.

I waited five more minutes before sneaking out of the room. The hallway was empty and completely still despite the commotion that had happened only minutes ago. Watching over my shoulder, I headed straight for the bathroom.

After I'd washed my hands, I retouched my lipstick and wiped the stray liner from around my eyes. Once I'd done what I could to touch up my appearance, I went back into the hall.

The study's door was now wide open. As I moved to pass, I caught sight of Sophie's blond hair inside. Before I could look away and continue my trajectory back to the party, she spun on her heels and saw me watching.

"Chloe," Sophie barked. "What are you doing?"

"Um," I said, jumping as if I'd been caught up to no good. "I was going to find Will."

"Come here," she ordered.

I gingerly stepped through the doorway. Inside, the room was mussed, books cleared from the desk and papers askew on the floor. A crystal vase lay shattered on the carpet. Next to it, a very flustered Lola knelt as she picked up the broken shards with a wad of tissues.

Lola looked up, and for the first time I saw imperfections in her appearance. Her makeup was smudged, a line of black tracing down her cheek. One of the straps of her silk dress was hanging loose, revealing her bare shoulder.

This was what I had wanted all along; to discover Lola Davenport's vulnerabilities, and to use them to take her down. But even so, it felt wrong to enjoy the moment. Not when I knew how her drunken boyfriend had terrorized her.

"You better watch yourself, Whittaker," Lola said, her words dripping with scorn, making me slightly reconsider my sympathy.

My mouth fell open in the most innocent way possible even though I knew exactly why she was mad. I'd confided in Maddy about her supposed affair with William.

"So you're spreading rumors to Maddy now." I remained frozen, and she continued impatiently. "If you want to keep dating Will, you better keep your mouth shut around her. She can't be trusted."

"And you can't be trusted either," Sophie added.

I nodded quickly, wondering if she truly had the power to overthrow me from being William's supposed girlfriend, even with my blackmail. I didn't want to push it, though, and it wouldn't help my agenda to try.

"I have something for you," I said feebly, hoping to redeem myself at least a little. I opened my purse, pulling out my card and the phone accompanying it. I knew this was messed up. I knew Stephanie would pay a price, and I could only hope it wouldn't be as severe as the one Monica had. "I know it's before midnight but . . . it's Stephanie Griffith's."

Lola's lips lifted into a devilish smile as her mood seemed to flip. "Maybe you are worth something, after all."

"And to think my card just told me to seduce the host," Sophie said, grinning darkly. "Go. We're done with you."

I didn't need to be told again. I straightened, exiting the room and strutting down the hall as fast as I could. I felt exhilarated. Lola's approval was the most expensive commodity in Wandemore Valley.

It was more difficult than I'd anticipated to find William. Still dazed, I maneuvered in and out of the upstairs crowd. It had grown larger as late night shifted toward early morning.

I noticed Claire gathered in a circle of Level Twos, her cheeks rosy with alcohol and her eyes lingering on someone behind me. I spun around, knowing that look would only have been used on one of the Level Ones.

Unfortunately, it wasn't quite the one I needed. It was just

Zach. He was at the center of a small crowd of people. I was ready to continue my search when I heard his voice over the crowd.

"Just because you're gay doesn't mean I need to talk to you," he said loudly, amusement clear in his tone.

I squinted, trying to identify the guy in front of him. Max Heath, a Level Four at best. A short boy whose parents were new money and had chosen to spend his hefty allowance on collectable vintage video games instead of designer labels. It showed with his bland ill-fitting wardrobe and terrible posture. What he was doing at a party like this, I had no clue.

Max was almost toe-to-toe with Zach, and by now I could see Maddy nearby ogling the situation.

"Did you hear me? Get out of my face, dude."

I couldn't see Max's expression, but from the looks of the partygoers, I could tell he was probably mortified. Had he advanced on Zach? It would be a bold move. Zach was royalty, and Max was openly disliked.

"Chloe."

William startled me, catching my attention just as the Level Four boy backed away.

"Is everything okay?" he asked. He looked toward the commotion. The people gathered were now dispersing.

I nodded once, but hoped he'd still get the clue that I needed him.

"What's up?" he asked, his voice low and slightly slurred with alcohol.

"Francis knew that I knew because Maddy said something. Lola's pissed and—" I took a deep breath. "I stole a girl's phone."

William eyebrows raised. "A phone?"

"It was a dare."

Just as I was speaking, William's attention was diverted to something over my shoulder. Lola had emerged from the hall, her makeup now freshly touched up and any evidence of tears long gone. Her strap had been removed completely, showing off even more skin than before. Her dark eyes were locked intently with William's, pulling out a whirlwind of conflicting feelings from my chest.

I was pissed. God, he was too good for her. I knew that now. From the week we'd spent in this fake relationship I knew that his soul couldn't possibly be as tainted as hers. How could she have a hold on him? And why did it make me so angry?

William placed an arm almost possessively around my waist, knocking me from my enraged thoughts. His eyes didn't drop from Lola as he pulled me closer to him. I was surprised that his touch caused a wave of heat to roll over me—probably from the alcohol I'd drunk.

I reminded myself he was trying to make her jealous. Using *me* to make her jealous. But even that thought excited me.

I studied his face, his moss-colored eyes still fixed on hers across the room. I didn't see affection or adoration within them. They were hard and cold, conflicted and vengeful, as if he wished his gaze could hurt its recipient in the way she was clearly hurting him.

His eyes found mine and softened. Maybe I imagined it. I felt an unfamiliar pull to move my head closer to his. But I stopped myself. I couldn't.

As time seemed to slow, his fingertips brushed my cheek, and before I knew it our lips collided.

THIRTEEN

Mon,

Guilt is eating me alive. I can't believe what I've done. It's like I've lost my moral compass since you left. Sometimes I feel like I'm really turning into Level One. That's stupid, isn't it? After what they did to you?

Though secretly, I will admit, I wonder if you'd have liked me better if I was more like them. You wouldn't have chosen them over me. This wouldn't have happened.

Love, Chloe

IN THAT MOMENT, I hated William Bishop.

My fingers scrunched around the fabric of his shirt where they had been resting between our chests. It took every piece of my willpower not to push him away—to shove him into the hordes of people around us and then slap him in the face.

Logically, this was a good thing. A *great* thing. Lola's jealousy—though dangerous—might be the perfect weapon to help bring her down. Only, I couldn't squash the childish part of me freaking out at William's lips on mine. I'd never kissed anyone before, and I hadn't exactly anticipated it to happen because of a fake relationship, and certainly not to make someone jealous.

My brain was screaming at me to end the kiss, to nudge him lightly, to giggle nervously and slap his shoulders in a way that wouldn't raise suspicion within our audience. But it was futile. My muscles were frozen in shock.

His lips were sweet and firm, warm and in control.

Stealing my first kiss.

I took a step back, my mind finally winning over my body—the part that was secretly indulging in the feeling of his lips against mine.

William looked just as shocked as I did. His hands reached out to stop me; I hadn't even registered that I was already walking backward. This would look terrible for our image, but I just needed to get away. Rage began to fill me so deeply that my breathing came in gasps.

I didn't know what to do. I didn't have anyone to confide in. Monica wasn't here. She couldn't hold me and tell me it would be okay. I paced mindlessly down the hall, wanting to cry out in frustration at the things I'd done just to get in with Level One.

I finally passed the door to the study. Inside, it was eerily quiet. I closed the door behind me, sliding one of the wooden chairs beneath its handle to ensure William wouldn't follow me. My lips still tasted sweet as my tongue ran over them.

This wasn't supposed to happen. I felt used and hurt. Despite how much time we'd spent together, how much we'd talked about, he chose her over me. Despite never agreeing to a kiss, he still took one from me to make her jealous.

He still stole *my* first kiss to hurt *her*.

Forgetting the makeup lining my eyes, I wiped a hand over them in frustration and buried my fingers in my hair. My head was aching. On top of that, my sobering mind was beginning to process exactly what I'd done. The possible hell I'd subjected Stephanie Griffith to.

Looking up, I saw a glint in the darkness. A sparkling pouch on the desk.

Opening it revealed the deck of cards Lola had offered to us earlier. She must have left it in here after she and Francis argued. I began sifting through them, my eyes barely making out the writing.

Remove a piece of clothing for each time someone asks you for a selfie

Double-tap on your crush's Instagram photo from at least two years ago

Collect a Richmond Prep boy's nudes

Seduce someone's boyfriend/girlfriend. Bonus points for pics.

I pulled out my phone from my purse and began snapping each one, the flash lighting up each piece of evidence captured. On their own, they were useless. There was no link to prove they actually belonged to Lola Davenport. But if I collected enough damning evidence, it would contribute to Level One's downfall.

I returned the pouch to where Lola had left it, before ordering an Uber, ready to be as far from this party as possible.

Sunday was spent in my room surrounded by textbooks and blasting my favorite music through my headphones, fast guitar riffs and loud vocals. It helped drown out my thoughts. I didn't know what happened to Lola after I left, or her reaction to William's grab for her attention.

It kept playing through my mind, the feeling of his lips on mine, one of his hands raised to my cheek, his fingers lingering in the roots of my hair while the other held my waist. His overwhelming scent and the heat of his body still felt as if it was enveloping me.

And on top of that, the most trivial, unnecessary thought of all: What did *he* think of it? Did he feel the same pull toward me that I had felt toward him? Or were his thoughts dominated by Lola?

What bothered me most was that tomorrow I'd have no choice but to resume normality. I knew this wouldn't be easy, but I hadn't anticipated that William Bishop would cause so much trouble.

Facing him was inevitable, but for now I could ignore him. Well, until my phone chimed on my bedside table.

I'm so sorry. I didn't mean for it to happen.

No, I thought in response, but didn't type. *Just leave me alone.*

Instead, I pushed aside the weakness of my feelings and reminded myself of my plan.

Don't forget what's at stake here, William.

Almost instantly, he responded.

I'll make it up to you. I promise.

I shoved my phone away, needing a day to stop pretending. To just be *me*. I didn't go to the gym or plan my outfits for the week like New Chloe would have been doing to keep her place on Level One. Instead, I abandoned my homework and headed downtown, strolling the streets and window-shopping. The more I walked, killing time in book exchanges and antique shops, the more I felt like I was escaping Arlington's superficial world.

But even so, the kiss never fully escaped my mind.

I certainly wouldn't go easy on William Bishop when it was time to take him down.

Monday came too soon. I was up earlier than usual, doing my makeup and trying to find a new jacket to match my plaid skirt and crisp shirt. Today, when I painted my lips with the color of a blooming rose, I wasn't reminded of Monica or the countless times we'd played dress-up. Instead, I was reminded of the way my lips had pressed against William's.

My first class was physics, and I took a detour past the populated corridors of campus, deciding to bypass my locker and keep my bag with me instead. The longer I could avoid William, the better.

But it turned out it was all for nothing. He was standing in front of my classroom, despite the fact that he didn't even take physics.

And if that wasn't unusual enough to spark speculation among onlookers, then the large bouquet of roses in his hands definitely was. If it wasn't for the crowd of people slowly gathering around us, I was sure I wouldn't hesitate to storm off fuming. Or shove his bouquet where it belonged.

But I couldn't do that with an audience.

The whispers of girls beside me caught my attention as time seemed to slow around our little spectacle. *He's so gorgeous*, I heard. *Why isn't she moving? What's going on?*

I knew I didn't really have an option. Not with Monica at the forefront of my mind.

Spreading the most love-struck smile over my face, I took another step toward William's outstretched arm, where the bouquet sat in all its blossoming glory.

It was heavier than it looked as I cradled it in my elbow,

careful not to meet his eyes again. Instead I studied the roses. The deep green leaves framing them almost matched his gaze perfectly.

Aware of the onlookers surrounding us, I tried to bashfully head toward class without a word, but then he pulled something else from his pocket. A *Tiffany's* box.

My cheeks reddened.

"I'm sorry," William murmured, only audible between us.

"You think this will win me over?"

"No," he replied. His gaze crossed the small crowd milling around us. "But it'll win them over."

I looked to the onlookers gawking at the roses in my arms. He was right. I gave him a glare that only he could see, before taking the box from him too.

"I need to get to class."

"Look inside the box," he said, pushing it into my free palm. "The flowers were for them. This is for you."

When I'd finally settled in the safety of my desk, the roses lying on the windowsill beside me—still managing to capture attention as students turned in their seats to ogle them—I opened the small box in my lap. Inside, there was no sparkle of jewelry. Only a folded piece of paper.

Three twenty-five at the boys' change rooms. Locker nine.

At lunch, the Level One table was alive with chatter about the weekend's party. I was sitting next to Maddy, who was feigning annoyance with me for leaving the party without telling her. She, and everyone else, seemed to be oblivious to whatever happened between Lola and Francis, or even Lola and William, who sat side by side opposite me, reserved looks upon their faces.

I wondered what punishment Lola was concocting for me. I started brainstorming methods to win her over. The phone was one thing but I'd need to try to cozy up more than that if I wanted more intel. In between ideas, I watched William from the corner of my eye, wondering just what information he had waiting for me.

The salad in front of me was busy suffering a brutal stabbing from my fork when the Level One table fell quiet. I looked up to see what had captured their attention, and my heart dropped when I realized it was Stephanie Griffith.

She looked terrified as Principal Neal led her out of the cafeteria. I never saw Neal leave her office, not unless it was serious.

Sophie began snickering, and William turned toward the girls. "What did you do?"

"Oh, we didn't do anything," Lola said, a wicked glint in her eye. It made me squirm in my seat to see her address him directly. Was I really still squeamish about their affair? "I heard a rumor someone reported her for having some pretty damning photos on her phone. You know. Drugs. Alcohol."

"Who would have known?" Zach added with amusement. If the boys were involved, then it was a whole new level of takedown.

My blood ran cold. This was my fault. I knew Level One would do something awful, I wasn't completely naive, but for them to do it so soon—before I'd had the chance to put a stop to them for good—left me feeling defeated.

But as much as my stomach turned with the guilt of what I had done, I couldn't squish the small trace of dark adrenaline circulating through my system. For the first time in my life, after never once causing a ripple in the student body, I felt a taste of what it must be like to be a Level One. I felt powerful.

FOURTEEN

Okay, Monica,

I admit. I'm starting to understand it, at least a little. The appeal of being on Level One. Everyone's attention on you, sitting at that table like you're on a damn throne. It's a power I've never had before, an adrenaline that puts you on a high.

The allure is a poison. But it's also a cure. I'm going to use the power it gives me as an antidote to their reign, to make sure they can't infect anyone else.

Love, Chloe

AT THREE O'CLOCK the bell rang, signaling the end of the day's classes, prompting the corridors to flood with students mingling and gossiping. It wasn't a minute too soon. I'd sat through the whole class of Claire's mindless babble about what Lola and Sophie were wearing Saturday night, and if I had to endure any more, I was going to lose my mind.

I was nervous to venture to the locker rooms. They were in an external building near the sports field. I hadn't set foot in the area since Monica dragged me to a lacrosse game last year.

I'd expected them to be bustling with activity. William might have wanted to meet me just before training, maybe his time was limited. Why else would he give such a precise time? At lunch, I'd been careful not to push the subject, worried I'd either raise suspicion or that whatever secret he held was just too sensitive to acknowledge aloud.

Whatever it was, it better be worth it.

I hesitated in the threshold of the building. What I'd expected to be an atmosphere filled with testosterone and Arlington's sweaty lacrosse team was an empty room lined with benches and tall metal lockers. I was reminded of my locker in the main school building, awaiting me with an overflow of budding roses.

Locker nine. Something about locker nine was supposed to hold my interest. I strode over to it, trying not to let my gaze linger on the less-than-clean surroundings on the way.

Locker nine was slightly ajar. Casting a look over my shoulder to see if he was waiting nearby, I pried it open. The door slung forward to reveal a navy uniform hanging on the rack. I pulled at the shirt, the back of the jacket reading *Bishop*.

Then something else caught my attention. It was a piece of paper taped to the inside of the door, the writing large and clear. *HIDE*.

I didn't have much time to decipher exactly what William meant by his message, because just as I'd ripped it from the door I heard the sound of footsteps outside the change rooms. In a split second I decided to follow William's instruction, and squeezed into the slim space of the locker before I could be busted.

Wedged between clothing, a lacrosse stick, and the smell of William's cologne, I was barely able to see through the thin slats grooved into the metal. My heart was beating hard now, both in anticipation for whatever was to be revealed and the fear that I would be caught.

The sound of someone entering the room made the hair at the back of my neck stand on end. Squinting my eyes, I could barely make out the face, but their dark skin and height gave them away. It was Zachary Plympton.

For a few long minutes the two of us were silent, Zach completely oblivious of my presence as he paced slowly around the room. I wondered what he was doing out here if practice wasn't on and the coach wasn't around.

Suddenly, he stopped.

"I know you're there."

I froze, almost dropping my cell to the floor.

"Hey, can't say I didn't try and catch you off guard."

I let out a silent breath of relief. He hadn't seen me. But the intruder brought me a new wave of alertness. Was that *Max Heath*?

What would he want with Zachary Plympton, especially

after their encounter at the party? And more important, what would the highly esteemed lacrosse star Zachary Plympton want with *him*?

"You're pissed at me," Zach said. "I know."

"Pissed is a complete understatement," Max responded.

"I've got an image to uphold, Max. You know what'd happen if someone knew."

Then it struck me. I suddenly understood their secret rendezvous.

"So you publicly humiliate me?"

"You gave me no choice," Zach said. "It showed *exactly* how much I care about you, and what I'd do to protect us."

Holy shit.

Silently, I opened the door just a crack. Enough for my phone's camera lens to poke through, ready to capture whatever scandal was about to reveal itself.

"I hated doing that, Max. I can't believe you'd make me do it."

"I thought you said you were ready to be serious with me," Max murmured.

"God, not like that. Not in front of my friends."

"You think keeping us a secret is protecting me? Your friends already make my life hell. This is about your reputation, isn't it?"

"No. Don't you understand? It would be so much worse if they knew I was dating you. For both of us. I don't care about my reputation. I care about us being happy."

I had to stifle a snort. That sounded like bullshit.

"Really?"

"Really."

And then I watched their figures become one as Zach drew his lover in for a kiss.

"You know I'd do anything for you, Max. I love you."

FIFTEEN

Monica,

Do you remember that time in elementary school when you asked me if I'd ever thought about running away?

I hadn't at the time, but you had.

I didn't understand what you meant when you said you hated the pressure your parents put on you to look good in front of all their friends. Now that we're older, I can see how that made you want to control things as we grew up. I think part of the reason we're best friends is because I let you be in control. I never minded, as long as I had you by my side.

But you can't control everything. I guess you know that now.

Love, Chloe

I DON'T THINK I took a breath for at least fifteen minutes after the newly outed lovebirds had left the room. But when I did, I erupted into motion, flinging open the locker doors and grabbing William's note before anyone else could find it. My boots slapped against the cobblestone footpath as I scampered to my locker.

What William was thinking, I had no clue. I was still in shock that one of the most yearned-for bachelors of Arlington had a secret Level Four boyfriend. Shaking the thought from my mind for now, I grabbed the roses and my bag from my locker before making my way to the parking lot.

Just as I'd hoped, a certain silver BMW was still idling by the exit. I didn't hesitate to open the passenger door and claim the seat which I'd sat in so many times this past week.

"Well, that was interesting," I said. What an understatement. A Level One having a secret affair with a commoner—let alone someone as low on the social ladder as Max—was unheard of. The fact that Zach had made a mockery of him at the party only made it all the more juicy.

"It worked out, then?" he asked, his eyes fixed straight ahead.

"How did you know?"

"I've stumbled in on them a few times. They meet there in the locker room on most Monday afternoons. I don't think they know I saw them. It's just something I've been sitting on," he said. "And then seeing what happened at the party . . . How terribly Zach treated him . . ."

"William Bishop, you and I have much more in common than I thought," I said, a small, hysterical laugh slipping from my lips.

"I knew flowers or jewelry wouldn't mean much to you as an apology. But secrets might. I hope you can forgive me. At least a little."

He was right. He could have showered me in gifts, but none were as valuable as ammunition to my plan. I felt almost gleeful.

"I'm still unbelievably pissed at you," I said, but my tone didn't match my words. For now, this new information had pushed William's misdeed to the back of my mind.

"You know, I really am sorry," William said. "I didn't even consider you in what I did—you've even told me before that you didn't want PDA. I wasn't thinking, and I don't ever want to do that to anyone again. Especially you."

"It wasn't just you kissing me," I reminded him. "It was because you did it to make her jealous."

"I know."

I bit my lip for half a second before deciding my next words. They came out fast when I finally found the courage to speak them. "And you stole my first kiss."

"First kiss?" he asked, looking genuinely surprised.

"Yep."

"I'm an idiot," he said. I studied his face, searching for any flaws in his apologetic expression. But I found none. He seemed genuinely guilty.

"Pick me up tomorrow?" I said, breaking the silence.

"Sure," he said, but I was already opening the door and

stepping back out into the school parking lot. I gave him one last small smile before turning and walking toward my Audi.

Unusually, my mother was nowhere to be seen when I arrived home. I hesitantly walked down the hall.

"Mom?" I asked, knocking my fist against the polished wood of her bedroom door. I heard a groan, giving me approval to enter.

She was lying in bed, her hand dramatically tossed over her forehead, her palm stuffed with tissues.

"What's wrong?" I asked, dropping onto the corner of the bed.

"I'm *fine*," she insisted, her words slurred. I looked to her bedside table to find an empty bottle of champagne. "Chloe, your outfit is so *cute*. When did you start dressing so cute? Is it for the mayor's son?"

"Mom," I scolded. "Where's Dad?"

My mother let out a rattled sigh. "He just left for New York to visit . . . a friend from high school. No, baseball. Actually, his cousin. He's seeing his cousin."

I let my lips sink into a straight line. Of course, this was because of Dad. Why didn't he at least try to cover up his shady "business trips" better?

"Look, Mom, I'm going to take a shower and then I'll come in here and we can put some movies on and go to sleep."

"Like when you were a kid, sleeping in my bed because you were scared of the monsters next door." This brought forth a drunken giggle. "Oh, the monsters. They were really the Barkers' greyhound puppies next door."

I smiled at the memory, thinking of how much my family life had crumbled since the days where my greatest fear stemmed from the pets next door. As I became older, I outgrew my rose-colored glasses. "I'll be back in a second, Mom."

"Don't take too long," she said. "I want to hear all about William Bishop when you're back."

SIXTEEN

Mon,

I can always go to my mom when I'm feeling down. I mean, I go to you about 90 percent of things, but there's always that 10 percent that only she can understand.

Sometimes I thought you were jealous of that. It's never been the same for you. Your mom would go ballistic if she knew half the things you keep from her. And add your dad, and the combined pressure . . . well, I know you're too afraid to ever talk to them about anything more than the superficial.

You know I've always been here, right? I know it's not the same. But it's something.

Love always,
Chlo

WHEN NEITHER LOLA nor Sophie made any clear attempt to take me down for the rest of the week, I started to wonder if the stolen phone had really redeemed me in their eyes after the slip of information to Maddy. Things were starting to go to plan. William would pick me up in the morning while my mother peeked nosily through the curtains. Then we'd separate and go to class, only to meet again at lunchtime.

On Friday, the conversations at the table revolved around that night's lacrosse game and heated debates on who was wearing what for the after-party at Maddy's. William and Francis argued over who played better in attack, Sophie chiming in with her opinion occasionally, while Zach and Maddy gave a detailed analysis of the other team's players. It sounded incredibly complicated.

And I stayed mostly silent. I smiled and tried to contribute at appropriate times, but I was mostly observing. *Sophie keeps looking over her shoulder toward the doorway. Is she waiting for someone? Lola and Francis look a little more affectionate today. Did Zach just openly glance over his shoulder toward Max?*

Like everyone else at school I was counting down the minutes until the bell rang, although unlike them, the start of the weekend meant my work was just beginning. When the afternoon finally arrived, I rushed home to change into what I was beginning to think of as my armor. Of course, I had a wardrobe disaster when the semi-casual dress I had picked decided not to zip up at the back. After tugging, sucking in my stomach, and swearing, I managed to break the clasp and ruin it.

By the time I found a new skirt to match the boots I'd been saving for the occasion, I barely had enough time to throw my cell and lip gloss into a purse before Mom dropped me back to campus. The parking lot was full of students, all sporting some kind of navy or gold, Arlington's team colors. I first cursed myself for not considering the color scheme, and then cursed myself again for leaving my jacket on the back of the chair in my bedroom.

I could already see William standing at the end of the field as I walked to the stadium. Even I had to admire how good he looked in his navy captain's jacket and shorts, his brow furrowed in thought as he discussed something with the coach.

When he saw me, his face brightened, and he jogged through the milling crowd to greet me. I had to admit, it felt special to see the parted students turn around and gawk as he wrapped me into a hug.

Don't you dare think about his lips, Chloe Whittaker.

"Why didn't you bring a jacket?" William asked as he pulled away. I hadn't even noticed my arms scatter in goose bumps. The temperature must have dropped ten degrees since classes had finished.

"I was in a rush. Didn't want to miss the game."

William smiled, the sun catching a dimple in his cheek as he shrugged off his jacket. "Here. I am your boyfriend, after all."

"Really, William, you're not my type," I joked, mimicking something he'd told me weeks ago. But even so, blush creeped to my cheeks. Taking William Bishop's jacket *did* label him as my boyfriend, loud and clear. I mean, it literally had his last name printed on the back.

"Anyway, I should get back to warm-ups," he said. "Enjoy the game, Whittaker."

He shot me a smile over his shoulder, a few of his teammates turning to slap his back and undoubtedly make idiotic remarks about how he was not only going to score in the game, but also with me tonight.

I hadn't attended many Arlington sports games. I'd watched a few of Monica's soccer matches in sophomore year, but she quit the team before the end of the season and I found myself pretty bored by them anyway, not that I'd ever tell her that. I wasn't exactly one for school spirit.

But lacrosse games were popular. People stood in clusters by the bleachers, some wearing clothing that was much dressier than a game would warrant. They were undoubtedly the students invited to tonight's exclusive after-party.

I was pacing around awkwardly, trying to spot at least one member of Level One, when I ran into Claire and Jack. Each of them was carrying a bucket of fries and sporting wide grins.

"Chloe!" Jack said enthusiastically, throwing an arm over my shoulder. "Nice school spirit. Want some?"

"No thanks," I replied meekly, casting a side glance to make sure Sophie wasn't around this time.

"Come sit with us," Claire said, her smile hopeful.

"Or you could go sit with your *new* friends," Jack said, the smile not faltering from his face.

I shot them a sympathetic look. "I might have to. We're

trying to get things ready for the party and they're expecting me to be there to help . . ."

Jack looked to Claire and raised a brow. "A party?"

"You weren't told?" I asked, then grimaced. Jack and Claire were usually welcome as Level Twos—Level One needed an audience, after all—but maybe this party was more exclusive than I'd thought. "It's at Maddy's house. You guys should come."

"Really?" Jack asked doubtfully.

"Sure," I said, my voice an octave too high. Then I spotted Sophie's ash-blond hair in the crowd. "Look, I'll text you the details, but I have to go now."

"Okay," Jack said, his voice wary. "We'll see you later, then."

I nodded quickly. I couldn't decide whether inviting them was a mistake, or if their presence could be comforting.

Sophie led me to Lola and Maddy. The three of them had their own exclusive area in the stands, a defined partition created with a row of empty seats on either side. Something told me there was an unspoken agreement that those seats stayed empty.

I was grateful to see a vacant spot beside Maddy. I didn't know what I'd do if they'd excluded me.

"Cute jacket!" Maddy said as I approached. "You two are so adorable."

I took that as a compliment to my acting, even if William and I being an *adorable* couple brought strange feelings to my gut. I figured my blush was fitting. "How long before it starts?"

"Five minutes," Maddy said. Then her attention landed on the field and she was back to gushing about her latest Richmond player crush. "Oh, see that tall one over there? Number two? That's the one."

"Hey," Lola interrupted, obviously tired of Maddy's infatuation. "Did anyone invite Desmond tonight?"

Sophie and Lola exchanged looks before Maddy let out a sigh. "Crap, no, I totally forgot."

"Desmond?" I asked innocently.

"He's our photographer," Maddy explained. "He usually puts together videos of our parties. He just got back from an extended summer break. He goes to Richmond, actually."

I needed to squeeze my nails tight into my palms to stop myself from betraying my thoughts. *The photographer actually exists?* Of course I'd pondered the idea, I'd even done a ton of research since I concocted my plan, but the only conclusion I'd ever made was that Monica was exaggerating. Level One wasn't *really* conceited enough to have their own photographer.

But maybe they were.

I begged my voice to stay level. "Oh, I've never seen one before. You'll have to show me sometime."

"We don't post them," Sophie said. "It's more a way we can look back on old memories. We don't exactly want to share *everything* publicly."

I could read through the lines enough to make my own conclusion. The footage was just another tendon bonding them into the highly coveted and unbreakable group they'd become over the years. Collecting videos meant group liability. One member couldn't break without the entire group breaking. Everyone had to keep their mouths shut, maintaining their exclusivity. When your friendship group contained cashed-up teens from the country's most influential families, there was more at stake than high school gossip when it came to insider secrets getting out.

I pinned my lips shut. My heart was beating fast. If footage of Level One parties did exist, and Desmond was in the right place at the right time on that monumental night, then there was proof of what really happened to Monica.

It had the potential to be the perfect weapon to take them all down, and finally get justice for my best friend.

I'd never realized what a brutal game lacrosse was. Our seats gave us a perfect view of the field, where navy-and-gold uniforms clashed barbarically for a white rubber ball the size of my fist. I could now understand why each player was dressed in what looked like a suit of armor.

Watching William made me uncomfortable. I swear I winced every time he collided with another player or their stick. It was obvious why he was captain, though. He scored four goals, leading the team to victory.

"Come on!" Maddy yelled over the crowd's applause. "We should go down there and congratulate them."

Though they didn't look half as enthusiastic, Sophie and

Lola joined us as we maneuvered between the cheering sea of navy.

"Everyone's looking at you," Maddy whispered into my ear as she linked her arm in mine. "You're wearing the last name of the best player."

I looked around to see a number of eyes pinned on me, darting away as soon as I noticed. One remained, though, and that was the cold stare of Lola Davenport trailing behind us.

The boys took a while to come off the field. They were too busy basking in the joy of the win. When they did, they were still breathing deeply and covered in mud and sweat, helmets and sticks in hand.

"Congratulations," Sophie said loudly as the Level One boys walked our way, flanked by the remainder of the team as they filtered through the crowd one by one.

"Thanks, Soph," Zach said. "Where were your pom-poms?"

"Must have left them in the car," she said with a smirk.

I looked between them. It must have been a private joke.

I jumped when someone's arm snaked its way over my shoulder and squeezed me close. "What did you think?"

William's eyes were bright jade against the flush of his skin. His hair was pushed out of his face, slick with moisture, and his scent enveloped me.

"It was rough," I said when my mind and lips finally found the ability to work together again. "I can't believe you can do all that."

William laughed, and I felt his chest rise and fall against

me. The way his arm rested around my shoulder could have either been for show or simply a friendly gesture. I couldn't tell which. Nearby, I could see Francis whispering in Lola's ear.

"But congratulations," I continued. "You played really well."

"Wow, a compliment from *Chloe Whittaker*?" he asked in mock surprise.

"Don't get used to it," I said, smiling despite my words.

"Wouldn't dare it. Anyway, we better shower. We'll see you girls back at Maddy's, right?"

"I think that's the plan."

He slapped the shoulders of the others before the three of them headed toward the showers. I turned to look for Maddy, who had been beside me moments ago, but she was already talking to number two from Richmond Prep.

It was almost dark when we piled into the chauffeured car taking us to the Danton house.

It was already crawling with caterers and cleaners when we arrived. Maddy's house was classic, giving off a rustic feel with its wooden panels and antique decor.

Maddy welcomed us into her home by retrieving two bottles of expensive wine and passing them to her guests. She laughed, tossing her curly black hair over one shoulder before finding a third on the shelf, pulling the cork and downing two large gulps.

Sophie rolled her eyes. "Such a show-off, Maddy."

After we'd each toasted to Arlington's win—despite the actual players having not even arrived—the girls went into Maddy's home makeup studio.

It was incredibly glamorous, lights framing the edge of each mirror and exquisite marble counters lining the walls. I stood in the threshold, watching as the girls laughed and placed themselves onto the stools surrounding the room.

"Come on, Chloe, sit," Maddy said enthusiastically, patting the seat beside her. I smiled and obeyed, swiveling on the seat and catching a glimpse of my reflection in the mirror.

"Shots," Maddy ordered to a caterer as they passed the wide entrance of the room. "An entire tray, one of every spirit you can find."

"Hey, Chloe," Lola said, her gaze eating me up. "Can you handle your liquor?"

I laughed nervously as the other girls gave enthusiastic grins, their attention locked on me. "Of course."

"Are you proposing a game?" Sophie asked, her interest piqued.

"We may as will kill time while we wait for the others." Lola's narrow eyes glazed over us, her attention landing on Maddy. "Equilibrium."

"Sounds fun," Maddy said, her smirk pulling to the side, dimpling her cheek. "In fact, perfect with a newbie."

I tried to convey enthusiasm as I tried to figure out what she meant.

"Right," Sophie said, her expression so full of glee I could only describe it as wicked. "I'll explain the rules."

I shifted in my seat, wondering how I could participate and still maintain control over the party.

"Equilibrium," she began, "is a game we designed ourselves. To get everybody on the same level."

I held my breath as she allowed for a dramatic pause. *Level One wants us on the same level? Ironic.* The caterer returned with a large tray of shots, their colors ranging from clear liquid to a minty green.

"It's a reversal of Never Have I Ever. The less experienced players get drunker. The innocent girls catch up to the"—her eyes landed on me—"not so innocent."

"Everybody is equal," Lola finished. "In *equilibrium*."

We moved our stools to a circle, the shots in the middle. My mind was already trying to calculate ahead of time. I needed to earn their approval, but I was also aware this game was specifically designed to target me. To embarrass me and remove my inhibitions.

"Right, I'll start," Sophie said with a smug smile. "Something simple. Sex."

I looked around with burning cheeks as each girl in the circle raised their pointer fingers to their lips, as if they'd never speak of their escapade.

I considered faking it, to blend in. But I had a feeling they'd question it, and without the support of William—the only one in Level One I could control—I felt my confidence to lie compromised.

Reluctantly, I reached forward to grab a shot. It was slightly brown. Maybe tequila. I gulped it, keeping my eyes closed as the fire trailed down my throat.

"Oh my God, seriously, Chloe?"

"A *virgin*?"

"Leave her alone," Lola's voice came, its tone tinged with amusement. "No shaming, right, girls?"

I ignored the embarrassment, trying to raise my jaw with confidence. "Next."

"My turn," Maddy said. "Hmm . . . Cheating."

I noted Lola's guarded expression holding Maddy's for a fraction of a second. Then her finger came to her lips, and Maddy did the same.

Sophie and I drank, again the burn enough to bring tears behind my eyes.

Lola didn't hesitate, her gaze still locked with Maddy's. "Screwing two boys at once."

Maddy narrowed her eyes as a manicured finger came to her mouth. The rest of us drank.

I hesitantly spoke my statement, glad to get a round of relief. "Uh . . . cheated on a test."

The girls laughed, not a single one drinking.

"Made out with a girl."

"Gone home with someone from Richmond Prep."

My stomach was turning by the time it was Lola's turn again. She cocked her head, her tone smooth. "Betrayed a friend."

I couldn't tell if it was my body protesting the shots or if I was just becoming drunk enough to reveal a vulnerability.

I brought a finger to my lips.

By the time I left the room, my feet were unsteady and my ears were ringing. The tray of shots had been devoured.

People had started arriving, including Arlington's lacrosse team. I was starting to feel dizzy from all the people, some I didn't even know, enveloping us all in hugs and introductions.

You're such an idiot, Chloe, a voice in my head whispered harshly into my ear. *You're here for Monica, and you went and got drunk. After all you've seen them do, now you're vulnerable.*

Just as my instinct was convincing me to run from the crowd, I saw William, his smile warm as he chatted with someone over the sea of heads. I immediately shifted through the people to reach him, his company feeling safer than anyone else's.

When he saw me he quickly excused himself and dragged me to the side of the room instead. "Hey, are you okay?"

I nodded quickly, then shook my head, then laughed and nodded again. I couldn't show my weakness in proximity of the Level One girls. "I'm fantastic! This party is so fun."

I was turning into a mess. You could clearly hear the alcohol breaking my tone.

"What happened?" he asked.

I didn't want to say. I was too ashamed to tell him I'd caved into pressure and consumed enough alcohol to make my feet stumble and my stomach turn.

But the look I gave him must have told him everything he needed to know, because he sighed in frustration and started leading me toward the back of the house. "How could you get like this, Chloe?"

I let out a giggle, the beat of the music somehow infiltrating my thoughts and making me want to dance, to rejoin the party, but William's serious look kept me put.

His hair was still wet from a shower, and he smelled of pine soap and fresh clothes. He was still holding my hand, despite hardly anyone being around to justify the intimate contact.

"Stay here. I'm getting you water," he said before dropping my hand and disappearing from view.

Despite my drunken euphoria, an anxious feeling was growing as a weight across my chest. I was frustrated by how much I was relying on William to be my safe person. And how much the memory of his lips on mine was like honey—sweet and warm and sticking in my mind hard.

I realized someone was pressing a cold bottle into my palm and that there were hands on my shoulders guiding me to a couch outside.

The air was cold on my face, helping to sober me as I gulped down as much as I could of the cool water.

"I'm an idiot," I said, and when I looked at him again, I couldn't look away. Maybe it was a combination of our closeness, his lips, and my significant intoxication, but the nearness of William was slowly overwhelming my senses.

He sighed, his eyes searching my face for something I couldn't quite place. "I shouldn't have let you go with them alone."

"Isn't that the whole point?" I asked.

He sat beside me, so close our bodies were pressed against each other. I was starting to feel drowsy and dizzy, like I could easily collapse from my seated position, so I instinctively reached out to grab his arm.

At first, he stiffened, but then he relaxed against my touch. His other hand moved to brush away the tangle of hair that had fallen in front of my face.

"How long will it take to sober up?" I asked.

"Maybe a few hours," he said with a chuckle that vibrated against my side. "You're going to feel like shit tomorrow."

I groaned, and then leaned my cheek against his shoulder when my neck became too weak. I could still hear the music inside, but outside seemed so peaceful. His steady breathing was the only thing I could feel.

God, when had I become so attracted to William? The alcohol was the only explanation. Under normal circumstances, there was no way my heartbeat would speed up just at the feeling of his skin beneath mine.

I raised my head, hoping that detaching from him as much as possible would help me think clearer, but it didn't. He was staring at me, looking concerned, his eyes burning into mine. And when my gaze dropped to his lips, I stood up abruptly.

"I'm going to use the bathroom," I muttered. Before I could do something stupid. Like kiss him.

SEVENTEEN

Monica,

I always wondered what it would have been like to be you. You were bright, from your hair to your smile. I was darker, darker hair, a darker sense of humor, a darker style. You could make anybody like you.

I'm different. I feel like I have to try so hard. I was always jealous of you in that sense. You're scared of nothing. How do you do that, Monica? You see something and you fight for it. I overthink to the point I just don't know anymore. You've really taught me a lot over the years. I don't know who I'd be if you weren't my best friend.

Love, Chloe

AS SOON AS I found a bathroom, I leaned over the toilet bowl and threw up. When the worst of it had passed, I feebly stood, my knees bumping together as they shook. I reached out to support myself on the counter and turned the tap on at the sink. Catching my reflection in the mirror almost made me throw up again. There was a trail of black mascara seeping down each cheek from the vomit-induced tears, and I was ghostly pale.

I cupped water in my hands and scrubbed at my cheeks and mouth, trying to rid myself of the dirty feeling that had crept over me. The ends of my hair felt gross too, so I ran them under water. I searched through the drawer below the basin and found a tube of toothpaste, which I put onto my finger in an attempt to brush my teeth.

I couldn't stay at the party looking like a wreck, not around Level One.

I was trying to control the uneven intake of my breath when the door flung open. I hadn't even thought to lock it in my haste to get to the toilet.

Platinum-blond hair and ruby red lips told me it was Sophie even before I could process the exuberant expression on her face.

"Oh, sweetie, I knew you had issues, but bulimia?" she asked, closing and locking the door behind us before plonking her purse onto the counter.

I couldn't even find the strength to tell her off.

"Aw," she cooed, cupping my cheek in her hand. "It's okay. Everyone struggles with their weight from time to time."

I gulped, trying to stop myself from projecting vomit

down the front of Sophie's cleavage. She reached behind her and into her purse, pulling out her phone.

The camera flashed. I moved to shield my face with my hand, but it was too late. The evidence of my drunken state was now in the hands of a Level One.

As my eyes readjusted, the blinding light leaving stains on my vision, I could see Sophie in the mirror touching up her lipstick.

"You know," she said, catching my eye in the mirror. "This wasn't exactly a party you could invite your own friends to."

"Wh-what?" I asked, my words involuntarily stuttering.

Sophie rolled her eyes. "The freckled girl and the Asian guy?"

Claire and Jack.

"I didn't think anyone would care," I said, my voice frail.

Sophie sighed dramatically. "Well, we do. You're so ignorant, Chloe. You honestly have no idea."

I was growing too tired to make sense of her words. I was now struggling to even keep my eyes open.

"Listen to me, Chloe," she said, her sweet tone growing sharper. "You might be hanging with us while you're dating Will, but just know that *none* of us are your friend. Not even Maddy."

My mouth opened weakly to respond, but Sophie pressed a finger against my lips to silence me.

"You should know that we all have Lola's back. If she

doesn't like you, then neither do we. You better watch it, because one wrong move and we'll destroy you, little Chloe. Will can't protect you forever."

"Sophie, I—"

"Shh, you don't have to talk anymore." Her electric eyes were wild, as if she was getting a rush from threatening me. "Nobody wants you here, anyway. You have no idea how stupid your fat thighs look with that skirt. Everyone's staring, Chloe. Everyone."

Sophie let out a humorless laugh as she straightened. The door closed behind her and I let out a rattled breath, a foul taste in my mouth.

It took a long time for me to leave the bathroom. I wanted to be home where I could cry in secret, my hopes of revenge seeming pathetic in comparison to the power someone like Sophie wielded.

I did my best to step out without attracting attention from the crowds of people laughing and drinking. The whiff of vodka as I passed a group of friends doing shots made my insides recoil dangerously.

All I wanted to do was find William and leave.

Sophie's words continued to run through my brain like razor blades. I was starting to suffocate with paranoia. *Everyone's staring, Chloe. Everyone.*

I let out a shaky breath, screwing my eyes shut for a moment. *Find William and leave.*

"Chloe!"

Thank God. "I need to go."

William's face was contorted in worry as he pulled me to the side of the party. "What's wrong?"

"Nothing," I said, my throat thick with emotion. "I just want to go home."

I could tell my dismissal bothered him. Thankfully, his obvious desire to interrogate me came second to his concern.

"Sure. Okay. I'll get an Uber."

We walked in silence through the crowd of people. I tried to keep my head down and avoid eye contact. I felt a few pairs of eyes follow me as William led me across the room. I wondered what it was like to go to a party to have fun. For Level One, it seemed like these gatherings were purely to torment people and enjoy the drama.

When the driver finally pulled up, William opened the door for me and followed me in. I found my shoulders relaxing into the heated leather seats.

William's lips were in a straight line. He wasn't saying anything, and it took a few moments for me to realize the silence felt abnormal.

"What are you thinking?"

He took a while to respond, and when he did his words came slow.

"I'm thinking that maybe it's my fault. Everything with Monica. After seeing how they can manipulate even you . . . I was in a perfect position to warn her, but I didn't. I let her get comfortable. I could have stepped in, you know? Saved her. But I always stick up for them."

My heart stopped cold, my complete attention now stolen to his words. "Why?"

"Because I grew up in this world, Chloe. I understand them. I understand *us*. And it's not all bad. I know all of us have some good inside, even if it's hidden. That's the part Monica saw, and it's all she wanted. To fit into our group. I couldn't exclude her." He was silent for a few more moments. "I don't know, I just never thought it would get so dangerous . . ."

I straightened in my seat, watching him in the darkness of the back seat. I couldn't tell him it wasn't his fault. Because, it partially was. That's why he was on the list to begin with. But I wasn't sure if that felt right anymore.

I couldn't find the words to continue the conversation, my voice stolen by a thick lump in my throat. We spent the rest of the ride in silence. When the vehicle finally stopped outside of my home, William stepped out to open my door.

"I'll be back in a moment," he murmured to the driver.

The air was cold, and my legs weren't very good at taking my weight again. William steadied me patiently as I swayed. Then he helped me unlock the gate before walking me all the way to the front door.

"There's something wrong," William stated. He must have noticed the pained look imprinted on my face.

"Tonight was a mess. I just want to sleep and forget about it."

William took a deep breath, his eyes darting over mine. "Are you going to be okay by yourself?"

I nodded in response, my hair blowing over my eyes. I tucked it roughly behind my ear. Was he . . . offering to stay with me?

My eyes sank to the floor, and for a moment, I considered it. If my parents weren't an issue, and Monica wasn't in the forefront of my mind, maybe I could have invited him in. He could have talked things over with me, maybe even shared the answers to the questions I had spinning through my mind.

But it was more complicated than that. We both knew it.

"Good night, Will," I said.

He chuckled. "You didn't even call me William."

I shrugged, I hadn't even noticed my slipup. He pulled me into a hug, the groove of his neck so comfortable against my cheek. *You make me weak*. So weak. And I didn't understand why.

Too soon, our embrace ended. He gave me one more smile before making his way back across the lawn.

As I unlocked the door and let myself in, I realized I was still wearing his jacket.

STAGE SIX

COLLECTION

EIGHTEEN

Dear Monica,

Let's be honest, you were always pretty obsessed with your appearance. More so than me, at least. You never saw how perfect you were, there was always something to point out in the mirror or comment on when you tried on clothes. I think I must have told you how good you looked at least a thousand times.

Now I see why. It's such a superficial world at Arlington. Your value comes from how much attention your social media posts get, how many faces turn to check you out in the hall.

It's enough to make anyone's self-esteem crumple. Even those as strong as you. What chance do I have?

Love, Chloe

ON SATURDAY I sat cross-legged, my body comfortably wrapped in cotton pajamas and an old fluffy sweater with bobbles on its drawstrings. Even after showering, eating, washing my mouth a million times, and resting, I still felt awful. It was like someone was running their nails down chalkboards on the inside of my skull, and my throat was a ragged trail of broken glass.

In front of me, on my laptop, was a newly developed list of all the things I could dig up on Desmond the photographer. It was time to collect tangible evidence that I could use. With my precarious status on Level One, I needed to move quickly.

After a sleepless night—and a lot of pondering—one problem became strikingly clear to me, one that I hadn't anticipated. My personal relationship with William Bishop.

I was good at planning. Well, at least I thought I was. I'd researched almost everything, from the correct pronunciation of fashion brands to each social media account controlled by Level One and their associates. But there was one thing I hadn't planned for.

How could I have known, having no prior experience with boys, that putting myself in an intimate relationship—even a fake one—would have an effect on me physically?

And no, I didn't *love* William. In fact, it could have been anyone. Just someone to bring out the teenage girl within me, who I currently wanted to strangle with the sleeve of William Bishop's jacket, hanging on the back of my desk chair.

I hated being out of control, and that's how I was starting to feel around him. As much as I wanted to blame it on alcohol, something about last night brought forward feelings that weren't going away in the light of day. I couldn't stop thinking about him. It was awful. And that was without even factoring in his relationship with Lola.

Pushing thoughts of him to the far end of my mind—which wasn't as effective as I'd hoped—I concentrated on the task at hand.

Things I may be able to use to take down Level One.

Zach's scandalous Level Four boyfriend. Well, that one was all prepared and ready to go, the picture's presence practically burning a hole in my phone, as well as the backed-up copies on my computer. I'd edited the photographs to make sure their identities were undeniable, and the stance I'd captured them in led only to one conclusion. A scandal.

When to unleash it? I wasn't sure. I'd hoped to gather as much intel as possible, taking down the group all at once, but I felt restless. I felt vengeful. Especially after Sophie's words at the party. Maybe it wouldn't hurt to knock down an easy target as a warm-up for the big finale.

Maddy's affair with Francis. Exposing that would be gold. It was one thing for Lola to know, but the *whole* school? Although, so far, apart from an overheard conversation in the toilets, I hadn't found anything solid. It was valuable, but I needed evidence. Something that made Francis look really bad, and preferably something that could be spread fast. A photo, maybe. Something someone could still find from a Google search in twenty years.

But what about Maddy? Why did the thought of destroying

her reputation bring me a pang of guilt? Maybe because she'd been nothing but nice to me.

She's the one sleeping with Francis, I reminded myself. And then there was everything she did to Monica.

That's who this was for, after all.

Lola and William. I wrote it, then tapped my pen against the notepad for a few moments before crossing it out. Not only would this bring down William, but I also knew the repercussions for Lola from Francis could be . . . awful. But then, after everything Lola had done to Monica, I just couldn't let it go.

And William. I closed my eyes, fighting an internal battle for a moment before opening them. *Focus, Chloe.* He was on my list too.

I wrote it again.

Sophie's secret boyfriend. *Maybe.* If I could find out who he was. I'd had almost no leads. Maybe it wasn't even relevant. But God, I needed to take Sophie down. Not just for Monica, but for myself. Her comments last night rattled me, particularly after everything I'd changed about myself to be beautiful enough for Level One. She was evil.

New list: to-do list.

To do: *find out who Sophie is sleeping with ASAP.*

Use the games.

The cruel cards stacked in Lola's little pouch. With enough supporting evidence, they were just another piece I could pin to Lola Davenport.

My phone vibrated beside me, making me jump. It was William.

I ran my tongue over my chapped lips. I wanted to ignore it, to take a break from our "relationship" and hopefully snuff out whatever weird attraction I felt for him. But something deep within me made me swipe the answer button.

"Hello?"

"Hey, are you okay? I haven't heard from you and it's almost two in the afternoon," he said. He almost sounded annoyed.

"Yeah, I'm fine, just . . ." My eyes grazed over the mess of lists in front of me. "Doing homework."

"Seriously? You can do homework after last night?" he asked, a doubtful tone in his voice. "Anyway, just wanted to make sure you were alive."

"Barely," I said. Talking to him on the phone was easier. I wasn't overwhelmed with his stupid emerald eyes.

"Do you want to talk?"

"About what?"

He let out a breath. "I don't know, about last night."

I shook my head, before remembering he couldn't see it. "No, I'm fine. Really."

"Okay." The line went silent. "I'll see you Monday morning, then?"

"Eight o'clock?"

"On the dot."

I pushed down the swell of contentment at the idea. I

lifted my shoulder to support the phone and reluctantly added to the list.

Maybe Bishop's blackmail.

As promised, William arrived at my house right on time on Monday morning. I had his jacket folded neatly in my hands, and I placed it onto the back seat as I climbed into his car. Ridding myself of the jacket was the first step to ridding him from my mind.

"Whittaker," he said in greeting.

"Bishop," I said with a nod. I straightened my skirt over my thighs and checked my lipstick in the drop-down mirror, consciously avoiding his gaze.

"Are you feeling any better?" he asked after a few moments.

I'd tried to act like I was feeling fine, but the way I was fidgeting with the strap of my bag and restlessly tapping my foot must have given away my turbulent thoughts.

"I just—" I cut myself off, before composing myself. "I just can't wait to do it. To take Level One down."

"Level One?" William asked, frowning.

Oh, right. The Level system. I shook my head. "It's nothing, just something Monica and I came up with to describe Arlington's social system."

"I'm intrigued," he said, looking genuinely curious. He'd pulled into the school parking lot, now, but he cut the engine and turned to face me. "Enlighten me."

I bit my lip. "We should get to class."

"You've said it now," he pushed.

I huffed, realizing that now that I'd piqued his interest I wasn't going to get out of it. "Fine. We divided up the students into five levels. Level One is the elite, like you and Lola and Francis and the others. Level Two is your gigantic flock of admirers. Level Three is the people who don't really care, but still hold a relatively good status. Level Four is the people who don't fit in, and Level Five is younger kids and the people you hate."

"Interesting," he said. "I mean, it makes us sound like . . . I don't know, celebrities."

"To most of the student body, you are."

"Seriously?" He looked doubtful.

I nodded, thinking of Claire and the dozen or so other students who'd tried to befriend me just for dating him.

"Huh." He tapped his fingers on the steering wheel. "Never thought about it like that."

"Yeah, you probably wouldn't have, considering you boys are only there to look pretty and pine over. It's the girls who do the law enforcement and make the system stick. You can't pretend you don't notice that."

William sighed. "Yeah, I can see that. But we wouldn't be where we are if people weren't obsessed with the idea of climbing the . . . hierarchy."

"That's true," I said. "Though God knows why anybody is."

"You are."

"That's for a different reason, though," I reminded him. "Monica."

He looked somber as he digested my words. Then he put an arm on the back of my seat to regard me more intently. "And how close are you?"

I looked at him with confusion.

"To taking down Level One."

His use of the term made me shudder. It was strange to hear it voiced aloud by anyone other than Monica or Jack. I blinked in frustration, the pressure of my task heavy on my shoulders.

"I need more evidence," I said.

Then I remembered. After the patchy memory of the girls' drinking game, I'd forgotten the most powerful resource of all. Photographs.

"Can you tell me about Desmond?" I asked suddenly.

"Desmond?" Will's brows furrowed for a fraction of a second before it dawned on him. "Oh, the photographer?"

"Yeah," I said. "There really is a private Level One photographer? I thought it was just a rumor."

William looked thoughtful for a moment. "I think I know where you're going with this."

"Then why do you have that look on your face?" I asked.

"Because it's a long shot," William said, letting out a rattled breath and leaning back in his seat.

I watched as students milled around their cars, dawdling before class and oblivious to me pumping William for information to destroy their hierarchy system.

"Desmond went to Richmond Prep," he continued. "He wants to be a paparazzi when he's older. The girls love him. He lives with two other guys in an apartment on the edge of Wandemore Valley. Rumor has it he was kicked out after he caught a snapshot of two teachers having an affair."

"Wow," I said, not expecting him to be so forthcoming with details. "You seem to know a lot."

"I'm not really a big fan of the guy," he admitted. "But the group has dragged me to a party or two he's thrown. He gets his income from recording and taking pictures at parties, he probably has hours and hours of footage. Probably footage that could get a lot of people in trouble."

"And possibly footage of Monica."

William stretched, deep in thought. "The night Monica . . . well, it's hard for me to remember. It's hazy because I was pretty drunk. I think he was there. I mean, I'm sure Monica would have wanted him there. It was her birthday party, after all."

My heart was beating rapidly with a newfound excitement. It flooded me with so much adrenaline that I needed to dig my fingers into the leather to stop from demanding he turn the car around and take me to Desmond's house right that second. I needed to be careful and thorough. I needed to meet Desmond.

"Class?" William asked when I didn't reply.

Right. With dread, I realized we'd need to head in now if we didn't want to be late. I nodded and gave a thankful smile as we exited his car.

At school, the student body was bubbling with speculation. It was as if everywhere I went, murmurs and curious looks followed. Apparently, Sophie's photo of me on Friday night had spread fast.

"I heard she's actually addicted to drugs, and Will's helping her through it," one girl whispered loudly to her friend behind me at my locker. I narrowed my eyes, wondering how they'd jumped straight to drugs.

For the first time, Level One was now targeting me. I'd watched them easily take down Stephanie over the period of a few days, and Monica after toying with her for a few months. How long would it take, to finally cross them off my list?

I slammed my locker shut. Maybe it was time to actually do something.

I was making my way to my desk when someone fell into step with me. "Chloe, hi!"

"Hi, Claire," I said a little cautiously as she took the seat beside me.

"Did you have a good weekend?" she asked.

"It was okay," I said, trying to decipher any sort of emotion she could be feeling. Was she pissed with me? I couldn't tell. "How was yours?"

She shrugged. "Pretty good."

"Good?" I pressed.

Claire sighed. "Look, Chloe, it's totally fine, but you should have just said the party on Friday was exclusive."

"I didn't realize," I told her. I shouldn't have felt guilty—I shouldn't have invited her in the first place. It was better for everyone if they stayed away from Level One.

"It's okay," she said, a smile lifting on her delicate features. "I forgive you. And I'm sure Jack does too."

I grimaced. "I should apologize to him."

"Um, maybe just avoid it for now," Claire said, scrunching up her freckled nose. "Sophie said some pretty mean stuff to him. He was a little upset afterward."

My heart plummeted. Poor Jack. What had I done? I wanted to protect the general student body by bringing these people down, not directly subject them to their evil. It only fueled me. "God, I'm so sorry."

"It's okay," Claire said again. "Anyway, it mustn't have been that private. There were so many people there. It makes me wonder if it's something more personal that got us kicked out."

It's because you're friends with me, I wanted to say. But I didn't. Because I needed my relationship with William to remain rosy to onlookers, and that meant that I was getting along with his friends. "I'm sorry, Claire."

She gave a small smile. "You could give me the answers to the physics assignment due tomorrow to make it up to me?"

"Sure," I said. But I hadn't even started that assignment myself.

I was walking to the library to prepare to undertake my first act of revenge when a hand suddenly wrapped around my wrist and pulled me into an adjacent hallway, too fast for me to process who it was.

"Chloe. I think we need to have a chat," he said.

My heart froze over when I realized it was Francis Rutherford.

I remained silent as he guided me away from the lunch rush, but not completely out of view to the handful of students walking by. I tried to keep a light smile on my face, both to shield my inner terror and to maintain appearances for the curious gazes of Level Twos.

What did he want?

"As you're apparently aware, my girlfriend is screwing your boyfriend," Francis said casually, his ice-blue eyes a mirror to Sophie's as they burned into mine.

"Straight to the point," I said through gritted teeth, putting some distance between us now that he'd dropped my wrist. I wasn't going to lie, Francis Rutherford terrified me. Ever since hearing him scream at Lola through the wall last week I had kept my distance. He was dangerous.

"I'm not playing around," he said. "Like you seem to be doing."

I froze. "What do you mean?"

Francis laughed, leaning backward against a locker, his arms crossing his chest. "I'm not buying it. The whole Will thing. I know him best, and it's not like him to lock down so fast."

"What are you implying?" I asked, proud that my voice didn't waver. I cast a glance over my shoulders, silently hoping that William might be looking for me in the halls.

"Nothing. That's your business. But the fact that Lola has decided to sleep with Will creates . . . issues."

"Sounds like they've already been dealt with," I said, trying to find a way to shut him down. "She and William ended it long before he started dating me. It's old news."

Francis smirked. "Is that what he told you?"

I watched with narrow eyes as his smirk widened in a disconcerting triumph.

"Lola's been sneaking out."

That doesn't mean anything, I thought. But the frantic expression on his face told me not to doubt him. Instead, I filed this new information away.

"Aren't you angry?" he asked, taking my lack of visible reaction as indifference.

I tried to keep my stance strong and my breathing steady. Right. What would I do if I *was* William's girlfriend right now? I'd never even come close to this situation before, but I imagined if I had, I'd be furious.

"Yes," I said, my tone clipped. I tried to make my voice sound as authentic as possible. "I can't believe he'd do that to me."

Well, that was true at least. Lying was easy if you just manipulated the truth.

"Neither of them realizes who they are hurting," he said with feigned sadness.

That was interesting, considering he was apparently sleeping with one of her closest friends. But I kept my mouth shut.

The Level One clique didn't act normal. They had a completely different set of morals. "What are you proposing?"

He chuckled. "You really are straight to business. You know, I can see why Will likes you."

The way his eyes raked up and down my body made me feel dirty and exposed. I scowled, wishing my skirt was longer. "That's not why you dragged me away."

"No, you're right. It's not. It's because I think we should work together."

I shifted my weight and crossed my arms to match him, skeptical of what the highly esteemed Francis Rutherford would ever need from someone like *me*. Apparently, his way of controlling Lola wasn't working.

"Tackling it from one end just doesn't cut it. We need to handle it from both ends. You keep your side in line and I'll keep mine," he said.

I scowled—why did he think that the only solution was to control William? If this were all real, and my boyfriend was cheating on me, I'd probably dump his ass, not manipulate him to stay.

"What if I wanted to break up with him?" I asked, playing with the idea. Although breaking up with William could be the end of my Level One status, it could also be my emergency exit. "What if I just wanted out of all of this?"

A flash of anger crossed Francis's face. "You won't. Because if you do, I can promise I will make your life miserable. Wouldn't want that, would we, Chloe?"

He made me sick. His expression lit up as he issued his threat, and the way my name rolled off his lips sent my skin crawling.

"No."

"Good girl," he said before sighing dramatically, as if our conversation alone tired him. "I want you to report anything back to me."

Then he took a step closer—so close that his whispered words were as clear as day. "Otherwise, the only way to keep him away might be to go after his girlfriend too."

Goose bumps erupted over my arms. I screwed my eyes shut as his laugh echoed through the hall.

"Chloe?" I heard behind us, causing me to open my eyes. Relief washed over me. He was here to save me.

"What's going on?" William asked, now storming to where we stood edged to the wall.

"Nothing," Francis said with a wide grin, daring to nudge me with his elbow. "Chloe and I were just having a nice chat."

I glared at him as I stood closer to William's arm. "Let's go."

We walked in the opposite direction of the cafeteria, toward the courtyard where students lay in the sun, books propped in their laps. A Level Three sanctuary.

"What did he do?"

I shook my head, confused. I knew Francis was despicable and a completely unreliable source, but I wasn't about to confront William straightaway either. Not if it was true, and he was lying to me about Lola. I needed to think. "Nothing."

To my surprise, he didn't push. Instead he nodded to an empty table. "Want to eat out here instead?"

I contemplated the idea of eating out here in the fresh air with just William, like we were two friends oblivious to the web of drama that held us.

But for now I was riddled with the suspicion that maybe I didn't know William as well as he wanted me to believe. After Francis's threat—raw evidence of the monster he was beneath his golden-boy charm—I was preoccupied with a new hunger.

"I need to go to the library and study," I said. "But I'll catch you after school."

The library, the oldest of Arlington's buildings, was empty save for a few students hastily cramming beneath lamplight. It was the only building in the school not framed with stained glass, a dark retreat for silent studying. But though studying was my disguise, I was here for something much more important.

I found a shielded space between the shelves and folded onto a beanbag, taking out my phone. The images of Zach and Max were saved. All it would take was a few taps of my thumb and I could release them to the world.

But it wasn't time for my revenge to be done with yet. I couldn't reveal my true motives to Level One until I was sure each of them would get the karma they deserved. I needed to do it anonymously.

I hoped the printer was stocked with plenty of ink.

Skipping classes was new for me. I'd never been one to sacrifice my education, but I needed a time where the halls would be clear. I doubted what I was missing in math was nearly as important as distributing my first piece of evidence. A taste for what was to come.

Level One better be scared.

I'd printed out three hundred copies of the photograph, captioned with *Aren't boys mean to the one's they like?* Maybe to anybody else the picture would be harmless. But to Zach? After the scene he made at the party embarrassing Max in front of the school?

I hoped it'd cause destruction.

I poked one in every third locker, notably skipping the Level Ones'. I wanted to keep them out of the loop. I wanted them helpless.

When my work was done, I crossed my arms over my chest, excited for the moment the empty hallway would become grounds for chaos.

For the first time since returning for the semester, Jack didn't speak to me in our final period. His head was down, his pen scratching at his notebook. I wondered what they'd done to him, and the guilt enveloped me. I hoped in the end he'd understand.

William found me straight after class. I was quickly trying to get to the lockers, eager to see the reaction to my work. His hand caught mine, steadying me. My heartbeats were already featherlight from the excitement, but his fingers looping between my own only accelerated them.

"Wow, slow down," he said, a smile dimpling his cheek, as if my excitement was infectious. "What's up?"

"You'll see," I said knowingly. I tightened my grip on his hand and led him into the hall.

As I'd expected, it was alight with conversation. People were already holding the pictures, some laughing, some pointing. I caught sight of Maddy, who was looking over Claire's shoulder. I saw her yank the picture from her hand, staring at it closely.

"Chloe . . ." William said beside me, letting go of my hand. "Is that—"

"Yeah," I said, adrenaline flooding me. "I did it."

It was hard to gauge the reactions of the remaining Level Ones. Because I'd chosen to place the revelation at the end of the school day, everyone was off home or to extracurriculars. I rode in William's car, silence between us for the entire ride.

"Are you angry?" I asked.

He hesitated before shaking his head. "No. Not at you, I mean. I just feel weird. It's like it may as well have been me, you know?"

I frowned.

"I'm the reason you had those pictures. And not just

because I was blackmailed. I chose to let you into the locker room. And I've known Zach for almost my whole life. My parents knew his parents. I was there when he came out, through the times where he was scared he'd lose everything. And I guess I've betrayed him."

"You've been with him through that, but you've also seen who he is," I reminded him. "You saw what he did to Max at that party. He's not a good person."

"I guess you're right," he said. "I mean, I *know* you're right. But what makes me any better than the rest of them, you know?"

I pursed my lips. I couldn't answer that.

Social media had been alive all evening with the gossip bouncing between Level Twos, the drama even attracting the interest of Level Threes and Fours. From the moment I got home I was glued to my phone, watching it unfold from the comfort of my bedsheets.

When I clambered into William's car Tuesday morning, there was a displeased look fixed on his face.

"What's wrong?" I asked, grimacing. Was he still acting weird about exposing Zach?

"That obvious?" he asked. His gaze was fixed straight ahead, his lips in a thin line.

"Well, you look pretty pissed," I said carefully.

William sighed. "I got a call from the coach this morning saying not to come to practice tonight. Apparently some strings are being pulled that he can't control."

"Oh God," I said. It was a whole other problem. "Francis."

"Yep." William turned a corner, almost propelling me into the window. "And with all this Zach mess, I doubt the team will be fit to play in this weekend's game."

"I'm sorry," I said. He was the team captain, after all. "I can't believe he's choosing all this drama over what's best for the team."

"I can. Because he can be a real manipulative bastard when you're on his bad side," he said.

I thought on it for a moment, searching for some way to make everything all right. "I can try and fix it."

He snorted. "How? What are you going to do?"

"I could talk to him. Maybe I could persuade him," I said, only half believing my words.

"Chloe," William said, "don't go anywhere near him. Please."

"You can't tell me what to do," I mumbled.

"No, but it would piss me off more if he managed to hurt you, okay? Just . . . let it go."

I exhaled and shrugged, still not convinced that letting things go was the best option. William's concern had created a flock of ugly butterflies jumping in my stomach. Instead I focused my energy on mentally killing them one by one.

Finally, as the bell to lunch period rang, I was put out of my misery and finally able to see the result of my takedown.

Lola, Sophie, Maddy, and Francis were already sitting at the table, the girls' legs crossed primly and Francis's posture lazy as he leaned back in his chair, one hand on the table and the other perched over the back of Lola's seat.

"Sit down," Sophie said—mostly to Will—as we approached the table. She upturned her nose in my direction before continuing. "We need to talk."

I pushed my nerves aside and pulled out a chair.

"What's going on with Zach?" William asked.

"Well, I for one had no idea he was screwing that loser," Francis said with a snort.

"It was obvious he was keeping something a secret," Maddy countered.

"I thought it was some dude from Richmond. But it makes sense. He seemed to have something against that kid," Lola said.

I looked to William, hoping it'd help remind him that this exposé was only for good.

"Whoever did it clearly had some beef with him," Maddy said. "Maybe even us."

I carefully assessed each of their faces.

"Oh, come on, it was probably Max himself. You guys heard what he did at the party," Francis said.

"True," Sophie said with a sigh. "My point is, it falls back on all of us. If we stand up for him, we look bad. They've made him into an asshole, and I don't want that bringing us down either. If we look bad, then people talk. A lot. We can't get involved in his scandal."

My satisfaction began to falter. Wasn't all of Level One meant to feel this? Wasn't it meant to make them scared?

"You're right," Lola said.

"We have to disown him, just like everyone else," Francis concluded.

Just to keep their reputation.

On cue, the cafeteria door opened to reveal Zach with his lunch tray. I watched as the room fell quiet, faces turning toward him. Some glared. Some chuckled.

He looked toward Level One. His clique. His friends. And when he saw their unwelcoming gazes in return, he turned and retreated.

Zachary Plympton could be crossed off my list.

At lunchtime the following day, Maddy took William's seat beside me before he could sit down, earning a suspicious look from him before he sat down on the other side of her. His jaw was tight. Being dropped from the team was still plaguing him. He'd been pissed off all day.

"So, Chloe," Maddy said, her eyes focused on pouring dressing over her salad. She looked as polished as always, hair neatly combed into a scrunchie. It was all as if Zach had never existed at this table at all. "I was thinking this weekend we could hang out. Just the two of us?"

I hesitated for a moment, my gaze instantly falling on

where the ice queen Sophie chatted with Lola. "Uh, I'm not sure . . . Maybe."

"Maybe?" She laughed, flicking her ponytail over her shoulder.

I stalled by stirring my coffee intently for a split second. It was risky, but if Maddy wanted to hang out with me, then maybe she'd share more secrets that could help me tick more names off my list. "Okay."

"Excellent," she said, her eyes lighting up in glee. "You'll need a fake ID."

NINETEEN

Mon,

I have a confession. I don't think you ever knew that I knew, but there was one secret I kept from you.

It was after you'd returned from a party. You were so drunk I don't even think you were aware of where you were, but you called me and asked me to come over. You still thought I was the kind of friend you could call at 3 a.m., even if at school you wouldn't speak to me anymore.

You told me everything. About how you slept with Francis Rutherford.

About how you knew it was only a matter of time before Lola found out and made you pay.

Love, Chloe

ON FRIDAY MORNING, Maddy passed me a yellow envelope. How she was so well acquainted with someone that she could have a fake ID delivered within three days had me in awe.

I waited until after lunch to open it, worried a teacher might see and confiscate it. Shielded by the door of my locker, I tore it open and the plastic card fell into my palm. *Chloe Whittaker.* Born in 1999. Twenty-one years of age. I'd taken the picture against my wall on a self-timer. I looked cold, my lips pressed into a thin line, my eyes coated in liner, daring someone to challenge me.

"What are you looking at?" William's voice rang smoothly from my side.

I looked around to make sure nobody was paying attention before slipping the card into his hand. "Maddy got it for me. For tomorrow."

She was supposed to be taking me to a club.

"Nice," he said. "You look terrifying."

I scowled at him. "Thanks."

"And you look terrifying now." He chuckled, leaning against the locker beside me.

"You're in a good mood," I noted. William had walked the halls of Arlington like a storm cloud all week. News of a supposed injury had been leaked as the cause of his suspension from the team. Though both went unspoken by Level One, that and Zach's scandal were all the other levels talked about.

"It's Friday," he said cheerfully. "And I don't have to see a smug-looking Francis for two whole days."

"Friday couldn't have come sooner," I agreed, thinking of all the moments I'd been stared down by Sophie or Lola.

"I'll see you here after school?" he asked, his gaze flickering to the clock on the wall.

"Yeah," I said, slipping the ID into my purse. We'd settled into an easy routine, and I'd be lying if I said I wasn't enjoying the human contact too. Some days our between-classes hug was the only nice thing to happen all day.

When William had said he'd see me after school, I expected that he meant the place he usually did, where he leaned against the wall by the parking lot each afternoon with a charming smile spread across his face.

I didn't expect to find him at the center of a crowd, faces eagerly watching some kind of commotion. I was just in time to see the first punch. And it was thrown by my fake boyfriend.

The *whack* of knuckle against cartilage was still echoing through the air as blood started dripping down the nose of Francis Rutherford, his eyes simmering with the kind of fury I'd never seen on anyone's face before. This was *not* good.

Well, not for William at least. I had to admit, seeing Francis slightly crouched over, the corner of his eye already swelling along with his previously perfect nose, was a little satisfying. A *lot* satisfying. But then he straightened and lunged toward William, his hands colliding with his cheek.

"You son of a bitch!" Francis yelled, pushing William back until he hit the stone wall.

But before Francis could gain any leverage, William shoved him back, punching him again. God, if William kept going, he was going to get expelled from the school, not just the lacrosse team. Most of the surrounding crowd had started cheering and taunting, divided almost equally in support for each Level One.

The ones who weren't were looking at me as if I was supposed to do something.

Bracing myself, I realized they were probably right. Girlfriend duties. I stepped forward, throwing my arms over William's shoulders and yanking him away with all my might.

"Stop!" I said firmly. "He is *not* worth getting kicked out of school!"

William was panting, a mark reddening on his cheekbone as his green gaze pierced Francis's over my shoulder. It was chilling. I'd never seen him look at someone like that.

"You start on me and then get your pretty little girlfriend to defend you," Francis spat from behind me. "That's not how this works, asshole."

"Like you have *any* problem beating on girls too," I said with venom, knowing he wouldn't dare touch me in front of the student body. His eyes locked on mine with fury, but with William beside me I didn't feel scared. In that moment, I wasn't considering the mess or the complexities of Level One, I was only considering the sheer hate I felt for Francis.

I looked to William, who was still staring at him with so much disgust it rattled me.

"Let's go," I said. "Before a teacher sees this."

I tugged at his arm, glad that we were in what was a quieter end of campus despite the hefty crowd that had grown at the drama. I couldn't see any school staff around us yet, but I knew a gathering like this would attract attention.

As soon as we were out of earshot, I turned to him. "What were you thinking? I had no idea you could be so stupid!"

"He's—" William started saying, but his breath caught. "He deserved it."

"What happened?" I asked, looking over his shoulder to make sure nobody had followed us. I saw the refuge of a half-open classroom door and pushed him toward it so we could be out of sight altogether.

"He was saying disgusting things about you, Chlo, in front of everyone. And on top of all this lacrosse bullshit . . . I snapped. And no, I don't regret it," he said, supporting his weight on a desk once I'd shut the door behind us.

"And whatever he said was probably designed to get to you," I said, still pissed at him for falling prey to whatever Francis had used as bait. "You do realize that you could be suspended for this when someone tells a teacher. *And* Level One are undoubtedly going to shun you."

"Is being with them all that matters to you?" he asked, his hand running over his jaw.

"You know it's not like that," I said.

"What's it like, then?"

"Monica is all that matters to me," I said firmly. I crossed my arms over my chest and let out a breath, trying to calm myself. "I had no idea you were the kind of guy to throw punches."

William laughed darkly. "I'm not."

"Then what was that?"

William looked down, his hair falling over his forehead as he ran a finger over his reddened knuckles. "I've been saving that punch for a while. Let's just say it was overdue."

I paced the short space in front of him, half worried that if I strayed too far away then he'd run back out there and finish what he'd started. His tense posture and wild eyes told me that attacking Francis was still on his mind.

Finally, I rolled my eyes, realizing that reprimanding him was silly. "Well, I won't say he didn't deserve it."

A half smile rose to his lips, and he looked up at me, the eyes that had been so filled with hate softening slightly. "So now you agree with me."

"No," I said. "Violence is never the answer. And to be honest, seeing you hit him was kind of scary."

"Still don't feel bad about it," he said. His cheek was swelling now, turning into a bruise. There was a shallow gash along his cheekbone.

"You know you probably won't get back onto that team," I said softly. That punch symbolized a lot more than his hatred for Francis. It was senior year, and this would definitely be going on his record.

"Francis wouldn't have let me back on it anyway," he said. Then he sighed. "He's pissed off because his girlfriend will never love him and that damages his ego."

I took a seat on the desk beside him, finally granted an opening. "Is it true you're still seeing her?"

William gave me a disgusted look. "What? No, why would you think that?"

His tone was enough to make me believe him, and it brought a relieving reassurance to my troubling suspicions. "I heard she's sneaking out. Maybe to see you."

He shook his head, a glint in his eye. "I don't know what she's doing, but it's not to see me."

I rolled my eyes, almost wanting to slap him for making a joke of it.

"Your cheek is starting to bleed."

William lifted a finger to the wound on his cheekbone. "Oh, shit."

I stood up and walked toward the teacher's desk at the front of the room, grabbing a box of tissues and taking a handful. Gently, I pressed a folded tissue against his cheek, careful not to apply too much pressure. William didn't wince or pull away in discomfort. Instead, he sat still, his eyes watching me as I tried my best to stop the bleeding. "I kind of expected you to be more of a germaphobe."

I scoffed. "You clearly don't know me very well."

"Hey, you're unpredictable."

"I'll take that as a good thing," I said. I needed to be unpredictable. I couldn't have people seeing through me.

"I'm lucky I get the real you, at least," he went on. "Not the one who's pretending to be someone she's not."

I raised an eyebrow. His face was so close to mine.

"Maybe I'm pretending right now," I murmured.

"I don't think so," he said. We were quiet for a moment, and then he spoke again. "How did someone like you get caught up with someone like Monica?"

I gave a small smile. "We just fit."

I didn't realize that I'd stopped dabbing at his cheek. William's hand wrapped around my forearm, lowering it from where it had been hovering in front of his face.

"You're a very complicated girl, Chloe Whittaker," he said fondly. Too fondly. He was still holding my arm so gently that it almost made my chest split in two. All I could think about were his lips on mine, and how easy it would be to rekindle that connection. To feel that closeness my insides yearned for.

Did this mean I couldn't cross him off my list if I felt this way? Could I do it?

There might have been many sacrifices I'd made to fulfill my plan, but falling for William Bishop would not be one of them.

The moment was broken when the classroom door was flung open, revealing Mr. Hammond, our bio teacher. Sophie stood beside him. She ignored my presence, frowning at William and his busted cheek.

"What's going on in here?" Mr. Hammond barked, looking from me to William, who had turned away to shield his injury.

"What happened to *you*?" Sophie echoed. Her scrutiny was heavy as I darted away from William.

"We were just talking," I said quickly. "Sorry, sir. We'll leave."

Before Mr. Hammond could question us further, we fled the room. I half expected him to follow us down the hall and demand answers, but he was apparently unconcerned by the fact William had clearly been in a fight. Maybe Sophie was covering for us, a strange Level One loyalty thing.

William was oddly quiet as we walked to our cars. Maybe it was the adrenaline wearing off, but he was suddenly distant. I'd driven myself this morning, so I didn't even get the car ride home to ask him about it. He didn't even pause to say goodbye, let alone give a parting hug as he headed for his BMW with a small wave over his shoulder.

As I sat in Maddy's makeup studio Saturday afternoon attempting to stick lashes to my eyes and trying to ignore the memories from a week ago, I couldn't help but worry about William. He'd ignored the few texts I'd sent him today to check if he was okay.

I wondered if his father had heard about the fight, or if the Rutherfords were already drawing up an assault charge. Even so, I had to admit, the fleeting image of Francis cradling his nose was bringing me satisfaction.

I thought back to that charged moment between us in the classroom. It was impossible to ignore the fact that William was a good guy . . . or that I'd started to develop some very real feelings for him. I had no idea what that meant for my plan, though, at least as far as it concerned him. As for the others . . . I could only hope tonight would prove useful.

Following Maddy's recommendation, I'd done my makeup extra dark to help me pass as older. I didn't feel prepared, and I began to feel the creeping possibility that I was walking into a trap. But before I could chicken out, in my head a voice desperate for secrets whispered: *What's the worst that can happen*? *Isn't it worth the risk*?

Yes.

Maddy was busy babbling about the fight as she held a curling wand to her hair, waiting for me to spill every detail as I dusted my cheeks with setting powder. Once I was done recapping, I reached for my phone, opening my Facebook app to check if William was active. The green circle next to his name confirmed my suspicions.

So he *was* avoiding me.

"Come on, let's go get our dresses," Maddy said, pulling me from my thoughts. We took our vodka sunrises and headed upstairs for her bedroom.

I was wearing a gorgeous Givenchy dress—tailored to fit the awkward curves and crevices of my body—and heels that would make my height almost comparable to Maddy's five-foot-eleven frame. I looked along her photo wall while I waited for her to do up the clasps of her shoes, Polaroids strung with fairy lights in front of her closet.

There were a lot of pictures from parties with large groups of people, but there were also a few close-up selfies of Maddy with other people.

"Is that Claire?" I asked, observing the picture of the slightly younger Claire and Maddy, who were arm in arm.

Maddy looked over her shoulder from where she was tying the strap. "Oh, yeah. We used to be friends."

Before she rose to power, of course. For some reason, I pictured what it would be like if Monica was still here. Would she have one lone picture of me left with her on her wall, cluttered among hundreds of others, our friendship a distant memory?

As if my thoughts summoned her, my eyes caught sight of her blazing red hair in a picture with Maddy and Sophie. Mon's smile was so wide it was infectious. There were a number of similar photos in the same area on the wall, all with Maddy in the same tight cobalt dress.

"When were these taken?" I asked, crouching so I could examine them better.

"Oh, I think that was at Zach's birthday last year. See the

cake in the background? It had a male stripper come out of it. Desmond took all those photos."

Just the topic I wanted to broach. "Is Desmond, um, around again?"

"Yeah, he was pissed he missed the party," she said, rolling her eyes. "He might be out tonight, though. He works at a lot of clubs."

"Oh, okay," I said as nonchalantly as possible. That would be extremely valuable. Then I tried to steady my voice to avert suspicion as I spoke my next words. "Is that Monica Pennington?"

Maddy looked to where I was pointing.

"Yeah, that's her." She shot me a half smile, not quite meeting my eyes. "Tragic, wasn't it?"

TWENTY

Mon,

You used to tell me Maddy Danton was nice. Friendly. Inviting. I knew it was all a part of their game, but I tried to believe you. Now I see it. You and she have more in common than meets the eye. Playing with Lola's bad side. Playing with her boyfriend.

I know it's been a while since we last saw each other, but you're still my best friend. I never judged you for sleeping with him, or when you told me it was intentional. You said a lot more than you wanted to that night. How you wanted to make Lola jealous, to maybe even control her. I figured it was drunken rambling.

Every day I wonder, maybe if I'd taken that seriously, it wouldn't be like this now.

Love, Chloe

WITH OUR OUTFITS perfected and our pregame leaving us lightly tipsy, Maddy and I piled into one of her dad's private cars.

"I'm so excited for our night out," she gushed. "It's going to be so much better without the others and their drama, especially after the fight, and everything with Zach. I'm so glad Will met you, Chloe."

That was strange. I'd never heard Maddy make any indications she didn't like being on Level One.

"What about Sophie and Lola?"

"Oh, they're bitches," she said. Though her tone was joking, her smile faltered a little. I raised a brow, surprised that all it had taken was one drink for her to admit this.

"Why do you hang out with them, then?" I asked.

"I don't mean it like that," she said. "I really like them. Everyone does. They're my best friends, we've been through everything together. They're funny and exciting and I love them . . . but I know they have stuff on me. I think sometimes they're scared. They need dirt on people as some kind of insurance they won't slip up, even me . . . I don't know. It can be pressure sometimes, that's all."

"Do you think they have dirt on me?" I asked, projecting innocence into my voice. I hadn't expected Maddy's honest answer, but I felt like the more naive I seemed, the more she'd show sympathy.

"I think you're in the probationary period for now.

Things between you and Will are still new, so you're not settled in yet." She began examining her lips in her phone's front camera.

"Should I be worried?" I asked with a lighthearted laugh, as if I was sure she was just being paranoid.

Maddy laughed with me, and I sensed it was mostly out of fear of being laughed *at*. "Definitely worried. Hope you don't have any skeletons in that pretty closet of yours, Chloe."

Let's just hope I can bring you all down before I have to worry about that.

The club we were going to was one of Maddy's favorites, which she'd been talking up ever since I'd agreed to go out with her. I humored her with feigned enthusiasm.

Club Aura screamed expensive clothing and cash-filled purses. The ornate building was illuminated with colored lights, and from the large line of people outside dressed in designer brands, I could tell it was popular.

"I have an arrangement with the owners," Maddy explained as she sauntered up to the VIP line. "Another perk of having a pop star daddy."

The bouncer raised an eyebrow toward Maddy, who slipped her ID into his hands without a word. In that moment, I was sure that I was about to be arrested. Thinking about it now, there was no way I could pass for twenty-one.

But once he was satisfied with Maddy's, he only took a mere glimpse at mine, his eyes darting from the plastic card to my face and then toward the entrance.

My whole clubbing knowledge was composed of scenes from movies and TV shows that Monica and I used to watch together, so I wasn't sure what to expect. Toward the end of last year, Monica had started sneaking along to clubs too, but by then it was past the point where we'd confide in each other.

Maddy's eyes flickered in the strobe lights around us, and the music thudded so loudly that to speak she had to scream into my ear. "Let's get some drinks!"

She led me toward where most of the crowd seemed clustered, and as we got closer I saw the huge crystal bar stretching out across one side of the room, people in black creating bright colored drinks in tall glasses as if it were an art. It didn't take long for Maddy to be served. She mouthed something to the male bartender, who nodded.

He had just retreated and returned with two of the elaborate-looking cocktails when Maddy leaned further to whisper something directly into his ear. I watched the exchange carefully, but as far as I could tell it was just some flirty remark.

The bartender disappeared again with both cups. Maddy turned to me, grabbing both of my hands and swaying them to the beat of the music. "I'm so excited to dance with you!"

There was no way my voice could carry over the speakers, so I just nodded enthusiastically as Maddy twirled beneath my fingers.

As the song ended and another one began, our drinks were placed on the edge of the counter, and Maddy slapped some cash back in return. She handed one to me before taking her own.

My attention had been distracted by a tall lady walking between us, her hair teased so large that it added an extra foot to her height. She yelled an "excuse me" before gently pushing through, and by the time she was out of my view again Maddy's expression had changed.

"Wait, I want to try that one," she said quickly, grabbing the drink from my hand and taking a dramatic sip through the straw. "Oh, yeah, he made yours *way* stronger, want to swap?"

I frowned, but took her drink in return, sipping it awkwardly. To me, hers tasted pretty strong itself, but I didn't exactly have the experience to judge.

Maddy linked her pinkie with mine and led us through the dancers and toward velvet-covered stairs, which were cordoned off by a scarlet rope. She disregarded this, unlinking it and gesturing me through.

Climbing the stairs was difficult with the tall drink in my hands, and some spilled over the lip of the cup and onto my fingers, the sweet and sticky liquid making my grip unsteady. Maddy had already drunk a third of hers, so she didn't have the same problem as she powered ahead of me.

The top of the staircase revealed another elaborate room, this one a little less busy and slightly more illuminated. It was clear that this area was more exclusive, an almost equal mix of girls and guys in pretty cocktail dresses and suits.

Maddy led me to a leather couch in the corner of the room where she dramatically threw her arm out for me to sit down and join her. I pulled my phone from my purse and checked it. No messages. I took another sip from my drink.

"And here," she continued, "is the prime position to check out guys. Well, not for you of course, but for me."

"I thought this was a girls' night," I mused playfully.

Maddy laughed. "Exactly. Which is why we have to find some entertainment."

I watched as her eyes scanned the crowd, dashing from face to face and up torsos and around shoulders, seemingly unsatisfied with her options. Her eyelids were cloaked in a smoky glitter, her lips a deep red as they curved upward in thought.

And then she downed the rest of her drink and straightened, her face scrunching as if she was nauseated by the taste. "I need some water. Want some?"

Since when was Maddy the type to request *water*? "Sure."

I sat still as she dived out of view. I fidgeted awkwardly in my seat as people moved around me, sipping my drink every so often, enough to give me something to do. I was still worried about William.

Two songs later, Maddy returned. I was grateful, having grown nervous that one of the many elite partygoers would approach me. She only had one glass of water in her hand, and she took a long drink before handing it to me. "Screw it, let's dance."

After taking a mouthful I had no time to object before she dragged me to my feet, my half-emptied drink forgotten on the table beside the seat.

Girls swayed their hips and ran their hands through their hair, laughing together, and guys watched them carefully from the sidelines. Maddy didn't release my hands as she started moving with the rhythm. It was reassuring. I felt less awkward moving with someone else, and I think she sensed that too.

A few songs past and I found myself smiling. It was fun to watch Maddy mock the other people around us with her hilarious moves—which seemed to be getting more and more clumsy as the night went on—and somehow the beat of the music was easy to dance to, making me even *enjoy* the sensation. I was becoming warm and breathless when a bright flash temporarily blinded me.

"Des!" Maddy squealed over the music before my vision could right itself. By the time it came around, I could see Maddy hugging the boy behind the camera with enthusiasm.

"I've missed you, Mads," he said, just loud enough for me to hear. "Pity you didn't invite me to your party last weekend."

"Hey, it's not like you gave us a date that you'd be back!" she said, her voice slurred but her smile bright. "I didn't realize you got the gig."

"I didn't," he said. "This is my job trial."

Desmond had jet-black hair and olive skin, his jaw sharp and his eyes dark, at least as far as I could tell with the lighting.

He didn't seem to notice me, until Maddy pulled me closer to her side. "This is Chloe, Will's girlfriend."

Desmond's attention turned to me, and he raised an eyebrow. "Didn't know dating was his thing."

"Well, it is now!" Maddy said. I hadn't realized how much her voice had slurred over the last half hour or so. "Hey, take another picture of us while we're *actually* looking!"

Maddy wrapped an arm around my waist and Des positioned the huge camera in front of his face, giving a quick warning before the flash went off again. I think I smiled, but I couldn't be sure.

"Hey, I—" Maddy paused, swaying on the spot. I let her throw an arm around me to steady herself. "I don't feel so good."

Then, before I could stop her, Maddy fell to the ground.

She almost pulled me down with her, but I managed to turn enough that I could half hold her up. "Maddy?"

She groaned and held a hand to her head as she tried to stand again, only managing to sway on the spot. Desmond quickly bounced into action, pulling her from under her arms and taking her unstable weight as he walked her off the dance floor. Around us, people were watching, some showing concern and others amusement.

Maddy slouched against the wall by the stairs as Desmond tried to get her attention. "Maddy, Mads, can you hear me?"

There was no response, and he shook her shoulders a little. "Madeline!"

She groaned and tried to shove him away, mumbling more to herself than us. "Maddy, not Madeline."

Des sighed, looking to me. "How much has she had to drink?"

"I—I don't know," I said, my mouth dry. "Two drinks in total, I think. She seemed fine—this is so sudden. Surely she can't be this drunk already?"

He had resorted to pulling Maddy up again as I rambled, and then a burly security guard approached us from the side of the room. "She can't stay in here if she can't stand."

"I think she's okay—" I said quickly, but the man cut me off.

"She's out of here. You too if you're her friend."

I was about to bring up the fact that her dad was a pop star—perhaps, like getting us into the club, it would get this guy to treat her better—but Desmond cut in. "I'll get her out as soon as possible."

It was lucky that Desmond was strong, because getting Maddy down the stairs was difficult. After a lot of maneuvering and swear words tumbling out of Maddy's lips, we managed to get her outside, the night air hitting me like a slap in the face as we went to the other side of the building to avoid the crowd. "What's wrong with her?"

Desmond sighed, slowly lowering her to the paved ground and lifting her chin. She grinned at him loopily, her eyes fluttering shut as if she were struggling to stay awake. "Maybe she was drugged. It's almost like someone messed with her drink."

"Are you serious?" I asked. "She got her own drinks. She had them the whole—"

But she didn't. She took my drink.

"Oh God," I said instead, crouching and taking Maddy's hand. She had taken my drink *for* me. The drink *she* had ordered. It didn't make any sense.

"Can you call a car?"

"Shouldn't we—shouldn't we take her to the hospital?" I asked.

"You can't take her to the hospital. The media would go nuts. Get her home and make sure her mom's there. Saves her having her face all over the papers tomorrow morning."

I looked at him with doubt, suddenly feeling a surge of protection for Maddy in her vulnerable state. But he was right, a hospital trip may be a last resort with her famous family.

I sighed. "Okay, I'll call the car."

After I'd called an Uber, I sank down next to Maddy on the pavement, Desmond hovering on the lookout for the approaching vehicle.

"So, you're Will's new thing, huh?" he asked.

"I'm hardly a thing," I said, my voice faint and vaguely annoyed.

"Well, obviously." He snorted, as if it were funny. "I was just curious. I've spent four years videoing these guys. I've come to know them pretty well."

"Really?" I asked, hoping he'd elaborate.

"Yeah, I literally have a box full of hard drives with footage of their parties. They pay a good wage," he explained with a chuckle.

I looked toward the club. "I thought you were on a job trial."

"I can afford to take a minute. Anything to look out for an old friend."

I looked to Maddy, her eyes closed and her lip popped in an uncomfortable pout. I was brushing away a lock of hair that had stuck to her cheek when the driver pulled up to where we were sitting. Des and I both straightened before hoisting Maddy to her feet and walking her into the back seat. My first night clubbing and I was going home just after eleven.

"Hey," Desmond said before I tucked into the seat beside Maddy. "It's okay. It's not like this is an unusual thing for Maddy. It's messed up, but she's always doing reckless things like this."

I nodded, giving a thankful look. But beneath the surface, his words bothered me. Just because she was reckless didn't mean she should just be waved off when things went wrong.

"And—" He regarded me carefully as he adjusted the camera strap so he could reach into his pocket. He pulled out a small business card. "If anything happens to her, call me straightaway."

I frowned. "Thanks."

He nodded farewell as I shut the car door, feeling oddly uneased by the seemingly friendly encounter.

Getting Maddy inside was difficult. Once we'd pulled up at her house, I pressed the buzzer to her gate, alerting the housekeeper I was with Maddy.

It was her mother who came to the car, her appearance goddess-like, a picture-perfect replica of Maddy with enough Botox to pass as her sister.

"I—I think she was drugged," I said.

She took Maddy under her arm, giving me a wary glance. "You girls at that school are a bad influence on her."

I gulped. I figured that was my cue to leave.

Once I'd ordered a ride and finally arrived at the gate of my house, I took a moment to check my phone again. No text. I felt a little ache in my heart, but I tried to ignore it. Now was not the time to be caught up on William Bishop.

TWENTY-ONE

Monica,

You broke my heart. You should know that.

I had no idea how little I'd prepared for the loneliness I felt when you first sat at that Level One table. I never made friends like you did. It never came as easy. I sat with your old friends—like we were last season's clothes.

I know deep down you missed me. But I wasn't cut out for Level One.

Not like I am now.

Love, Chloe

I WOKE UP to a vibrating sound against the bedside table. It took me a while to process that it wasn't my alarm. No, it was the demanding droning of a call. I groaned, my hand lazily swiping the answer button and bringing it to my ear.

"Hello?" I asked, my voice groggy with sleep.

"Chloe, hi." It was Maddy.

Suddenly, the events of last night came rushing back and I sat up straight in bed.

"Maddy," I said when I had my bearings. "Are you okay?"

Maddy laughed musically on the other end of the line. "Yeah, I'm great. I just wanted to say sorry for last night."

I hesitated. "How did it happen, Maddy?"

"How did what happen?"

"How did you get drugged?" I asked, diving straight into the question she was clearly trying to avoid.

"Drugged?" She laughed again. "Oh, Chloe, I wasn't drugged. I just ate something bad, that's all. Des overreacts sometimes. I was fine."

I frowned. She definitely wasn't fine when she'd been mumbling incoherently in the back seat. "I think it was more than that, Maddy."

"Well, whatever, I'm fine now, and I owe you a huge apology. I can't believe our night was cut short by *that*."

Was she seriously going to pretend it didn't happen? "Maddy, are you sure it wasn't something more?"

She hesitated, but only for half a second. "Yep, I'm fine now. Anyway, I have to go, I'm on my way to Lola's to help with homework. I'll see you tomorrow!"

I hardly managed to utter a goodbye before the line disconnected. I stared at the blank screen, empty of notifications.

My mind reeling, I fumbled for my purse and checked its pockets. Inside was the fake ID, as well as Desmond's business card. On it was his phone number and email, and on the back a postal address, which looked residential.

Taking down the remaining names on my list seemed easier to visualize now, with a treasure chest of potential material lying in Desmond's grasp.

On Monday morning, I woke before my usual alarm, preparing my schoolbag and doing my makeup quick enough to be almost an hour early for school. I'd taken extra care to wing my liner and wear an outfit that clung to my waist, the white blouse cropped close and the plaid skirt grazing dangerous territory.

Today, my place on Level One would be rocky, and looking the part was the least I could do.

William still hadn't texted me all weekend, save for a message late last night explaining he'd meet me at school. I wasn't satisfied with that, though. I wasn't about to walk into Arlington without him, especially if we weren't on good terms.

I made my way to William's home. I'd never been inside the mayor's estate, but I'd driven past numerous times, always gawking at its high fences and the towering building behind it. It was bright and crisp out, the lawns still glittering in a fresh coat of dew.

I'd sent William a text, hoping he'd see it and feel alarmed enough to come outside. I killed the engine and waited.

It was five minutes before the gates opened, revealing a tall figure with mussed hair. I wound down my window.

"What are you doing here?" Though he sounded annoyed, I thought I saw relief flicker across his face. I wondered if my mind was just playing tricks on me or if it was really there.

"You ghosted me this weekend," I said as he climbed into the Audi. "That's not part of our deal."

He let out a sigh, his hands moving to rub his eyes. On closer inspection, it looked like I'd woken him up with my message. It was crazy to think the boys of Level One could just roll out of bed and head to school, while I spent an hour just on makeup alone.

"Look, Chloe," he said as I killed the engine. We needed to sort this out before we reached campus. "I just . . . I'm not sure if this is all a good idea."

My heart sank, and I tried to keep my gaze straight ahead. "You can't just decide you don't want to do this. That's not how it works."

"I know." There was a long pause. "Sometimes I forget that all that's between us is my dad's corruption and your revenge plan."

My fingers burned as I clenched them around the wheel.

"I just—I need this, William," I said. "I'm so close—I know I am. I'm so close to exposing them, to getting the revenge Monica would have wanted—"

"Would she?" he interrupted. "Is this what Monica would have wanted?"

I clenched my teeth. "You didn't know Monica."

"Well, from my experience, she would have done anything

for attention, especially Lola's. Maybe even worse things than Lola herself would do."

I wanted to slap him. I glared at him, fury blinding my vision.

"Chloe . . ." His tone told me he almost regretted his words. His hand reached out to touch my arm, but I dodged his touch. "We need to talk about her—"

"No," I said harshly. "We don't."

"Okay." He held his hands up, as if posing himself as harmless. But right now, he was doing so much harm. He was my strongest asset. No, my strongest ally.

"It's not true," I said. "About our deal being all that's between us. I thought we were friends."

Through these few weeks of fake dating we'd developed a friendship. A complicated one, admittedly, but for him to disregard it as nothing hurt.

"Then listen to me."

I turned away, crossing my arms over my chest.

"I can't keep doing it, because I'm starting to care too much to see you self-destruct like this. To see you play their games and try and win them over."

William *cared* for me?

"At first, I saw Monica all over again, a girl desperate to be popular. To break into our group of friends so everyone in the school would like her. But that's not it. You're just holding on to someone who left you behind, long before she really left."

His words cut me, because they were partly true. Monica and I had argued so much before she cut contact altogether. The last time we spoke was an argument. I'd ignored the invitation she left me in my locker to her birthday party. We were in a rough patch.

"I've seen more than the Chloe you're trying to be—I've seen more than who you are when you're trying to be like them. I've seen your loyalty to your best friend tear you up, the guilt of talking badly about people plague you all day. The way your face lights up when you change the radio station on the way to school and blast your favorite music. I've seen you put Monica first even when she's let you down. You deserve better than this."

"Will—" I tried to say, to stop the words pouring from his lips and splitting me open, leaving me bare. But he cut me off and continued.

"That's why I can't keep doing this," he said finally. "The fake dating. It's too confusing for me—for us. I can't keep waiting for something to go wrong. For those girls to get ahold of you too."

"But Monica—"

"Chlo, Monica wouldn't have wanted you to repeat her mistakes."

I looked down to my hands in my lap. "You're on my list too, William. I'm supposed to be taking you down for doing this to her."

Silence. I'm not even sure why I said it. I knew this could

be the end of us now. I could see the pulsing in his jaw as he stared me down. "I thought I was protected."

"I lied," I said, my voice thick. "I've told a lot of lies for her."

"Still doesn't mean you have to do it," he said. "But if that's how it is, then I am out, Chloe. It's over."

Could I lose William now? Logically, maybe. I had almost all I needed from Level One in terms of intel. I just needed to collect it. Even though the others would turn their backs the second William deserted me, I still had a chance.

But if I let down my walls to the influx of nonlogical feelings held at bay, I knew losing William now would affect more than my plan. I cared about him too, and I needed him more than I should.

"I won't hurt you," I said, my voice cracking. I was ashamed at my vulnerability.

William looked at me carefully. Maybe he was searching for any signs I was lying, or maybe he was just seeing how pathetic I was. Then his hand reached out, and this time I let it find my arm, pulling me close and against his chest.

"You better not, Whittaker."

TWENTY-TWO

Monica,

I always wondered if you were capable of the kind of things they were. My heart told me you weren't—that you were better than them—but now I don't know anymore. I feel like I stopped knowing you when you started going to their parties, when you started changing yourself just to impress them. I don't know who to believe now. My memories feel blurred.

Please tell me it isn't true.

Love, Chloe

"ONE MORE WEEK," William said as I pulled into Arlington's parking lot. "As of Friday, no more pretending."

By second period William and Francis had been called to the principal's office. The halls, though currently absent from the reigning king and his newly defined rival, were abuzz with their drama. And by default, this meant that everyone's attention was on me too. I kept my chin high, attempting to keep my dignity intact, as if I was totally unconcerned with the looks I was getting.

The tension was turned up a notch when Lola, trailed by Sophie and Maddy, strolled over to my locker. I tried to keep my cool as she sauntered through the hall, her eyes training lazily on the ogling students before they found their way to me.

"Chloe," she said, as if she were surprised that she'd made her way directly into my path. When she spoke, her voice was injected with a sickly sweet dose of false friendliness. "I hope things are okay between us with everything going on. I mean, boys will be boys, right?"

"Right," I said, my tone too high as I tried to go along with whatever she was playing at. *Boys will be boys*, what bullshit.

Her voice dropped even lower. "I can't help that they're fighting over me."

I narrowed my eyes. Not even Sophie and Maddy were in earshot to hear that one. There were so many retorts I wanted to hurl at her perfectly smug face, preferably ones that the whole school would hear. But I couldn't waste my progress on pettiness. There was a bigger picture here.

"Must be hard being Lola Davenport," I replied sarcastically, making my way past her.

She seemed disappointed that I hadn't taken the bait. That

was clear when she called out after me, her voice laced with venom. "See you at lunch, Chloe!"

I headed to my next class early, suddenly feeling dirty from the pairs of eyes that clung to me. Everyone was talking about the fight. The stories about it had become so exaggerated that some people were saying Francis was in a coma and William was being held in jail.

I wasn't the only one early to class, though. "Hi, Jack."

Jack looked up from the textbook he was reading and smiled, acting as if he hadn't been avoiding me for the last week. I still hadn't managed to catch him on his own since the party. "Hey, Chloe."

"How are you doing?" I asked. I wished I could reassure him by telling him I was going to take them down, that Level One would pay for being mean to him and everyone else.

"Fine. Busy with school," he said with a shrug, his brown eyes lingering on the floor. "You know, sometimes I mistake you for Monica, sitting with them."

I swallowed. I remembered the days where Monica would sit between Lola and Sophie, laughing at freshmen as they pooled into the cafeteria. It stung to think Jack saw me as just the same. "I'm sorry about the party."

"So Claire said," he mused. "It was shitty, but it's in the past. I just want to be done with it."

I nodded, but I could tell things weren't quite resolved.

By lunch, my stomach was in knots. Between being nervous for the outcome of Will's meeting with the principal and the prospect of joining Level One without him by my side, I was dreading entering the cafeteria. And so I dodged it, making a beeline for the quad, sitting beneath a tree and pulling out my phone.

I began my usual routine, scrolling through Instagram, checking for Facebook updates and viewing the Snapchat map. That's when I noticed something I'd missed this morning. An account leaving a comment on Sophie's latest selfie—one taken with an angel filter and a wide smile.

Click here for lols

I clicked the username, *@jackoffjack*.

The profile was filled with screenshots and pictures. I scrolled back to the first one, posted a week ago. The timestamp told me it was from messages sent in freshman year.

Love you, Soph. I know we've only known each other a week, but I know this is it. I think we're meant 2 be.—9:12am

U don't have to worry. I won't tell anyone.—9:46pm

See u at school tomorrow xx.—9:53pm

All were from Jack Thomas.

I looked at the next one. He'd sent a picture, a mirror selfie with his shirt off. Prepuberty Jack was scrawny, ribs showing as he bit his lip.

Do u want to see more?—10:20

Ur so pretty. Want u so bad—10:26

I couldn't believe it. How could Jack have ever thought it was a good idea to send Sophie these messages? And on closer examination, it seemed like Sophie's responses had been cleverly deleted. I could have bet my entire family's fortune that it was her who set up this account.

Each photo contained a plethora of comments and likes, some handles I recognized as people from Arlington, some even from Richmond Prep. Although there were one or two standing up for him, at least 90 percent were making a mockery of his extreme freshman crush.

And all of this, I was sure, was because of me. I'd invited him to that party, and Sophie had seen enough in the hallways to know he was linked to me. He was an ally.

And if I was isolated, I was easy to take down.

TWENTY-THREE

Monica,

How did you do it? Hurt people like this? It's easy to forget how dangerous Level One can be with their charm, but when it comes to their victims, they hold nothing back. They can destroy anyone's reputation in an instant. Did you feel this? The guilt? You must have. You were best friends with them, after all.

It confuses me, what you must have done to be in so deep. I'm trying so hard to understand what led to this. I just want to do what's best, to give them what they deserve.

And I will, I promise. The more I see, the more determined I am. I'll do it. For you, and for everyone they hurt.

Love, Chloe

AFTER SCHOOL, I avoided Lola and the others by sneaking around the side of the campus to my car. I was almost there when someone caught my attention.

"Chloe! *Chloe*, there you are!"

I looked over my shoulder to see Maddy Danton scampering after me, clearly struggling in her heels.

"Are you okay?"

I frowned. "Why wouldn't I be?"

She hesitated, and I could tell she was biting something back.

"Oh, you know, Will getting in trouble and all."

"I'm fine," I said. William had gotten lucky with only detention instead of suspension.

"Okay, well . . ." Her voice trailed off. Her wide brown eyes were plagued with something.

"What's wrong?"

She let out a pent-up sigh. "It's Lola and Sophie. They're royally pissed with me. I messed up."

"How?"

She shook her head. "I can't tell you. You'd probably hate me. But I wanted to warn you, in case they come for you too."

"Maddy, what did you do?"

"I have to go," she said quickly, giving me a sympathetic look before heading toward the drop-off zone, where her daddy's private car was waiting.

If I wasn't already sure Lola was ready to destroy me, now I was certain. I cursed, Maddy's encounter only fueling the anxiety I felt returning to school tomorrow.

Once I was in my car, I pulled out my printed copies of Google Earth images with shaky hands. They showed the exterior of Desmond's unit from every available angle. Then I made my way to the other side of town, a wide pair of sunglasses covering half my face

I was nervous. Mostly because it was broad daylight, and even though I blended in with the other cars crowded around the housing development, I felt out of place in my red Audi. Why hadn't I considered taking my mother's less conspicuous black sedan?

Luckily, a nearby elementary school finishing up for the day meant that I wasn't alone in hanging around the street with an idling car for the first half hour or so.

The house was small compared to the extravagant mansions of my classmates. It was three bedrooms, all one floor, from what I'd gathered on the floor plan from the real-estate website advertising the unit next door. Which room was Desmond's, I wasn't sure.

I'd need to scout the house more closely, possibly at nighttime. I doubted the security was extreme, especially if it was owned by three teenagers living together to share expenses. Maybe a lock on each of the bedrooms, but those could be easily disabled . . .

I waited outside of Desmond's house for two hours. Two hours of my stomach grumbling from skipping lunch and my nerves running haywire, paranoid that someone would see me. I tried to do some of my physics reading while I waited for something to happen, but I couldn't focus, my eyes darting from the page to scout out every detail; the angle that the curtains were pulled at over the front window, the array of envelopes poking out of the letterbox. Anything that could be a useful detail.

At half past five the first car pulled up the driveway. It was a middle-class car, its driver a tall blond boy who I recognized from Desmond's Facebook page.

As he stepped out of the vehicle and collected the mail, my heart leapt from my chest and I hurriedly looked in the opposite direction. It was too easy for him to see me, I was too suspicious in my car—I had to leave.

I drove home, unable to shake the feeling that someone was following me.

I found myself struggling to get out of bed the following morning. Maddy's warning had me terrified, and William had lunchtime detention, leaving me vulnerable.

I finally mustered up enough courage to drag an outfit from the closet and pull on some ankle boots, my head still groggy from my unsettled sleep.

I was late to class, which wasn't good considering how much my work had been suffering. In fact, I'd received my first ever B since freshman year, and I was still riding on a two-week extension for an assignment in math. I fell into my seat next to Claire like a zombie. Her eyes searched my face, as if trying to uncover whatever drama was causing my haggard state.

The tired fog that was cloaking my mind quickly cleared when I saw Maddy in the hallway on my way to lunch. She was dressed as glamorously as always, her hair in a tall ponytail and her lips a deep plum.

"Hey, Chloe," she said absentmindedly as I stopped beside her. Something seemed to have changed since yesterday, she seemed defeated.

"Hi, Maddy," I said. I hoped she'd at least shield me from Lola and Sophie. "Coming to lunch?"

She nodded once before closing her locker and turning in the direction of the cafeteria. She seemed tense.

I looked at her, about to ask what was wrong when I sensed it myself. The atmosphere in the cafeteria was different. The whole student body was quieted, their eyes turning to Maddy and me as we entered. Instead of mingling between friend groups and standing up to get more food, everyone was seated, their attention directed toward the middle table.

Maddy lifted her chin and walked in front of me, and I couldn't help but feel as if we were walking toward our execution. Perhaps we were.

It was then that I noticed what had drawn everyone's attention. Sophie was pacing the area around the table like a lioness stalking her prey, her hips swaying slowly with each step and her smile wide. In her hands was a bell, its chime now silent. She'd already caught the attention of the whole lunch hall.

And that's when Lola climbed up onto a seat and then up

on the table, her stilettos sharp as they sat dominantly beside Level One's lunch trays. By now, she had the attention of every single person in the room, except perhaps the teachers. They'd conveniently deserted the cafeteria as if anticipating her announcement.

"Sorry to interrupt your lunch," she called, her sickly sweet voice hardly needing to be elevated as she addressed her subjects. Everyone was holding their breath in silence, anyway. "I have a surprise to share with you."

Her eyes fell on Maddy and me, her teeth shining with menace as she grinned.

"I hope you all enjoy it. Feel free to share it with the world. It's a gift from me to you."

And then, as if we were in some kind of excerpt from an episode of *Gossip Girl*, the whole cafeteria erupted in a synchronized emission of text tones and vibrations. Even my own phone chimed in my pocket, and I pulled it out and unlocked it as fast as possible, my fingers clammy.

My hand flew to my mouth just as the student body flicked their switch from deathly silence to deafening noise.

Thin bronzed legs were stretched across two boys, black strappy heels barely clinging to each foot as they arched with euphoria. Her body was clad in lacy lingerie, but it may as well have been nothing with the way it was stretched across her chest. In one hand dangled what looked like a cigarette, the other cradled the cheek of one of her companions.

The faces of the guys were blurred out. Their hands were

all over her, and from her expression, she reveled in it. Maddy Danton's face was captured for all the world to see, oblivious to the camera pointing in her direction.

I couldn't tell how old the photograph was, but I guessed it was the one Sophie and Lola had been talking about in the bathrooms. The one they were saving for her as punishment for jeopardizing Lola's prized reputation.

Tearing my gaze from the picture, which had been sent in a bulk message to all 921 of Arlington's students, I took in the horror-struck expression of Maddy standing beside me.

"You promised you wouldn't." Her eyes were cold with rage, her breath coming quickly. "You told me if I dealt with her you'd protect me."

"Oh, babe," Sophie said, clicking her tongue. "But you didn't, did you?"

"I did everything you asked, I just needed more time—"

"We don't have forever, Madeline." A smirk brightened Sophie's baby-blue eyes. "And your time is up. Good luck with your life, you alcoholic *slut*."

Maddy leapt forward, grabbing the collar of Sophie's blouse. "After all I've done for you! Do you have any idea the shit I've gone through for you?"

I didn't know what to do. I was standing frozen as the student body watched what was likely going to be the high point of this semester's gossip, right up beside Francis and William's fight and Zach's secret boyfriend.

One thing was clear to me, though: I was the girl Maddy was supposed to *deal* with.

Maddy let Sophie go abruptly, apparently realizing her smug smile wasn't going to drop. She glared hatefully at Lola, before spinning on her heels and fleeing the room.

I quickly followed her, having to double my stride to catch up.

"What's this about?" I asked as soon as we'd vanished from view.

Maddy's face had paled. Her arm slackened in mine as I let it fall. "What does it look like, Chloe?"

"It looks like you didn't hold up your part of a bargain," I said coolly, the sympathy I felt for Maddy canceled out by the possibility of her plotting against me. "What was the bargain, Maddy?"

She pulled at her hair and screwed her eyes shut, as if giving up. "If I gave them something to use on you, they wouldn't use what they had on me."

My heart ran cold. That meant they were actively trying to destroy me. "Why didn't you?"

"Because I couldn't," she said. "I tried but I couldn't give you that spiked drink on Saturday and I couldn't let Des film it. It's like this endless cycle of bringing people down. I don't even know what you did to make them hate you so much. The scandals, the rumors, God it just felt like Monica Pennington all over again."

My heart splintered. Did she really just say her name aloud? Emotion came thickly, and I didn't even know how to decipher it.

"I had no choice, Chloe," she continued. "It was you or me, and at this school, you have to save yourself. But in the end, I couldn't. I thought maybe if Des saw me roofied he'd tell Sophie and Lola I'd accidentally just mixed our drinks, but I guess they knew. This is why you can't have a conscience at Arlington. As soon as you put someone else first, you lose."

The bell rang through the hall, signaling the end of lunch. Maddy's eyes were swimming with rage, her expression both forlorn and furious.

"I'm going. I have to do damage control before this spreads to my family. Or worse, the press."

And with that she stormed off. Had a Level One just sacrificed herself for me? Or was it Monica that was responsible for Maddy's change of heart? I couldn't help but admire her, at least a little. I was sure if our situations were reversed, I would have burst into tears back in the cafeteria. Although I considered myself determined and strong, to be humiliated in a public setting was a whole other story.

I couldn't let myself continue to worry. Not right now. Like she said, I should be thankful.

But even so, my thoughts kept spiraling back to her, to the fact she damaged her reputation and her health just because she decided last minute she didn't want to hurt me. It made my chest heavy. I was supposed to be destroying Maddy Danton, not *liking* her.

There was a whirlwind of messages from the newly created school group chat. I tried to avoid opening them, but I had to gauge the reaction. One thing was apparent: Level One themselves had crossed the third person off my list.

Knew she was a whore, but didn't realize she took two guys at once omg

I'd be so embarrassed, lmao no dudes gonna wanna touch her again.

Gross she so dirty!

Just posted it on my Tumblr, it's hot af

I cringed at the sexist, horrific comments that just kept coming. I muted the chat. This was the student body I was trying to protect by taking Level One down. And yet, despite the fact that so many of them had been tormented by people higher up on the social ladder than them, they fed off of Maddy's downfall. Whether they were delighted or disgusted, everyone was talking about it.

I blocked the chatter out of my mind and tried my best to focus on my chemistry lecture. But all I could think about was the photo, and how Level One had beaten me to the punch. To ruin Maddy Danton's social status. And it clouded me with sadness.

When school ended, nobody left campus straightaway. People lingered in groups, exchanging phones and devices, countless memes and photoshopped versions of Maddy's picture going viral through the student body.

I couldn't go home. I had a test tomorrow morning and I hadn't even done the homework on the topic, let alone started to study it. I knew if I went home, then I'd fall into the trap of planning what my next move should be. Despite the new urgency to finish my revenge quickly, I needed to pass senior year.

I entered the library, walking down the open area of seats, enveloped by tall shelves, hoping to find an isolated table to sit at and somehow forget about Level One and its drama for a few hours.

I'd found a small nook to drop my books, but I'd only just opened my chemistry text when a shadow crept onto the desk.

"Chloe. We need to talk."

It was Jack Thomas.

I remembered the Instagram account Sophie had made to bring Jack down. With his social status a level lower than Maddy's, his scandal was hardly making a ripple. It was more bullying than school-wide gossip. Still enough to make sure nobody would want to be his friend, though.

"I'm sorry," I said. I wasn't sure if I meant for the Instagram account, or Sophie's wrath, or the fact I *really* needed to study. I shut my book and started to move toward my bag.

"Not you too," he mused. I narrowed my eyes. He almost seemed . . . cheerful.

"What's going on?"

Jack pulled out the chair beside me, folding his arms in front of him and regarding me with a curious gaze.

"I think we have the same motive here," he said. "When it comes to taking down Level One."

TWENTY-FOUR

Monica,

An endless cycle. Is that what this is? An endless cycle of taking people down? I remember in sophomore year when we would watch people rise and fall from afar like phases of the moon, every month or so a new victim.

You know, it was only a few weeks after everything happened that I realized they'd get away with what they did. Just like they got away with everything else. I started to piece together a plan.

I promise you I'll make things right. I promise.

Love, Chloe

"HOW DID YOU find out?" I tried to act unfazed, but beneath the table my fingernails bit into my thighs.

"I'm not stupid, Chloe," he said with a smile. "Did you really think I'd believe that you just started dating one of them? I know you better than them. I've known you longer. Your loyalty is your biggest fault. I could see right through the act. And when I saw you were the one who'd printed off all those pictures at the library after hacking the password to the school's system? I knew for sure."

"What are you going to do?" I tried to sound calm, but I felt ice-cold. My entire plan was exposed.

"I haven't decided yet," he said. His tone was snide. "But for now, I want to help you."

My entire time at Arlington, all I'd seen was Jack trying to fit in. For Level One to like him. From parties to tutoring to spreading around their gossip, he'd always been happily on Level Two. It surprised me that he suddenly wanted to take them down.

"Level One needs to pay," he said. His smugness had now dissipated, leaving his jaw tight and eyes intensely boring to mine. "I want them to pay."

"Is this because of Sophie?"

I swear I caught his poker face falter.

"It's because of all of them," he said. "I was the smartest kid in my elementary school, you know. I earned a full scholarship."

"I know," I said. Everyone knew. As much as he tried to blend in, he was different. His family might have had connections, but they lacked the wealth the other Arlington parents oozed.

"You don't get it. I was the *smartest*. I aced all my classes first semester. But I was outshining people like Francis and Lola and Will. The people who were supposed to be the success stories."

I could see where he was going. I wouldn't be surprised if the Level Ones were even able to control everyone's grades.

"Francis was the first to threaten me. He was scared of his parents. Being outshined by some nobody. He said he could have me expelled in an instant if I beat him. And I would have been stupid not to believe him. A mediocre graduation at Arlington is worth a thousand valedictorian titles at any other school."

He was right. There was a reason politicians and pop stars chose to send their kids here.

"And they mocked me for it. For being the scholarship kid, for having to listen to them. For being powerless. And all I wanted was for them to accept me. I was so awkward and naive back then. I thought I loved Sophie Rutherford because one day after English she told me she liked a poem I wrote."

Jack's eyes seemed far away.

"Ice on a sea breeze, like she looked at me, a queen's scornful smile, worn like silk draped upon her skin."

I remembered that day, the day everyone had laughed at Jack's speech impediment as he read to the class. He'd hidden it well since then. It was almost undetectable. Another side effect of being a Level Two: you'd do anything to conform. Like Monica had done when she shed me. Like I had done when I joined them.

"She thought I wrote it about her. How conceited." He seemed to return to the present, crossing his hands in front of him, all business. "Anyway, point is, they've taken every opportunity I should have had, opportunities I worked for. And I'm tired of playing nice."

"They took Monica," I added quietly. He was right. We really did have the same motive.

"I'll give you what I have, if you give me what you have," he said. "Then we can negotiate."

Could I trust him? What he said made sense, yes, but also selling me out could elevate his status, giving him the boost he needed.

"I promise I have valuable intel," he said.

That got me. At this stage, I needed anything I could get my hands on. William wanted this over by the end of the week, and with Maddy out of the way I didn't know how much longer I'd be able to hold on to my position.

"If you can give me something new," I said. "Then I'll tell you where I'm at in my plan."

"Deal."

Jack held out his hand. I shook it.

"I hacked into the school's system and found deleted surveillance footage," he said. "I gave them a chance, you know. I tried to play nice. But after what Sophie did, kicking me out of that party—it was the last straw. I had to do something."

"Seriously?" I asked, unable to stop from gaping at him. "How?"

He waved me off, like it didn't matter.

"I was hoping to find something to use against the school, to blackmail them into doing something. But I found something even better. Someone deleted a video of Sophie sneaking around with someone."

"You know who Sophie is seeing?" I gasped, my voice a barely contained whisper.

He nodded. "And it's a scandal and a half."

At this point, I was almost out of my seat. "Who?"

"Let's just say she's been getting anatomy lessons from our biology teacher." Jack's lips lifted in a smirk. "Mr. Hammond."

TWENTY-FIVE

Mon,

How did we get here? Don't you remember making the promise to go to college together? It seems silly now, forecasting things so far away, especially after so much has changed. I felt safe with you. Maybe too safe. Maybe that's why I never really bothered making any other best friends. I had you. We had each other.

I have to admit, it's left me pretty lost now. I used to think that no matter what, I'd always still have you.

Love, Chloe

JACK SENT THE thirty-second clip to my phone. Sophie and Mr. Hammond last Friday. William and I had been leaving the classroom just as they entered. Though the surveillance system was only capturing the hallway, Sophie and Mr.

Hammond's shadows, cast by the afternoon sun, were projected onto the tiled floor through the doorway.

Both figures moved toward each other, their movements showing enough to work out that they were undressing. I guess *that* was how Sophie maintained a perfect GPA.

In exchange, I'd divulged my side of the plan. Once I'd started, I couldn't stop, pouring out my secrets. William's blackmail. His love triangle with Lola and Francis. The games. Desmond's footage.

"After what they did to Monica," I said, "I can't bear it. They deserve to pay."

Jack looked deep in thought as he propped his chin on his knuckles. "You know, you had me worried for a little there."

I looked at him questioningly.

"Like I said, I knew you wouldn't be pining to be part of Level One after Monica. But after seeing you with Bishop . . . I wasn't sure."

"What do you mean?" I frowned.

"It's just, the way you guys look at each other." Jack shook his head, as if clearing the images from his mind. "Never mind."

I opened my mouth to say more, but then closed it. He thought I'd fall for William Bishop and forget about Monica.

"I'm here for Monica, and her only. She was . . ." My throat was suddenly dry. "She's my best friend."

"Chloe . . ." Jack's eyes were swimming with sympathy I didn't need. "You know you're not alone. It's not easy to—"

"I don't want to talk about it." I gave him a sorry smile when I saw his face fall. "I have to go."

"Wait—" Jack said. For a moment, I saw the vulnerability in his eyes as they searched mine, looking for something. But then they hardened. "I want you to promise, Chloe. Promise me that you will go through with this."

"I promise," I said. Of course I would. Couldn't he see what I had sacrificed for this plan?

He nodded. "I'm counting on you, Chloe."

After leaving, I accelerated out of the parking lot, studying for the test long forgotten. I had one thing on my mind now, and that was revenge. For Monica. For Jack. For me. Now, with a new alliance, exposing Level One was so close I could taste it.

Hours later my entire body was still buzzing from everything Jack and I had discussed. It was like I had just downed ten shots of espresso, my thoughts running a hundred miles an hour. All I needed was the final piece, the footage from their parties. I *knew* it would be valuable, especially if Maddy trusted Desmond enough to use as a pawn in her plan to drug me. What else had he been told to record?

I'd drawn up a dozen plans, running them through my head over and over. Now that I'd confided in Jack, there was the increased probability that I'd be exposed as a double agent. The more people that knew, the more likely they'd discover my motives. William was right. This couldn't go on much longer. I needed to act fast.

My mom was away, leaving the house empty tonight. She was accompanying Dad to some gala in New York. He liked to act like a family man when he could, at least when the press was involved. It was the perfect opportunity.

My fingers were dialing William's number before I could stop them, bringing my phone to my ear just as it started ringing. He answered almost instantly.

"Chloe?" he asked. "Is everything okay?"

"Yes," I said, letting out a long breath. "I'm just . . . planning."

"Planning what?"

I took a deep breath. "I want to break into Desmond's house and steal his footage."

William gave a long pause. "Breaking in and stealing? Really, Chlo?"

"Really."

"That's a big deal."

"Yep."

"And very risky."

"So is what I'm already doing."

"Not just lose-your-social-status risky, but go-to-jail-get-a-criminal-record kind of risky," he reminded me.

"Not if I'm careful," I said.

He sighed. It was frustrating to be discussing it in a phone call. I hadn't realized it would bother him so much.

"And you think this will finish it?"

"I have more evidence," I said. "About Sophie."

I filled him in on my encounter with Jack while he remained silent.

"You *told* someone?"

I was taken aback by his disapproval. "Well, yeah, he's on my side—on our side—he wants to expose them too."

"Aren't you worried this is going too far? I mean, now a teacher's involved. I don't think it's a good idea," he said finally.

I couldn't help but feel disappointed. "I know it's crazy, but I've thought this through. If I can get my hands on what I need, then it doesn't matter if I'm caught. I'll have enough evidence against Desmond himself that he won't report me. This will be over."

"I get where you're coming from," he said, "I really do, but I think it's extreme."

"So is what happened to Mon."

I could almost feel his look through the phone. That wasn't an appropriate response. "Chloe, seriously. Just consider the repercussions."

"Of course I've considered them," I said. I'd done my research. William didn't know that over the weekend instead of working on a math assignment I'd downloaded floor plans of the identical units for sale besides Desmond's and drawn out an entry plan, going as far as to undertake extensive research on the schedules of him and his two housemates. "Why are you trying to stop me?"

"Because this is a completely different league, Chlo." I waited for him to continue. "I don't know if I can afford to be involved. After the fight and all."

My disappointment only grew. Why had I subconsciously assumed he'd be in on this with me? It wasn't like I was going to blackmail him into it. Besides, I shouldn't need his help anyway. I could totally do this on my own. "I was just running the idea past you."

"When are you going to do it?" he asked.

"Tomorrow morning. Early." I couldn't wait any longer, not if Jack knew, only increasing the probability that I'd be caught. "If things go to plan, this will be a piece of cake."

"Right. And if they don't?"

"Then I go to plan B," I said, grimacing. "And it's going to involve finding a whole lot of blackmail material on him, something big enough to get him to help no matter what the girls have on him, whether that be cash or secrets."

"That *does* make breaking in sound easier," he said dryly. But then he dropped the sarcasm. "You know it's not too late, Chlo."

"For what?"

"You can stop this. Stop the whole revenge thing. Let Monica go. She made her decision. I'd like to see them suffer for what they did just as much as you, but this is crazy. Can't you see what it's doing to you?"

Maybe he meant the fact I was falling behind in my classes, or maybe it was stealing Stephanie's phone. Of course I was making sacrifices. That's what best friends did for each other. I was doing this to make things right.

"And, Chloe, I know you don't want to hear it, but . . . can't you see? Can't you see what happened since that night? We haven't gone unchanged. Monica changed us. We've been paying too even if you can't see it. Did you know—"

"It's because they're your friends, isn't it?" I asked, cutting him off. "You're on their side now. You want them to get away with it."

"No," William said. Though he wasn't physically here, his voice still managed to sting. "I'm on *your* side, which is why I'm telling you this. This isn't just a one-stop revenge job. They'll come for you after. They won't let you get away with it."

Of course I knew that. And I didn't care. "If you're on my side, then help me."

"I *am* trying to help you. Not Monica, but you."

William's words made my heart skip a beat. Not Monica, but *you*.

But a distant memory hit me, from one of the last times Monica and I spoke. I didn't like to remember our arguments. Or the times toward the end. When she'd started hanging at the Level One table, she started to resent me. I was holding her back, I guess. I'd caught her drinking at school, intoxicated with Lola, Maddy, and Sophie by third period, during one of their junior-year math-class drinking-game phases.

"Don't you get it, Chloe? I'm the only one who really sees you.

Probably the only reason you have any friends is because people want to be close to me."

"She's my best friend."

"And what about her?" he asked. "Would Monica have done the same for you?"

I thought about that. Toward the end, maybe not. She'd walk down the halls as if she didn't see me while heading straight to Lola Davenport's side. But he didn't know Monica before she became one of them.

"Yes," I said. "But it doesn't matter. You don't know her like I do."

"I think you're delusional," he said. His tone softened, as if he felt sorry for me. "I don't think you realize what you're getting yourself into, and I'm worried."

"Well, you won't have to worry much longer," I said, scowling. I couldn't even tell if my anger was justified anymore. All I felt was my heart breaking. "This will be over by the end of the week."

"What time?" he asked. "What time are you doing it?"

"I'm leaving here at three thirty."

"And if you get caught? What's your backup plan?"

There wasn't one. "I won't."

"Chlo?" I closed my eyes, trying to imprint his tone into my brain, to make sure I remembered how warm his soft use of my nickname made me feel. I might not hear it again, after all. "Be safe, okay?"

I squeezed my eyes shut just for a second longer, as if clinging to his words. I almost hated that he cared, even if it felt like a tether holding me together. "I'll do my best."

Neither of us knew what to say. After a few long moments, the line went dead.

I wanted to cry once my cheek hit my pillow, but nothing came out. I hadn't really been able to cry since Monica had gone. I'd let out a few tears of frustration, but my chest still felt like a bottle filled to the brim and ready to explode, and somehow that was so much worse.

My chest was so heavy I wanted to reach into my heart and throw it out. There was no reason for me to feel so betrayed. I tried to fill my mind with memories of Monica and me, back when things were good. But it only made me sadder. It was so unfair.

In the few weeks of senior year, my mental health had plummeted. The Level One girls had ruined any self-esteem I had, both from Sophie's snide comments about my body and the way they were constantly tearing apart the girls around us.

Every time they picked apart someone's appearance, I wondered what they thought of my own. I stared at the defrosting pizza waiting for me on the stovetop and pushed it toward the trash. Even if I could stomach food in my state, the last thing I wanted was to feel guilty about the calories.

I became a robot. I mutely went through a list of things to take with me, from binoculars to a black scarf to cover my face. I had a lock pick, thanks to a handy investment I made over the summer when I wanted to get into my father's locked desk drawer. I even packed a crowbar from the garage, in case I got desperate.

Sleep was impossible to find, no matter which way I lay or how hard I tried to ignore my whirling thoughts. I couldn't stop thinking about William, and how cold he'd been on the phone. Really, it was a luxury that he'd been nice to me at all. I should have expected this.

But even that revelation didn't make it easier. Especially since the moment I stopped thinking about William, I was reminded of something else. Stephanie Griffith's horrified face as she was led through the hall. Maddy Danton switching our drinks. Monica's gaze skimming past me in the halls.

At three thirty, I rose from bed, grabbing the black jeans and leather jacket I'd prepared. I laced light boots around my feet and swept my hair behind my ear with Monica's hairpin for good luck. I was feeling determined, the low having worn off, leaving behind a desperation to make this right.

I was grabbing the keys to my mom's car from the hook when headlights filtered through the silk curtains and into the room. I shielded my eyes for a few seconds before they switched off, the night feeling even darker than it had before.

It was no coincidence that a car was outside of my home at this hour.

I walked closer to the window, squinting. It was hard to make anything out in the night, but when he stepped out of his car and under the streetlight my heart hammered in recognition.

Wearing dark clothes and exhaling chilly clouds of condensation as he shoved his hands in his pockets was William Bishop.

TWENTY-SIX

Monica,

What would you have done for me?

During freshman year you told that boy to back off when he flicked a rubber band at my hair. One summer you gave me your ice-cream cone when mine fell to the floor. You'd spend hours doing my makeup, plucking my brows.

But you wouldn't sacrifice popularity for me. You wouldn't even try to have both.

I know, I'm naive. You couldn't have both. It was them or me.

But I'd have done anything for you, Mon. I still would.

Love, Chloe

MY BREATHING HITCHED as I stepped out of the door.

"You changed your mind," I said, my voice sounding faint in the quiet night air.

He raised his lips in a humorless half grin and crossed his arms over his chest wordlessly. I pursed my lips shut and headed to the car where he gestured, hoisting the duffel bag of tools over my shoulder and climbing into the passenger seat.

"Why?" I asked. My voice was croaky from the restless few hours of sleep I'd managed. I still wasn't quite sure if this was a dream.

"Because I couldn't live with myself if you went by yourself and something happened," he said. "I'm still frustrated, Chloe. I think you're being reckless. But I also know you're smart, and I believe you can do this. That's what scares me."

"You want to be on my good side when all of this goes down?" I asked jokingly. I wanted to ease the tension slowly developing.

He sighed, rolling his eyes.

"Thank you," I said. "I know this is a huge risk, with everything going on . . ."

"Which is why we can't get caught," he said.

I swallowed. "I just don't want you risking everything because of me. I know I asked you in the first place, but if something *did* go wrong, you're already in trouble with school. If you get arrested or—"

"We won't." His frown was set deep, and I could tell that even if he was quick to dismiss me, he was worried about it too. "Do you want coffee? I brought coffee."

The idea of caffeine had my mouth watering, and William nodded to where a thermos sat in the cup holder. I opened the metal lid and took a sip, before screwing up my face and passing it to him. "I hate black coffee. Gross."

"Hey, no complaining. You dragged me out of bed this early," he pointed out before taking a mouthful. "That being said, I wasn't getting much sleep."

"Neither was I."

William pulled onto the road and followed my directions toward Desmond's house. The streets were empty, and our journey was so quick that it wasn't enough time to settle my nerves even the slightest. I didn't realize how much I was starting to dread my mission.

"Whose car is this?" I asked as we rounded the corner onto Desmond's street. Instead of his usual flashy BMW, he was driving a smaller black one, which—although still luxurious—was a lot less conspicuous.

"My sister's. She'd kill me if she knew I took it, but she won't find out," he said.

"You don't talk about her much," I said, desperate to fill the space between us with chatter. Something about him going against everything he'd said before—even when I was attacking him—had created an atmosphere that was hard to ignore. He cared about me, and now he was showing it with more than just words.

And, meanwhile, I continued to deceive him and shove him aside for a best friend I didn't want to admit wasn't here. If only it were a simple choice between her and him.

"My sister?" he asked, oblivious to what was brewing in

my mind. "We're not really that close anymore since she left for college."

"I always wanted a sibling," I said as he pulled up under a tree behind a large truck. Conveniently, it was parked in a position that let us blend in with the other cars on the street without obstructing our view.

"Funny, I used to try and convince her to run away from home so I'd be an only child," he mused, a fond smile playing across his lips.

"That's awful."

"Not when she used to cut my hair in my sleep—or when she threw my pet lizard into the garden from the second floor. And once she ran over my new bike and blamed it on the fact that she was *learning to drive*."

I laughed. "She threw the lizard out of the window, really?"

"I think it was because I melted one of her Barbies in the oven by accident."

I pursed my lips in amusement and tried to see through the darkness to the unit closest to the street. I hadn't considered that there were no streetlights providing clear illumination onto the building. "I used to think Monica and I were supposed to be sisters."

William hesitated. "She'd have been lucky to have you as one."

We were silent for a little while. "You probably think I'm obsessed with her."

"Not obsessed," William said. "Just very protective. But yeah, I think you might be holding on a little too tightly."

Maybe I was. "It's just—after everything they did to her, how they just walked away from it . . . it makes my blood boil. I can't just back out because it's getting too complicated."

"I understand that," he said. "There was a reason I agreed, Chloe. I know what they did, it wasn't fair. What *we* did. And if revenge didn't mean taking risks like this, then I'd still be all for it."

"You don't agree with me, but you're still here for me," I translated. My heart swelled.

He was quiet, his expression thoughtful as he pressed the backs of his fingers to his lips, leaning his elbow against the window.

I returned my focus to the house. Fear was starting to nibble at my mind. What if his neighbors thought we were suspicious and called the cops? What if one of the housemates stayed home sick today and we couldn't get in? What about that test I was supposed to take in just over seven hours?

"If you could go back," William began after a few moments. "Would you do it all again?"

"What?" I asked. "Take down Level One?"

"Yeah."

I thought about that. Sure, everything had become a lot more complex than I'd imagined, but where would I be if I didn't? I'd be nobody, blending into the background with Jack while they ruled the school, letting Monica go without justice. I wouldn't have started this whole thing with William. I wouldn't have come to know him.

"I would," I said. "What about you? If you could replay the night I came to you with blackmail, would you still go through with it?"

"Well, I know you better now. I know that you wouldn't use it," he said with a wry smile. "I don't know. I don't think I'd let you into our circle. I'd protect you from their bullshit. I'd get whatever you needed myself instead."

"I'd still use it," I mumbled half-heartedly. His answer irritated me, as if I was incapable. But I knew from his tone that's not what he meant.

"No, you wouldn't," he scoffed. "Not now. Not after all we've been through."

I sighed. He was right.

We were quiet again when William's laughter broke the silence that had developed as we slowly became engrossed in our own thoughts.

"What's funny?" I asked.

He gestured to the space between us. "This. It's, what, five thirty in the morning? And we're sitting here staking out some guy's house."

Now that he said it, my tired mind also found it funny. Hilarious, in fact. I laughed with him. "If you'd told me six months ago that I would be sitting in a car alone with you at five thirty in the morning, I would have thought you were crazy."

"Really? I'm curious," he said, leaning in a little. "What did you think of me before all of this mess?"

I narrowed my eyes. "I thought you were just another Level One guy who had slept with at least half the school."

He laughed again. "Really? My reputation is impressive."

"I don't know if that's a good thing," I pointed out.

"And what do you think of me now?"

What did I think of William Bishop? Right now, in some ways he was all that was holding me together. I was sure that if I was alone the silence would eat me alive. It would amplify that little voice in my head that loved to remind me my failures.

"I think you're a good guy," I said honestly, averting my gaze away from his. "I think you're too good to be on Level One."

When he didn't reply I assumed he'd dismissed my words, but when I looked toward him he seemed lost in thought.

"That means a lot that you said that. When you found out about me and Lola, I thought for sure you'd hate me," he said.

Bringing up the image of William and Lola made me go from feeling sentimental to slightly repulsed, but I shook it off.

"You weren't in a good place last night," he pointed out. "I know you're stressed, but it's like you're losing it, Chlo."

"I felt like I was," I admitted. "After everything that happened with Maddy—I'm sure you got that picture too—and then Jack . . . I was overwhelmed . . . desperate . . ."

My voice trailed off and I screwed my eyes shut before continuing.

"Just being in this position, trying to put on this costume to be someone else; this intimidating, skinny, and rich Chloe who fits in with them—it just stresses me out *all the time*. It's taken away every piece of me. Everything I do is for the revenge, and the more I think it over, the more it drives me crazy."

"I think you have more of yourself than you think," he murmured. "I still see a girl who is everything those girls aren't. You underestimate yourself, Chloe."

Maybe if it wasn't for the tightness weighing in my chest, I wouldn't have spoken to him about my insecurities, and he wouldn't say things so nice they made my boundaries dissolve. Maybe his eyes wouldn't burn into mine in a way that made me yearn for him.

But they did.

My breathing had become shallow when his fingertips grazed my cheek, gently trapping the wisps of hair that had fallen from my ponytail and brushing them behind my ear. All I could think of were his lips, and the way he'd pressed them so urgently to mine. How exhilarating it had felt. For a moment, it felt like we were frozen, each one of us unsure what our next move would be.

But then a light switched on in a window across the street.

"Someone's awake," he said a little too quickly. We moved apart.

"It's Brad, I think. He should be waking up to get ready for work now," I said, my tone just as rushed as I checked my watch. "The others should be up soon too."

"You really have done your research."

My heart was hammering in my ears.

Minutes passed where we didn't say anything. We watched anxiously as the sky turned from an inky black to a murky gray. More lights popped on, both in the unit and the ones surrounding it. My gut was twisting at the knowledge that we'd soon be entering that house.

I was becoming acutely aware of the rise and fall of William's chest beside me, and I had to stop the urge to reach out and touch him in some way. To feel his skin burn against mine.

Hormonal teenage girl, I reminded myself.

This wasn't a good time for weaknesses.

The first car left the garage, followed by a second just before seven. Our conversation had died, each of us had hit a wall that we were too scared to break through.

The small space in the car was quickly becoming unbearable.

At seven fifty, just as I sensed William start to doze off beside me, the roller door opened and a truck pulled out. I could identify Desmond's profile as the driver in the dull light of the freshly risen sun.

I took a deep breath, the movement enough to stir William beside me. It was time.

TWENTY-SEVEN

Monica,

When I was young, all that mattered to me were you and my parents. I thought you were perfect, and I thought my dad was a superhero. Piece by piece, that image of him was destroyed when I grew up and saw him for what he really is.

You were different.

I never stopped seeing the best in you. Even now.

Love, Chloe

WILLIAM AND I exited the car simultaneously, him with the bag thrown over his shoulder and me on the lookout as we crossed the road.

"The front door?" William whispered, his lips barely moving as he spoke under his breath.

I nodded, watching as a car pulled up a hundred or so yards away. My breathing hitched. "No, wait, backup plan.

We don't have time to pick locks—we'll go to fence, where we're hidden from the street."

William, who appeared just as anxious as I was, led us around the side of the house. Time seemed to slow, each second exposed increasing the probability of something going wrong.

The fence was tall, much taller now that we were right up against it. I looked to William, who looked to me. Time was ticking.

"Here," he said after half a second. He crouched over, holding out his hands. "I'll hoist you up and follow."

I sized up the fence. There was no way I was tall enough to pull myself over it, but he probably was.

Following his instruction, I placed my foot in his hand, and on a silent count of three I jumped upward, hitting the metal of the fence with a loud bang. A wave of panic washed over me, and it took all my concentration not to slip. With my breath hitched I caught my balance, and after one more look at William, I slid over to the other side.

I didn't anticipate that there would be a dog.

The fluffy shih tzu didn't bark. Instead it merely tilted its head curiously before running toward me. I was about to freak out before I realized its intention was only to lick me.

"I'm tossing the bag over," William said seconds before the duffel bag flew through the air.

"Okay," I said, stopping it from hitting the dirt below just in time. "Um, just warning you, there's a dog."

William fell to the ground with a grunt. The dog, which was barely the size of a large cat, had been scratching at my leg. Now his adorable attention was on William.

"Not much of a guard dog," he noted.

"Shh," I said, looking around at where the top of the building met the gutter. "There might be cameras."

The garden was small, barely large enough for a patch of lawn and a clothesline, matching what I'd seen on satellite imagery. There were some outdoor pieces of furniture that looked like they'd seen better days, and an assortment of cigarette butts and beer bottles in a pile by the back door.

I couldn't spot any surveillance systems, but I didn't want to take the risk. I checked again.

"I can't see any," William said after a moment, confirming my thoughts. "Come on, we have to move."

I nodded in agreement before unzipping the bag and removing a pair of black gloves. I didn't have any for him with me, but I handed him the black material I'd intended to hide my face instead.

"We should have put these on before we jumped the fence," I said with a frustrated sigh. *Stupid.* I moved to the back window that I'd seen on the floor plan. It was the lowest to the ground and was also unlikely to come with heavy security, being at the back of the house.

"Prints won't stay for long," he reasoned. "It will probably rain in the next few hours. And we could always leave a front window ajar so they think we got in through there."

I nodded, convincing myself that his argument was reassuring. I ran my fingers along the window frame.

"As long as the dog doesn't tell anyone." He gestured to the dog sitting at his feet.

Ignoring him, my mind far from joking, I found the latch that removed the mesh screen from the window and pulled at it. I let out a sigh of relief when it gave way.

I looked to William, whose eyes were fixed on me with a look I couldn't quite comprehend. "What?"

"Nothing," he said, shaking his head with a smile. "It's just you're so professional, like you've been breaking into houses your whole life."

"Who says I haven't?" I challenged, pulling the window across the pane with triumph. I grinned. "And guess who keeps their windows unlocked?"

We'd gotten lucky when it came to getting in. But even with the glass pulled to the side, the gap wasn't big enough to easily climb into. It would be a squeeze, especially for William.

I slipped through first, sitting on the sill for half a second to assess the interior. It was a laundry room, obvious from the pile of clothing scattered over the tiles beside a washer and dryer. My feet hit the floor soundlessly and I turned to Will. "We're good."

After handing me the bag, William stuck one leg through the opening and hoisted himself up. I took his hand when I realized he wouldn't be able to balance while swinging his other leg over. It was warm in my grip, even through my gloves.

There was no time for my thoughts to linger, not when my paranoia had shifted from worrying the neighbors would see us to there being someone left inside the house. I did my best to push the growing anxiety away.

"We have to figure out which bedroom is his," I said as I prepared myself to open the laundry door. "We need to work as fast as possible—we'll split up and search."

He nodded, his expression wary. "What exactly are we looking for?"

"Hard drives. Cameras. Computer storage. Maybe even computers themselves," I listed. "We just need to find which room is his, first."

William nodded curtly, and with that I took a deep breath and opened the door, revealing a darkened hallway. It was quiet, almost too quiet. The sound of our breathing seemed to echo throughout the rooms, bringing a chill to my spine.

I threw him a flashlight. "Don't turn on any lights, and make sure you keep your hands covered."

"Got it."

"You go to the end. I'll start with this room," I said, nodding to the doorway closest to us. "Meet in the middle."

I didn't hesitate to barge into my allocated room. It was dark, the curtains drawn. I turned on my own flashlight, deciding where to begin. I could see that there were no decorations immediately identifying the owner, save for a poster of a car hung across the wall. I went to the top drawer of the bedside table, figuring that that was usually the most personal.

Inside were a few watches, a dozen or so condom wrappers, and receipts. I picked up something small and plastic. It was an expired bank card, something someone definitely shouldn't keep around. Unfortunately, the name on it was not who I was looking for.

After returning the bank card to where I'd found it, I backed into the hallway.

I wanted to call out to William again, but I was paranoid that someone would hear, so I went straight to the next room instead. Much like the previous one, it was dark and untidy. This time, though, I instantly knew it was Desmond's. In one corner of the room was a stack of camera equipment, a few different-sized tripods leaning against the wall, and boxes spilling with random straps, cords, and lenses.

This bed was unmade, but on the walls were photographs rather than posters. I examined them. They seemed to be pictures of parties; dance floors filled with movement and people grinning wildly.

A figure appeared in my periphery and I jumped. But luckily, it was just William. He must have cleared his room too. "Is this it?"

I nodded, moving toward the camera gear stacked in the corner. "I'll start here. You start by the chest of drawers?"

He obeyed, walking over and kneeling by the space I'd indicated. I didn't waste any time, pulling the boxes from their stacks and flipping through the contents.

I didn't understand any of what I was seeing, but it looked

to be more recording equipment than removable computer storage. I wondered if he somehow just kept it all on his laptop, uploaded to some highly secure online drive. I didn't want to resort to stealing anything as huge as a computer, but if that was our only option, then so be it.

Just as I was considering boxing up everything and taking it with us, William spoke, his voice in disbelief.

"Chloe, look."

He was kneeling in front of a drawer he'd just pulled out, its contents a jumble of thick plastic devices and wires. I dropped the box that had been on my lap and stumbled over to him, my legs weak.

I grabbed the first one I saw. They were all different sizes and brands, but I could see the one in my hand was a terabyte large from the engraving in the corner. I flipped it over, my gloved hands landing on a set of grooves at the base. I shone the light over it. A year was engraved into the case. *2015 Part One.*

"They have dates," I said. "Or periods of time, at least."

"This one has too," he confirmed. "Twenty seventeen."

I scrambled to find the next one, my heart thudding as I read the date. "Two thousand and nineteen." Last year.

William looked at me, this time hesitation in his eyes. "I'm not doubting you or anything, Chlo, I swear, but are you sure . . . are you sure you really want to see this?"

I swallowed, turning it over in my hands. It might not even have anything useful. He might have deleted every piece of Monica from it, just like Level One had done with their lives.

"Yes," I said. "I need it. I need all of them. Take as many years as you can."

We loaded them into the duffel bag, even the ones engraved with *family holiday summer 2018* and *Christmas 2017*. He could have saved them anywhere. I sensed a guy like Desmond wouldn't destroy anything as valuable as the demise of Monica Pennington. It had to be in there somewhere.

"I can't believe we actually found this," William said as I zipped up the bag, the last of the hard drives loaded inside.

"Let's hope our luck doesn't run out," I muttered, casting a glance around the room. There was nothing else valuable to me. If what I thought was on the drives was correct, then I had everything I needed.

Desmond was stupid to leave himself so vulnerable. I should have left a thank-you note.

"Let's go."

Our trip out went as smoothly as our trip in. We left the rooms as we'd seen them and fastened the screen back across the window. The dog whined as we passed through the gate at the other end of the house, locking it behind us.

I peeled off the gloves as we crossed the road, refastening my hair with a tie from around my wrist, and then we slipped into the car and drove off as fast as possible.

We'd done it. And now I was desperate to unlock whatever secrets the files could reveal.

"Can we go back to my house?" I asked. "I can't go to school yet—I need to find out what's on these."

"You could be searching for hours, Chlo," he pointed out as he pulled up at a light. He was flushed, his cheeks visibly warm, and I figured he was just as relieved as I was. "Don't you have a test?"

"No," I lied, dismissing him. I didn't want to be snappy, but I was growing tired and desperate. "Just take me back to my house."

William did as I said, pulling up on my street after minutes of silence. "I'll help."

I frowned. "Are you sure?"

He nodded.

I went straight upstairs once we'd arrived, ignoring any qualms I felt about bringing William Bishop into my bedroom. I'd been filled with a new energy, a new *purpose*. Even with all the planning I'd put in, I still couldn't comprehend that we actually came out of it successful.

I tossed the bag to the floor and pulled my laptop onto my bed. William perched beside me on the duvet. "Want me to grab twenty nineteen?"

I nodded, typing in the several passwords I had protecting my computer. He plugged in the hard drive as I waited for the desktop to launch.

William's eyes met mine in anticipation, their green illuminated by the light filtering through the curtains. The joy in my chest only grew with the small smile that formed on his lips.

Back up external hard drive?

I clicked yes.

This morning's victorious streak was broken when it reported it'd take an hour and thirty minutes to copy across the content.

William looked disappointed too. Maybe he'd also hoped we'd have immediate footage to show for our efforts. "Well, you could leave it running while you go to—"

The rest of his sentence was cut off by the distinct sound of the front door opening.

"Crap," I hissed. In one slow second, I managed to do multiple things at once. With one hand, I shut the laptop and forced it—and the hard drive—under a horde of cushions. With the other, I grabbed the duffel bag and William's arm before lunging into my closet.

Our breaths were coming fast as I heard footsteps below the stairs. My mom was home. I didn't even realize she would be back so early.

"It's my mom," I whispered, looking away. If I looked directly at him, our noses would touch. There wasn't much room between the designer labels. I was experiencing déjà vu, flashing back to when I was trapped in William's locker. Only, instead of his lacrosse gear pressed against me, it was *him*.

"Let me guess, she can't know you're skipping school?" he asked, his breath landing on the top of my hair.

I ran a hand behind my ear. "Obviously."

I could hear her downstairs, humming to herself among

the rustling of shopping bags. It was lucky William was driving a different car, or the model on the street would have definitely caught her attention.

I let out a frustrated groan. "We might never get past her."

"So we better get comfy?" he joked, shifting his weight slightly, only managing to come even closer.

"I'm trying to think."

But I couldn't think. He was all around me and my heart was still pumping from the break-in. My mind was giddy, high at the thought of having everything I needed in the bag by my feet.

He was too. I could tell by the rate of his heart against my chest. God, why did I have to choose the closet? Why not, I don't know, out of the window and into the bushes? Or under the bed? Somewhere I could think clearly—about more than his lips being so close to mine.

"Chloe . . ." he whispered, his voice strained. He felt it too.

My lips parted, but I couldn't answer him. Not with everything going on in my head—in my *body*. He was so close, and I was still soaring with euphoria. I felt impulsive, and I felt an attraction growing almost impossible to hide behind my logic.

But even with my inhibitions derailed, it still surprised me when my fingers laced through his hair to pull him toward me. Then his lips were hard against mine.

TWENTY-EIGHT

Monica,

You used to tease me for not having a boyfriend. I teased you for having too many, so we were even, but I didn't know back then how lucky I was to have you to talk to about anything. Liking someone is so confusing, and I don't have anyone to confide in. It's like you could know every logical fact and it could still be demolished by a feeling in your heart. You can build up so many walls but it only brings you closer.

You can try and protect yourself as best as possible, but they can still see inside. And it's the scariest thing in the world.

Do you know what that's like?

Love, Chloe

THUNDER RUMBLED THROUGH my body, an untamed animal that had broken free from its reins. Like a match meeting flame, a spark had erupted, so hot and wild that it overcame me entirely. I was a puppet to an animalistic instinct manipulating my fingers to wind through his hair, filling me with a desperation, a *need,* to close the distance between us.

The small space between us had ignited.

William's hands were hard against my waist, the tips of his fingers digging into my skin in a bid to draw me close, even closer than the chest-to-chest standing space already brought us. His lips were fast against mine, deepening our kiss in seconds, fueling the fire that I had started.

The whispers in my mind that reminded me I shouldn't be doing this had been dulled by euphoria. I was captive to William's scent, his shoulders, his hot breath against my skin, his *everything.*

This wasn't for show; there was nobody here to see us. It was just us. Just him and me and an impulsive decision.

"God, how do you do this to me?" he whispered as our lips broke away from each other momentarily. His breath tickled my ear.

How was I doing this to begin with? I asked myself, but then his mouth was back on mine and his hands were slipping lower, behind my thigh, pulling me even *closer.* I was sure I was going to explode. Sure that, somehow, something in my physiological makeup had shifted and turned me into a completely different person.

I'm making out with William Bishop. In my closet.

This was not part of the plan. No, this was a physical

reaction to close proximity and our giddy high after the roller coaster that was this morning. *And* the attraction, which I couldn't deny I felt for him anymore.

"Will," I whispered just as his lips started tracking down my jaw and across my neck in a way which made goose bumps rise on the most sensitive pieces of my skin. It felt electrifying, arising a whole new surge of feelings. "William."

He stopped. My chest was rising and falling against his at a quickened pace.

"Just Will," he murmured with a glint in his eyes.

"What are we doing?" I squeaked, having to consciously stop my hands wandering from around his neck to down his chest. "We can't do this."

"Why not?" he challenged, somehow moving even closer. "I don't think I've seen you lose control before, Chlo. Just let go."

He was right. And that was why I needed to regain it. I deflected his kiss, even if it made my heart lurch in yearning. "We need to get out of here."

"Didn't realize how fast you wanted to take this," he joked, his lips brushing against my ear.

"I mean out of the house," I whispered, not wanting to think any further about what *this* was. It was too complicated, and guilt was already starting to wind its way through my chest. "We're still hiding in my closet."

"I don't know, I kind of like it," he said, the flirtatious edge still thick in his voice. In the faint light creeping through the edge of the wooden doors, I could make out the crook of his smirk.

I heard the clamoring of my mom in the kitchen, and then the blaring of a radio as she switched on the speakers in the downstairs hallway.

"But," William said with a slow sigh. "You should probably get to school."

Shit, I thought, suddenly reminded that I was currently skipping my test, and now my mom was home I'd *definitely* be in trouble.

I swallowed. "I'll pretend to be sick, if I go down there now looking ill . . ."

William's fingertips ran down my arms, leaving a wake of electrifying currents bursting beneath my skin, distracting me.

"You can sneak out," I said a little forcefully as I tried to get a grip. As much as I wanted to grab him again, it was only a matter of time before my mom came up here, and the thought of her finding us like this was terrifying.

"Classy," he said. He gave a rueful smile and managed to put a few inches between us in the confined space. "We probably shouldn't rush into anything, anyway—not that I don't want to—it's just, this has all been . . . a little intense."

"Intense is an understatement," I muttered.

"At least neither of us got arrested," he said cheerfully, but something in his tone sounded distant. "Call me soon, okay?

When you get to the footage. Or if you . . . if you don't want to watch it alone."

I nodded briskly. I wanted to know what this meant for us, which felt silly. Was that even something I could ask? Suddenly nothing was adding up anymore—the deal, the revenge, the blackmail.

It wasn't supposed to be real, but that kiss certainly was.

"Chloe," William said, his hand cupping my cheek. "I . . . You know I really care about you."

"Yes," I whispered. He'd shown that.

"It was out of guilt at first. For everything that happened to Mon. But it's more than that now," he confessed, before dropping his hand, only to run it through his mussed hair instead. "That's why I wanted to stop fake dating. I can't tell what's real anymore."

"Me either." I shook my head, as if that'd be enough to clear it. His words were only leaving me more confused. "We can't talk about this now. I'm going to go downstairs. Come down when you hear us talking. I'll distract her and you duck out the front door. Quietly, okay?"

"We did just rob a house," he reminded me. "I know what I'm doing."

Tentatively, I opened the door to my closet and stepped out. I hoped putting some distance between me and William would calm my racing heart, but it was futile. I tried to focus on anything other than his lips.

I realized I couldn't exactly go downstairs in jeans and a

jacket. I looked back to where William was leaning against the doorframe of the wardrobe and flicked my head. "Back in. I need to change."

He gave me a wide grin before retreating. I shook my head, feeling silly. I was just glad that there was no way he could see through to where I was pulling off my jeans and replacing them with pajama shorts.

While Mom yelled at me about not telling her I was home sick, William snuck out of the front door. Luckily, though, the lecture didn't last long. It was only a few minutes before she was brewing me a hot chocolate and making me lunch, insisting on calling the school while I lay in bed with feigned cramps.

I'd never been so relieved to have her as my mother.

When I returned to my room, I couldn't help the weird feeling weighing me down. It was all done, and now I was alone. And so tired.

I opened my laptop to start the transfer again. When I was sure it was all on track, I nestled under the covers, my mind disobediently returning to what happened in the closet.

And then I was drowning in the memory of William against me. And God, it wouldn't stop. My body was ecstatic, the experience playing on repeat, even more so than it had when he had first kissed me to make Lola jealous.

Remembering that even then—mere weeks ago—he'd still

been hung up on her had me reeling in my own jealousy. But even then, if I was the Chloe I was a few weeks ago, I'd be planning on using our encounter to my advantage. But I wasn't.

Something had changed. We had changed.

In another world, maybe William would've been my crush. Maybe I might've been his, and maybe we'd date. But it was much more complicated than that. I couldn't ignore that he'd once loved the girl I loathed the most. He'd sworn himself to secrecy to prevent justice for my best friend, just like all of Level One had.

I had to stop. I couldn't grow feelings for him, not now. It wasn't realistic. He was part of a world I could never grow content with existing.

When sleep finally found me, it didn't let me go. I woke late in the afternoon. As soon as I gained consciousness I reached to check my laptop, my heart thudding. The files were mine.

I fell back into bed, my chest now filled with a new emptiness as I realized the weight of what I was about to do. I was disorientated by sleep. I hadn't texted William like he'd asked, so I sent him a message. I could still taste him against my lips, erupting an erratic beat to my heart.

It could be everything I needed, or nothing useful at all. I couldn't get my hopes up. Nerves wrapped around me as I pulled the laptop in front of me, the light of its screen illuminating the darkness. I entered the removable storage, hundreds of folders appearing on the screen.

Like the hard drives themselves, the folders were organized by dates. I scrolled through them slowly, there were at least a hundred. But there was only one date I cared about right now. I just wanted the world to know the truth about what happened to my best friend.

But the date was missing.

I let out a curse. It made sense that he would hide it. The thought of him deleting it brought a wave of fear, until I came across an unusual folder name at the bottom. Unlike the others, it wasn't labeled with an organized date.

Escarlate. In one quick sweep, I highlighted the title and entered it into Google Translate. Scarlet.

Like Monica's hair.

My heart froze, cloaking in a sheet of burning ice. Though I was numb with anticipation, my fingers somehow managed to double click.

The folder revealed thirty or so media files, the thumbnails making it look as if they'd all been taken in the same place. The same night. Darkness, green and purple films of light.

With bated breath I highlighted them, my stomach squirming with a knot so tight I thought I was going to be sick.

I pressed play.

TWENTY-NINE

Monica,

Happy birthday. I never actually said that to you. I was too angry. Of course, I never made it to your party either. I wish I had. Maybe things would have been different.

I know you would have looked beautiful, and everyone's eyes would have been on you. They always were on you, anyway.

That's probably why Level One hated you.

Love, Chloe

"HEY, SCARLET," I heard from behind the camera.

Monica twirled for Desmond, and for a moment, with her eyes staring directly down the lens and her red hair flowing in spirals down her back, it felt real. It felt like she was grinning at me, like she was really here.

It was her birthday party. Her parents had abandoned her

family mansion for their beach house in Miami so she could host her own party, inviting only the most popular of Arlington's student body.

At that point, we hadn't spoken in weeks. But I still found the invite in my locker that afternoon, as if I were an afterthought.

"Are you going to get ready for Mon's party?" my mom had asked, having seen the invitation discarded in the trash.

"I can't," I'd said. There'd been a lump in my throat. I'd cried a lot back then, mostly in secret. I felt so lonely once she started hanging with them, maybe even lonelier than after she'd left.

Of course I'd thought about going. But I knew what it'd be like. Monica would have invited me out of guilt, and I'd stand by the sidelines watching as she tried harder and harder to be a Level One.

Desmond's camera followed her around as she embraced Lola and Sophie. I saw Monica pause to whisper something in their ears, but all the audio registered was some loud pop song blaring from the speakers she'd set up in the living room.

I skipped through the first few clips, the ones of Monica posing and dancing with people as they arrived. It made a painful knot grow in my stomach. One of those people could have been me. *Should* have been me.

One clip stood out to me, a black thumbnail among the colorful lights.

The first few seconds, the screen was dark. I could hear

distant music and Desmond's breathing; he must have been outside somewhere. Then figures appeared, silhouetted a few yards away. Desmond was adjusting the camera, bringing them in and out of focus, until stopping on the perfect setting. I could clearly see who it was.

"Being difficult?" Francis's whisper barely registered. I had to turn up the volume, so the background noise was blaring through my headphones.

"You wish," Monica said back. "You *love* it when I'm difficult."

"Actually, it frustrates me," he said roughly. "A lot."

"Then show it," she challenged.

"Out here?" he asked, gesturing to the house. "It's almost like you *want* to rub it in my girlfriend's face."

"Who cares," Monica said dryly. The tone of her voice was so familiar it made a shiver run down my spine. "It's not like we haven't done it before."

"Careful," he cooed, leaning in so close that his chest pressed against hers, her back against the hedge framing her backyard.

"Careful," she mimicked. "If you love her so much, then why do you want me so badly?"

"We all have our weaknesses."

And then he kissed her.

I was ready to exit the clip, bile rising to my mouth, when there was the sound of a branch snapping and Francis's face flipped toward the camera.

"Desmond, I'm going to kill you!" he said with fury.

"Wow, sorry, man," Desmond said from behind the camera as he straightened, the lens pointing toward the ground. "I honestly didn't know it was you—I saw the birthday girl and thought it would be—"

And then the camera was snatched from his hand and thrown to the ground.

But it kept recording, capturing nothing for a few moments before someone picked it up. Desmond sighed, and I could hear him brush the microphone off.

"I can't believe he saw you!" Monica said in a loud whisper. "You were supposed to stay hidden. That was our agreement."

"I know," Desmond replied. "But it's okay, I think it's fine, there's probably still footage—"

The clip ended.

I let go of the breath I'd been holding. Was Monica trying to record her and Francis to attack Lola?

The next clip featured Lola. She was beaming devilishly to the camera, huge earrings clipped to her ears and a plunging halter-neck dress showing off all her curves. She beckoned Desmond to follow her, leading him upstairs.

The five other members of Level One were gathered in Monica's bedroom. I recognized the butterfly fairy lights and the embroidered cushions. Maddy was on Zach's lap and Lola went to sit on Francis's, but his attention was on Desmond behind the lens as he glared with narrowed eyes. Sophie and William sat side by side, Will's ankle propped to his knee as he leaned back with a drink in hand, as if he didn't have a care in the world.

"Okay, go," Maddy said, as if they'd been waiting for Desmond.

"What are you guys doing?" he asked, the camera moving across each of their faces. Francis scowled at him. Desmond did have quite some nerve to keep doing his job after being caught.

"Playing a game," Monica replied, bringing her drink to her lips. "Truth or dare?"

Lola laughed.

"Here I was thinking you'd forgotten our game," she mused. Beside her, the eyes of Level One twinkled with entertainment.

"It's your turn, Monica," Sophie reminded her, leaning on her elbows so she could gaze at the redhead leisurely. "And I think your answer is dare."

"Dare, then."

Level One gathered in a group, deliberating her fate. Monica raised her chin and painted amusement onto her face, glancing toward Desmond as if checking he was still recording.

Finally, they'd reached a decision.

"We dare you to take a dip," Lola said carefully, testing her. She cocked her head to the side. "A skinny-dip."

"Fine," Monica said with a clipped tone. "Deal."

"Didn't your mom say the pool was off-limits?" Maddy said with a snort.

"Rules were meant to be broken, Mads."

She downed the remainder of the tequila.

"We'll be watching," Lola said, gesturing to the view from Monica's bedroom.

Monica blew a kiss as she stepped onto the balcony, looking over the crowd of people—Level One's kingdom—and out to the eerie calm of the pool.

After one more calming breath she spun around, her mask a vision of confidence and her smile one that belonged on a billboard.

"Don't miss me too much," she said, before taking off her necklace and throwing it to the bed, the first layer to be removed as she undertook her journey to the pool. She gestured for Desmond to follow her, the camera watching her every move.

People watched with curiosity as she strutted down the stairs and across the house, some gathering behind her in some kind of pageant. She kicked off her heels one by one, basking in the attention.

Only a few dared to follow her all the way to the pool, most stopping to settle in for the show. She gave a glance to the balcony, as if checking that Level One was still watching, before pulling her dress over her head, revealing expensive lingerie.

She smirked at the camera and gave a spin, almost losing her balance as she staggered to the edge.

By now, the crowd was cheering her on, fueling her high

as she danced around the perimeter of the pool. One foot in front of the other. She'd always been a perfect diver, and an even better swimmer. I knew that. I'd practiced diving with her at the swimming hole, had spent so many summers racing her along the shoreline at the beach. This challenge should have been a breeze.

Only, it wasn't.

With one more devilish smirk to the crowd, Monica turned on her heel and stretched, her arms raising above her.

She leaned onto the front of her feet, bending her knees and propelling herself into the air, arching perfectly. Her guests roared, all running forward to watch closer.

But none of them seemed to realize she'd jumped at the shallow end, her skull colliding with the surface below.

The students of Arlington Preparatory waited and waited for Monica Pennington to emerge from the glittering water, holding their breaths in anticipation for the finale of her show.

But when she did, many moments later, her face was down, her shoulders loose and her fingertips floating. The camera cut out quickly, and I was left with an empty screen.

THIRTY

Monica,

I first heard the news through Instagram.

Instagram, of all places.

The post had already been liked a thousand times. I'd woken up on that Sunday morning, the screen burning my half-asleep eyes. The first thing I did was open the app, hoping to devour the pictures from your birthday party the night before, eyeing you with scrutiny as you posed with the Level Ones.

But this post was different.

REST IN PEACE MONICA PENNINGTON. *Taken too soon.*

But you shouldn't have been taken at all.

Love, Chloe

TEARS WERE RUNNING thickly down my cheeks. They were the kind of tears you couldn't really feel. They just sort of gushed silently from your eyes.

I guess now my body decided I could cry.

In some ways, I felt as responsible as Level One. I'd been home that night, consumed by sadness at the first of our birthdays apart. If I'd gone, maybe things would be different. Maybe I'd have been able to talk sense into her—to do something—*anything.*

I hated them for taking my best friend from me when I couldn't stop them. I was powerless back then, but not anymore. Not now.

I'd heard the stories that had trickled down over the following days, that it had been a game initiated by Level One. It had fueled the rage that started my plan for revenge.

Now that I'd started crying, I couldn't stop. I crawled into a ball beneath my covers, the tears soaking my pillow and my breathing turning into sobs.

The therapist my mom had forced me to see had said so many times that I needed to accept what happened was nobody's responsibility. I needed to accept that she'd made a bad decision, and forgive her for it, but how could I when it was all their fault?

In that moment, the revelation that I had damning footage was nothing compared to the devastation flooding through me. Not only had I refused to accept that Monica had caused her own death, I'd refused to accept she was dead at all. To me, she was still there, on the other side of the ink as I wrote to her. Reachable by just a letter.

I wiped my nose on the back of my sweater sleeve and reached for my phone. I couldn't trust my voice, so I typed out a message, my vision blurred. William was right. I didn't want to be alone.

Can I come over?

Almost immediately my phone dinged with his response.

My parents are touring for dad's campaign atm, so yeah, okay.

I crept downstairs after changing into jeans and a shirt.

"I need to grab notes from my friend for the classes I missed," I told my mother, grabbing my keys from the counter. I wondered if she'd detect the tears in my voice, but if she did she didn't acknowledge it.

"Okay, honey. Don't be out too late."

He was waiting for me, sitting on the front steps, wearing sweats and a white cotton shirt. I tried my best to inhale deeply and reset my breathing, but my exhale still came out shaky.

"Hey, Whittaker," William said. His tone was sad. He must have known.

I stepped out of the car. I'd brought my laptop and I hugged it tightly to my chest.

"Here, come inside."

William led me into the living room. The ceiling was high, a modern chandelier low over the coffee table. I perched on the edge of a sofa.

"What did you see?"

I opened my mouth, but nothing came out. He searched my face, his eyes filled with concern, before pulling me into a hug.

"It's okay."

But it wasn't okay. She was gone. The tears erupted again, overflowing onto his shirt.

"I'm sorry," I said through a sob. I was so embarrassed. This new Chloe was supposed to be a strong Level One girl. They weren't supposed to show weakness.

"You have nothing to be sorry for," he said simply. "I should be the one apologizing . . . I should have done something. I'll never stop feeling guilty for that night."

I straightened and wiped my eyes. Feeling his gaze on me made me insecure. I shouldn't care what he thought of me, but I couldn't stop thinking about what he was seeing. Dark circles, puffy eyes, and bare skin.

"I just . . . it was so easy to pretend she wasn't gone," I said. "It's so stupid, but I feel like that's changed. I'd heard all the stories but now I've seen with my own eyes that it's true."

"It's not stupid. Everyone processes things differently, Chloe. It's a big deal what you went through. Losing her, I mean."

His words made me want to cry more, and I had to avert my eyes to the shag rug in the middle of the room. Though I'd broken from our hug, his hand still rested on my knee.

"I just need to talk about her," I said. "I know I never wanted to before, but . . . I need to be sure before I do this. Take them down."

"I'll tell you anything you want to know," he said.

I took in a rattled breath.

"You said once that Monica changed Level One," I said, my voice wavering slightly.

William's jaw pulsed in concentration as he traced his finger along my kneecap "She did. Of course she did."

I waited for him to gather his thoughts, silence stretching before he continued.

"I think everyone changed after that night," he said, his gaze out of the window. "None of us wanted it to happen, Chloe. I don't think we even knew that it could. It's easy to feel untouchable—like nothing can hurt you—when you live life with everything at your fingertips. We made a pact . . . not to talk about the game."

A pact. So they wouldn't be held responsible.

"Maddy," he said, his voice catching a little. "She hasn't always been so reckless, it doesn't make sense. You'd think she'd have toned it down. But it's like she's . . . taken Monica's place. She's self-destructing. I think she's using it to mute something."

"What do you think she's trying to mute?"

"Guilt," he said.

She was supposed to be Monica's friend too.

"Zach's always been a dick, but it's worse now. He lashes out, even at us. Monica always liked him, they were good friends, and now it's like he resents the world. He's bitter, he has a lot of anger at himself for not doing something to stop her, and he takes that out on other people."

I hated him. I hated him for being close to her, and still letting her die.

"And Sophie," he continued. "Ever since Monica she's become protective over Lola, even more than before. I'm sure you've seen it. She's scared. I think everything she puts into her tough exterior takes a lot of effort. Beneath it she's really nothing anymore. She used to be warm, you know? *Warmer*, at least. Now she's Lola's cold shadow."

I thought back to the way she threatened me in Maddy's bathroom. She was definitely protective over Lola. Had Monica made her feel threatened? Or brought her even closer to Lola with her death?

"Lola," he said, his voice quieting. "She didn't talk for a week. To anyone. Not even to me. She took a long time to come around, it really got to her. And then it was as if she snapped back to normal in an instant. She was loyal to Francis again. She just wiped her memory clean. Her way of coping, I guess."

I was angry. It felt wrong that Lola could be tormented by *my* best friend. I was jealous even, that up until her last moments, Lola had known her better than I did. Than I ever would.

"Francis has gone off the rails. But he was heading there, anyway," he said with a sigh. "I don't think he's made it to even half of his classes this semester. And it's senior year."

In a way, I felt a pang of satisfaction that they were at least suffering in some way. But they weren't suffering for the same reason I was. I was suffering because I lost my only friend. They were suffering because they killed her.

"I keep thinking there was something I could have done," William said. "I told you about the others, but she changed me too, Chlo. It destroys me to think about it. All the times I tried to help her—it was like she didn't care. I had no idea this would happen, if I did . . ."

His fingers tightened over my leg as he spoke.

"But she still made those choices. She wasn't always the victim. She was playing her own game too."

She was. She was trying to control Lola. That's the only reason she'd want footage of her and Francis. She used to joke about what it would be like to be queen of Arlington, to sit in Lola Davenport's shoes. Maybe that was exactly her aim all along.

She'd pretend she didn't know me in the halls, just to keep her image intact. All she wanted was to be one of them, and it had extended past most people's goal for popularity. She wanted the power.

Monica's parents were rich, yes, but it was mostly by inheritance and investments. They weren't influential. It didn't give Monica instant status in the school like the others. She had to work for it—and she was hungry to do so. Her mom tried to control her so much it made her desperate to break rules. It was written into her persona since before I even met her.

"I write to her," I blurted. "I mean, I know she won't reply, but I keep having this stupid hope that maybe it isn't real. Maybe she will."

William pulled me toward him again, so that I was nestled into his chest. I closed my eyes and let myself become lost in his warmth, his scent, the pace of his breathing. We stayed like that for a long time. I wanted to be mad at him. He was in that video too. But somehow, I couldn't. He'd done so much for me. For Monica.

"I told my dad about what happened, you know," he said, his breath catching in my hair. "I wanted to tell the police everything. I mean, we were just kids. I didn't think we'd get in trouble for telling her to do it. But he wouldn't let me. He said if I did, I'd destroy the family. That because I was involved, it'd bring him down too."

"Would you have done it?" I asked. "Taken that fall?"

"In a heartbeat," he said quietly.

Now it was our chance to make things right.

We sat through hours of footage, sprawled on his couch with the laptop in my lap. Most of it was boring. The boys playing beer pong at parties, the girls clinking champagne flutes and air-kissing one another. Drunken dancing. Happy group shots.

But there were snippets interlaced within that gave me hope that we'd actually have something. It was finally time for the next stage. The exposé.

Between clips—even with everything I was trying to process—I couldn't stop imagining what it would be like to kiss William again. I'd look at him out of the corner of my eye, hoping he'd catch me and bring his lips to mine again. But he didn't. I was starting to think that he didn't want to.

Maybe it was all in my head.

I hadn't realized I'd fallen asleep until William nudged me gently.

"Hey, Chlo. Wake up."

"What time is it?" I looked around us. Through the windows I saw the sky had darkened.

"Almost eleven."

I bit back the lump in my throat. It was still dry from the tears I'd shed. I was so comfortable leaning against his chest. I didn't want to leave.

"What's up?" he asked, his fingers moving to brush through my hair. I don't even think he meant to do it. He stopped midway, his hand dropping to his side.

"I just . . ." My voice trailed off, and I felt a blush creep to my cheeks. "I don't want to leave."

William hesitated as he observed me with thought. He must have caught what my tone was letting on. "You know, I didn't think you'd feel that way after the footage."

I frowned.

"I was scared that when you saw how much I was involved with them last year, that you'd hate me."

I was supposed to hate him, yes. But the footage was one thing, and the real-life William was another.

"I should," I said. "But I can't."

I leaned forward slowly. Never in my life would I have defined myself as brave, but it took all my courage to open my heart to him in that moment. My lips met his softly before pulling away.

"You really feel that way?" William said, swallowing. "After everything?"

I was too scared to speak, and so I just kissed him again. He kissed back, and for the first time in months I felt whole, like all the disembodied elements inside of me were working in sync again.

"You should go home," William said, his voice husky when we finally broke apart. "I want you to stay, but I don't want to take advantage of you. Not again. I know you're upset, Chlo. And we can't miss school tomorrow."

"Why do you have to be a good guy all of a sudden, William?" I asked with mock disappointment. It would be so much easier if he was the obnoxious Level One I'd imagined.

"Will," he said, a chuckle lacing his tone. "Will you ever listen to me?"

"Never," I said triumphantly, pulling him down by the base of his neck to kiss him again. Before it was because I was trying to distance myself from him, and now it seemed like a fun thing to do out of spite.

He *was* a good guy. If he never got muddled up with Level One and their secrets and lies, maybe I'd have crushed on him long ago.

It just took blackmail to see that.

STAGE SEVEN

EXPOSÉ

THIRTY-ONE

Mrs. Whittaker,

As Chloe's physics teacher, I continue to grow concerned with her ability to complete assessments to the high standard expected of her with her affinity for mathematics and science.

I'm concerned she's found the wrong crowd, and as much as she is an asset to this school, I'm beginning to ponder whether she requires extra support, especially after the tragic passing of her friend just before summer.

Please call me as soon as you can.

Regards,
Ms. Neal

ONCE I WAS home, nestled under my covers, William's parting kiss still fresh on my lips, I managed to watch the rest of the footage, some of it on triple speed, gathering little pieces. I reviewed the list of videos I'd deemed useful, including the clip of Francis and Monica after editing it to conceal her identity. The last thing I wanted was to taint her memory. It was them I wanted to cast in a bad light, not her. I compiled them with the photographs of Lola's playing cards and Jack's stolen footage of Sophie and Mr. Hammond.

On Friday morning, I reveled in the victory of my completed video, transferring it onto a flash drive ready to be uploaded. Though I had a backup on my phone, I decided loading it onto a computer and sending it as an attachment to a bulk email would be more dramatic—and would give no opportunity for the teachers to excuse themselves when it was shoved in their faces. For Monica, I wanted the best show of all. I stood before my full-length mirror, my blouse tucked into my plaid skirt and socks pulled high. This would be over now. I didn't need to be this Chloe anymore, I didn't need to be like them.

I kicked off my heels and pulled on my boots, switching my cashmere cardigan for a denim jacket.

Mom had insisted on driving me to school. I was in trouble. She was suspicious of my supposed cramps the other day after Ms. Neal emailed her and told her about my dropping grades. It wasn't ideal, but I could work with it. I just needed to get to Arlington with enough time to drop my bomb.

In the car I fidgeted with the USB in my pocket, flipping it over and over, replaying in my head the videos that were collated together, ready to be mailed to every student in Arlington.

On the night of junior prom, the night that I'd spent sitting at Monica's vanity watching her get ready, Desmond had been filming the preparty at the Davenport mansion. He'd also captured an argument never meant to be overheard.

"What are you doing in here?" Sophie asked with venom, oblivious to the camera that had been left recording in Lola's sitting room. I'd learned Desmond was sneaky, often trying to grab footage that was definitely not included in his payment. Or maybe it was, and it was designed to be leverage within Level One to bind them together.

"I should be asking you the same question," Francis sneered.

The Rutherford twins were standing opposite each other, arms both crossed over their chests defensively.

"You need to stop," Sophie said, regarding him carefully.

"Stop what?" Francis asked, clearly amused as he began circling her at a leisurely pace. *"Sometimes I think you love Lola more than I do."*

"Maybe I do," she answered. *"Wouldn't be very hard, would it, France?"*

"Now, now, Sophie, you know the only reason you're in her life is because I let *you be there. Don't want things to change, do we?"* he'd asked, his smirk switching to a devilish grin. *"All it takes is one wrong move, Soph, and you'll be toppling down the social ladder before you can utter another word."*

Sophie had scowled at him. If it had been anyone other than Francis on the reciprocating end of that glare, they would have burst into flames. But he only looked amused.

"You're not as powerful as you think," he said. *"And I won't hesitate to destroy you if you get in my way."*

After that, the footage cut out, for what reason I wasn't sure. But the contents would still be enough to send ripples around Arlington. It was taking sibling rivalry to a new level.

And then there was a compilation of videos from different parties scattered throughout the last twelve months.

The truth-or-dares. Kept behind closed doors, rituals performed within Level One. Whispers had trickled around the school of their crazy antics, but nobody really believed them. Nobody had any evidence, after all.

Lola's cards. Lola giving Francis a lap dance in front of the others, Maddy making out with a sophomore girl, Sophie locking a freshman in a basement. The girls making a Level Two girl strip with the threat of shaving her head. A clip of Francis, Lola, and Sophie in Francis's new Ferrari—Desmond filming from the back seat—as they drifted around the corners of suburban streets, a bottle of vodka passed between them every time they veered. Sophie strutting across a tabletop with cash stuffed in her underwear and navy-and-gold pom-poms in her hands.

Francis cheating with an unknown girl—her face and red hair censored to make her anonymous.

Sophie and Mr. Hammond making out in the empty classroom.

And the final scene. Level One gathered in Monica's bedroom, about to give the orders that would end her life.

This is your royalty.

The video finished with an eerie black screen.

"Try and concentrate today, Chloe," my mom said, her voice gravelly with concern, shaking me from my thoughts. "I'm serious. No boys or chitchat about parties. Just try and catch up on work, okay?"

"I will, Mom," I lied. Schoolwork seemed so distant, especially when I was about to take down the popular clique. Who knows what they would do once this was unleashed.

"I'll check in with your teachers after school," she warned, reaching forward to pat my knee. "We're going to fix this, okay? I'm here for you."

I looked at her, her unconditional love for me apparent on her face, and for a moment, I believed I could do this. That things would be right. "Okay."

I took my first step through the halls of Arlington, wearing my favorite shade of cherry lipstick, the one that reminded me of Monica. Now my smirk took a little more effort, my perfected armor worn with grief. But I was ready.

I opened my locker as if it were a normal school day, shoving the flash drive safely behind the door. I needed to wait until lunch, when everyone would be together and I could be sure to gain the attention of every single student.

When I turned around, I caught sight of Maddy Danton, who was looking past me with horror. My confidence faltered at her expression.

I turned to see who she was looking at.

For the first time, Lola Davenport didn't have anyone by her side. She was wearing not a trace of makeup, clear by the circles under her eyes and the lack of her signature lipstick. She looked stressed. Worried.

And then I saw why.

There was something glinting in her hand, a golden sparkle. The hairpin. *Monica's* hairpin.

My hands instinctively flew to my hair. How could I have been so stupid? It must have fallen out at Desmond's house—my adrenaline preventing me from even noticing—and somehow it had ended up in the hands of Lola Davenport.

Which meant *she knew*.

"Chloe," she said, her tone sharp, as if she wanted to waste no time. Her dark eyes stared me down. "I can't let you do this."

THIRTY-TWO

Monica,

We lit candles for you and set up a shrine in the halls. The teachers put up posters telling us not to drink. The school hosted assemblies. All Band-Aids to the bigger problem: their students have too much power. An imbalance of it, where those with less can be exploited and manipulated until there is nothing left.

Even now, I guess I can't blame the school. After all, it's us—the students—who crave the power. Us who laughed and made sexist slurs as Maddy Danton was publicly embarrassed, cheered when Lola and Sophie sent Stephanie Griffith walking out of the cafeteria in her underwear. And that's only in the past few weeks.

Something needs to change, Mon. And I'm going to make it.

This is for you. All of it.

Love, Chloe

"PLEASE—JUST—TALK with me," Lola continued when I didn't move. Her gaze was starting to grow frantic and her fingers wrung the corner of her untucked blouse. Was she nervous?

My lips opened and closed, no words escaping. I was so close to revenge I could taste it—so close to ruining her just like she ruined Monica. I didn't need to listen to Lola Davenport anymore.

But something about her lack of makeup and unkempt state stirred me. Maybe it was all part of the act. I could stand my ground. After all, there was nothing she could do now. The tables had turned.

I finally nodded, my gut twisting in warning.

"Let's go somewhere private," she said, grabbing my wrist and leading me away.

My heartbeat accelerated. Her appearance could be to her advantage. Maybe her vulnerability was just a ruse to lure me into some twisted fate she'd prepared. I knew she'd probably go to huge lengths to keep her secrets, after all. I started calculating how quickly I could call for help.

I wished I released the video while I had the chance. Now I was exposing myself to new attacks.

"I don't want people to overhear," Lola muttered, her black hair falling from her braid as she scoured the people around us. Was she making sure nobody was eavesdropping?

Probably making sure there will be no witnesses to your untimely death.

"Overhear what?" I managed to ask, my voice much too feeble. I cleared my throat, trying to maintain my demeanor.

She sighed, running a hand through the thin strands that fell to her face. "We just need to talk, okay?"

I raised an eyebrow. With a small pang of guilt, I realized I'd be skipping my first class. I could already hear my mom's impending lecture.

My mind was so busy turning over my options that I didn't realize Lola had led us up a flight of stairs and was making a beeline over the mezzanine for the fire escape.

"Uh, should you be opening that?" I asked as she tugged at the heavy door. I was sure it would set off some kind of alarm and our whole secret meet-up would be announced to the world.

"Relax," she said, her tone tinged with bitterness as she glanced my way. "We used to come out here to skip all the time in sophomore year."

Sure enough, there was a little platform of metal railing that we could stand on, sitting us above the main courtyard.

Lola lowered to the ground, dangling her feet off the edge of the platform and looping her arm around the banister. I looked over my shoulder one more time. The door was shut. Warily, I joined her.

"That girl is still finding ways to haunt me," Lola said once I'd properly joined her, pushing her palms into her eyes before taking a steady breath and clearing her throat. Her eyes fixed on mine. "Monica, I mean."

My mouth went dry. I couldn't speak. Hearing Lola say

her name was like falling face-first into ice, a freezing slap across my cheek. She must have pieced it together. Desmond must have given the Level One girls my hairpin, knowing they'd be the victims of the stolen footage, and Sophie must have told her it was mine. Connecting my motive to Monica would have been easy considering the most valuable clips on that hard drive were proof of what they did. What they were hiding. And if I had stolen the footage, then my plan would be clear. I wanted to take them down.

"She was your best friend. I don't know how it didn't click sooner," she said, the statement hanging in the air, crawling over my skin. The words coming from Lola's lips sounded wrong. Monica was sacred to me. I wanted to snatch her from Lola's memory and keep her to myself.

"She was," I said, my tone defensive. I shifted my weight in discomfort.

Her lips popped open and closed, like she was about to say something but then something stopped her. She looked down again, collecting herself. When she did speak, her tone was cloaked with emotion.

"You want revenge for what we did that night." She took my silence for confirmation. She looked sadly over the quad and nodded. "It all makes sense now."

"You're not going to stop me," I said. "The whole world needs to know the truth. It wasn't just a freak drowning. It was your games. You guys killed her."

Saying the words aloud cut deep. I tried to hold back tears

of my own. I wouldn't let her see them. She didn't deserve my vulnerability.

"Yes. She died." She paused to catch her breath. "She died. And I'm going to live with that guilt until *I* die. And maybe we deserve what you have planned for us. I'm sure it's awful. We're awful."

Her gaze met mine again, and for a second Lola Davenport looked a little human. She didn't look like the unattainable goddess she usually did with perfect makeup and a perfect grin. She looked tired. Her expression was fractured with remnants of grief.

"I didn't know her before she started coming to our parties," she mused. "I didn't know if she was a good person. I didn't care. And yes, she might've been innocent back then, but she was never naive."

I let my eyelids flutter shut for a second, Monica's face filling my vision. Again, jealousy burned my insides. All the moments that Lola had shared with my best friend should have been *mine*.

"She was playing a game, Chloe," she said. "None of us were clued in until it was too late, and she had control. She was strategic. She knew what she wanted, and that was to be in charge of whatever power we have here at Arlington."

Monica never hid how much she envied Lola's position as the head of Level One. I just never thought she was serious about taking it over. It was all supposed to be a joke. I had more faith in her than that.

Until I saw her make a deal with Desmond to film the clip of her and Francis. Maybe she was planning to bring down Lola Davenport long before I ever was.

"It was me who told her to do it," she said, her voice quieting so that I almost struggled to hear her words as they trickled away with the wind. "I told her to dive into the pool. Monica was always pushing the limits. I didn't even consider that it could be so dangerous, I really didn't think . . ."

I waited for Lola as her eyelashes fluttered and she blinked away tears. I couldn't tell if it was an act, and my grip tightened on the cool metal I was leaning on.

"We thought it would be funny. We knew she'd regret it in the morning, that she'd be embarrassed, or she'd maybe give up—she'd learn her lesson and stop messing with me. I had no idea she was that drunk. We—we thought she knew what she was doing."

My mind was screaming at me to shut her out. She didn't deserve the chance to explain herself. But I was captivated, clinging to each word, wanting to understand.

I knew Monica was never pushed into the pool. They didn't force her, not physically. That was the point. It was never forced. It was a mirage of glitz and glamour and exclusivity cast around them. They harnessed their allure for their own entertainment. For their own evil.

"I just wanted to tell you I'm sorry. We never thought she'd die," she said, her voice sharp. When I looked at her,

I realized there were streaks of tears tracing down her cheeks. "I just wanted to say it before you do whatever you're going to do. I don't care what it is. We deserve the worst. I just want to try and protect Will."

I stiffened. "What about him?"

"You know if you do this, they won't come for you." I stared at her blankly. "Oh, come on, Chloe, you must know us well by now. Francis—he'd do anything to protect his reputation. Sophie too. When Zach finds out it was you that spread those pictures—which I'm sure he'll put together straightaway—they'll find your weakness. And it's him."

I narrowed my eyes.

"You're clean as a whistle. You didn't grow up like us. So instead of your reputation, they'd come for what you care about most."

Confusion swept through me. "William?"

"You care about him," she said. "We all see that. Not to mention he's all you have."

My breath was coming fast now. I could imagine it so easily. Francis already had a rocky relationship with him, and all of them would back him up if they knew I was planning on taking them down. I was sure William had enough dirt with all of his time on Level One as well as his family corruption. They could easily ensure his future was destroyed. Their own kind of revenge.

And God, it hurt to think about it. She was right. I did

care about him, I was past denying that now. If they ruined his life because of what I did, then I wasn't sure I could live with the guilt. My chest constricted painfully.

"It was fake," I said, my bid to his protection. It was the only thing I could think of to detach myself from him. "Our whole relationship wasn't real. It was all a lie."

Lola's lips lifted a little. "That's not true. You know it and I know it. I know Will maybe better than anyone."

She should be trying to destroy me right now.

She went on. "He really does like you, and the way you look at him . . . the others have seen enough to know that hurting him would hurt you. And they'll use it."

I let out a long breath. If what she was saying was true, then I had left a gaping, vulnerable hole in my plan.

"Why are you telling me this?" I asked, suspicious.

"Because I care about him too much to let that happen," Lola said, her eyes darting away again. She took a breath. I'd assumed that Lola only saw William as an object, someone she could use to rebel against Francis. Another *thing* she could play with and control.

It would be so easy for her to say that, to hide the fact that she was protecting herself by using my feelings against me.

"Why?" I asked harshly. If she was going to play on my emotions, then I wanted to know hers.

"Why do I care about him?" She sighed heavily. "It's a long story. One I don't even understand. I love Francis. Or, I loved him. I'm not so sure. He's everything a boyfriend should be, charming, handsome, from a good family . . ."

She shook her head, as if dispelling whatever thoughts had entered her mind.

"But he's . . . a locked cage. A sealed deal, with the way our families are tied together and all. His way of caring about me is caring about what people think of us. He terrifies me as much as he makes me fall for him. Sometimes I sneak out just to clear my head and work it out. Escape it. It's like everything he does he apologizes for so well that it doesn't matter anymore. I'm an idiot."

I thought back to the sound of the vase shattering through the wall.

"Will was my attempt to find *his* weakness. To get back at Francis for all the things he does to me. Cheating. Yelling. Controlling. That's when I saw how good Will is, and I realized how bad *I* am. How messed up this world has made me. After Monica . . . I couldn't pretend anymore. I let Will go, because I only deserve Francis. Pretty on the outside, evil within."

"That's . . . messed up," I said after a long silence, letting my thoughts simmer. An abusive relationship as self-punishment. I almost wanted to reach out and touch her—to comfort *her*. But then I remembered who I was talking to, the whole spectrum that was Lola Davenport. "So why do you manipulate people if you know how bad it is? Why do you bully even your own friends?"

“Isn’t that what you’ve been doing this whole time? Manipulating people?” she asked, giving me a sad smile. “Maddy adores you, you know. She really thought you were friends. The rest of the school is obsessed with you for dating Will, and obviously he’s crazy about you too. You have a lot of people wound around your little finger.”

To a degree, she was right. My whole plan involved manipulating people. And it wasn’t hard to understand the gratification of popularity, the rush of having people interested in you. I sighed, tucking my hair behind my ear, my gaze fixated on the flagpole opposite us.

“As for the control, it’s the only way I can keep things from falling apart. We were all thrown under a pact after Monica. Those tapes were always supposed to be fun, another secret that brought us closer together—the dirt from parties and the stunts from our games. It let us do crazy things without worrying about who would slip up when it came to having each other’s backs. I know. It shouldn’t be like that. But in our world, we can’t take any risks. When Monica . . . well, things got scary. Our parents pressured us to keep quiet. I can’t give you an exact answer, but every day it feels like the only way to survive is to keep together. Francis and Sophie, William and Zach. Maddy.

“You have every reason to do it. To just release it. But I don’t want you to. I don’t want Will to be the one who suffers for her. I can promise you that despite whatever masks you see on our faces, the guilt of what happened to Monica Pennington eats at us every day.”

I clenched my jaw, the piece within me so desperate for revenge coiling around my stomach, begging me to attack. But I felt numb. Now I had the weight of William on my back too. I had to choose between him and my revenge.

My thoughts were bouncing around so fast in my mind that I almost felt like screaming. The weight on my shoulders felt enormous. I was literally playing with people's livelihoods—their reputations.

"I need to think," I said quietly. "I need to be alone."

Lola hesitated. "Are—are you sure?"

I saw her fidget from the corner of my eye. There it was. She *was* scared.

"Above all, you should know this won't fix it," she said. "It's a cycle. This whole thing. Before us there was some other clique and after us there will be a new one. Fresh meat. People *always* want someone to adore, to idolize, to feast on when it comes to gossip. It's just another part of human nature."

The Level Twos were part of the problem, after all. The rest of the school who fed the drama, fed the insanity.

"Do the right thing, Chloe," she said. She unlinked her legs from under the pole and straightened, looking down at me where I still sat with my legs dangling.

"Don't you even care what I have to use?" I asked. Did she even know about Monica and Francis? Of Sophie and Francis's arguments over her? Of Sophie and Mr. Hammond's affair?

"I was forced to pretend Monica never happened, but you've brought it all to the surface. Maybe one of the others will slip. It's inevitable. I'm tired of maintaining this after everything that happened. I want to be human."

I blinked, feeling both frustrated and relieved. Frustrated because the fact that Lola didn't care meant that she didn't have anything left to hide, and relieved because, somehow, something in my universe had become balanced. Of course, I was more stressed than ever now that I had William to consider in all of this. But still, I felt like . . . like some of the blame that plagued me had dissipated.

"Oh, and I think this belongs to you." Lola paused to drop the hairpin into my lap.

I stayed there looking over the courtyard for a little longer after she left, turning the pin over and over in my hands. What would I do if they came after William, furious at me taking them down, for ruining their reputations? Would they even go that far, or was Lola planting the idea in my head, using my own feelings against me?

And the most confusing thing of all: for the first time in my life, Lola Davenport seemed human. Even with all her messed-up relationships, she still seemed traumatized by what happened to Monica. In some ways, she was like me. Was she more than just the worst thing she had done?

And God, would this do anything, or was it just a cycle like she said? Would revenge fix this, or just cover the surface of the chunk of me missing ever since Monica died?

I wanted to confide in William, to hear his voice of reason.

Maybe prepare counterattacks to protect him. I even wanted to talk to my mom.

I was dreading what would be waiting for me at lunch, especially with my mind undecided. Maybe I should have done it while I had the chance, back when my choice seemed simple.

My thoughts were far away when my phone vibrated, bringing me back to reality. I was confused when I saw it was from the school-wide group chat Lola and Sophie had created to share the picture of Maddy.

Only now it was being used to expose *them*. The video file uploaded to the chat was instantly familiar.

It didn't matter how I felt anymore. My revenge had been unleashed.

STAGE EIGHT

COLLATERAL

THIRTY-THREE

Chloe,

I believed your promise. I trusted you, in fact.

But then I saw your car outside Will's house last night. Yes, you're not the only one who can do surveillance. And then I saw you and Lola heading to the fire escape and I knew it was game over. If she had the chance to get to you, then they won.

And they won't win. I want them to pay. I want Sophie Rutherford to pay.

Don't forget, I'm doing this for us. For Monica.

Jack

"NO WAY."

I stared at Jack's profile picture for a long time, the severity of what he had done sinking in. The group chat had gone silent, nobody knowing quite how to react to the bombshell.

The lunch bell broke my trance, blaring across the empty quad. It threw me into action. Damage control.

I had to find William.

My boots clattered down the mezzanine steps and into the cafeteria. It was empty. There were still a few minutes before students would start heading to lunch. My mind was haywire, trying to work out what class he was coming from.

I darted into the hallway, running head-on into a wave of students who were all talking excitedly. I heard whispers about Mr. Hammond, gasps about Lola and Sophie's games, Francis's secret hookup, but, most important of all, Monica's name. People were talking about her again—of that night again. It wasn't just a drunken stunt. People knew the truth.

I saw Sophie's Barbie-doll figure walking determinedly down the hall, her glare aimed directly ahead. A phone was pressed to her ear. I was ready for her to attack me, darting out of her way as she passed, but she barely registered my presence.

"Yes, Daddy, a *lawyer*. We need a lawyer. And you need to send a car to get us right away—"

Behind her, students gawked, some even laughing.

Nobody ever dared laugh at a Level One.

Pandemonium continued, my eyes searching every face hoping it was William's. From behind, arms flung around me and I stiffened.

"Chloe!" It was Maddy. "I'm so sorry. *So* sorry, Lola told me you were friends with her. We didn't mean it, what we did. I can't believe that video exists."

I couldn't form words as Maddy hugged me tight. I wormed my way out of her grip. "You're not mad?"

"*You're* not mad?" She looked at me, confused.

Of course. They didn't know it was me behind the video. Maddy probably didn't even know about the hairpin. Jack had posted it under his Facebook account.

Did this mean William was safe?

"Maddy, I need to go," I said. I didn't know how to feel. Her eyes shone with guilt. She mustn't have realized I already knew she played a part. I'd known this whole time.

I couldn't believe the takedown was really happening, the control I'd tried so hard to gain yanked from my fingertips. I found my locker, and sure enough the lock was busted, people darting past it obliviously. Did that mean Jack wanted this more than I did? Did the constant torment of never being enough drive him to stealing it from me anyway? I shook my head in disbelief, backing away and continuing on down the hallway.

A commotion blocked my way. Standing in a clearing of students was Lola Davenport and Francis Rutherford.

"Francis," Lola said sternly. Her bag was slung over her shoulder, her jaw tight. She must have been just about to leave. *"Move."*

"You're not going anywhere," Francis said. He looked furious, his black eye from his fight with William still far from fading. "You can't just walk away from this."

"Do I have to say it again?" She threw her hand in the air, turning in a circle so she could address the crowd surrounding her. "I'm leaving. We're *over*. I can't believe you. Of all people, it was her. Monica."

Francis grabbed her elbow as she attempted to pass him.

"Let her go, Francis."

Finally. William Bishop walked forward, nudging Francis aside.

"Out of my way, Bishop," he said. "Unless you never wanna play another game again."

William didn't flinch. He stepped forward, making Francis drop Lola's arm. "I'd leave her alone. Unless you want another black eye."

Francis scowled, but I saw him falter as he took a step backward. "This isn't over."

William looked unconcerned as Francis disappeared into the crowd. I wondered if Francis had seen the footage—the damning evidence of his sister and the potential of his own downfall driving him to the edge.

I watched as William moved closer to Lola. "Are you okay?"

She nodded, before looking over her shoulder and finding me in the crowd. "I'm fine. In fact, I'm great. You should see your girlfriend."

His eyes finally met mine, and a tension within me was immediately relieved.

Then it finally started sinking in. Jack had taken responsibility for the video, leaving me intact. Even if Lola knew I was behind it, nobody had any proof that it was really me. I could erase everything I had in an instant, destroy the hard drives.

William would be safe.

"Finally," he said, moving toward me and taking me into a hug. I could feel the eyes of students around us watching. "I've been trying to find you."

I pressed my cheek to his chest, inhaling deeply, as if his aura could relieve the panic that had been running through me as my evidence was leaked to the world.

"Attention, Arlington Preparatory."

It was Jack's voice blaring through the intercom, silencing the halls. He must have hacked the PA system. I looked up at the speakers in wonder.

"Your royalty aren't who you think they are, and now the whole world knows. And yes. You're hearing correctly. It's me, the one you mocked. The one you stomped on so you could shine."

"How did he do it?" William whispered.

"Is that *Jack*?" I turned to see Claire, her eyes wide and lips parted in disbelief, nearby.

"I hope you're listening. I hope you know nobody could really love you for what you are, and after this you're worth no more than your pretty faces. Nobody will be pushed aside again. I know everything. And I won't hold back."

My mouth was agape. I couldn't believe it. He really was taking responsibility for it. All the acting, the lies, the planning—now it was all his.

"Play nice, Arlington."

After that, the student body was never really the same. Just as fall started changing to winter, the Rutherford twins were unenrolled from Arlington Preparatory. After Sophie's affair was exposed and Mr. Hammond fired, their parents were desperate to cover up the scandal. Not to mention, with Francis and Lola's relationship over, they didn't want to face any more embarrassment.

Zach Plympton had lost his bad-boy reputation. I suspected Max had dumped him, considering he'd openly criticized Zach as an ego-driven jock. Now Zach only seemed interested in sports, rarely showing up to any school parties. Not that the parties were anything like they used to be, with everyone unsure of exactly who might be waiting to expose them for what dirty work happened within their circles.

Maddy Danton had worn her mistakes, filming a teary YouTube video confessing everything, from the contents of the exposé to what it was really like to be a Level One girl. Across the world, her story resonated with thousands of girls—both being bullied *and* being a part of the bullying just to save face. It had stirred a viral movement to improve the social system. Apparently, Arlington wasn't alone with its queen bees and peer pressure.

Lola Davenport changed the most since the video was unleashed, falling off the radar and rebuilding her entire character. She didn't resent me for creating the footage, or even seem to care. It was a secret kept between us. She was suddenly free—abandoning the pressure associated with her rich family and deactivating all her social-media accounts. She didn't try to hide her vulnerability. Having the Rutherford twins exposed and their grasp on her destroyed was the best thing that happened to her. Even I found it hard to hate her anymore.

That being said, Level One didn't go unpunished.

The six of them, along with Monica's family, the school principal, and police, met for several meetings, where—according to William—each of them confessed their part in Monica's death. I wish I could have been there to listen to their accounts—not just of their responsibility in her death, but of what Monica had become too. I was starting to learn my best friend wasn't the angel I wanted to see her as. She really was trying to become one of them, and if she had it her way, maybe she'd be the one enforcing the hierarchy today.

But I didn't need to think about that. I could remember her as the best friend I grew up with and be at peace. I knew who she was beneath all of that, after all.

I didn't regret my revenge plan, but now that the dust had settled I couldn't help feeling guilty. Every piece of my plan relied upon a rage so uncontrolled and so personal that I lost part of me in the process. Since losing Monica, I had to rebuild, and I couldn't do that while I was lost with grief. Instead I was busy formulating someone else, the Chloe that let me blend in with my worst enemies. The Chloe that past me would have hated.

I'd done things that made me feel so guilty to blend in with Level One, things that I think left some permanent marks, like the guilt I felt for Stephanie, or talking badly about Jack just to get the Level One's approval. I'd gone to the principal's office just that afternoon, confessing my part in Stephanie's phone scandal. I'd earned detention, but it felt superficial in comparison to the torment Level One had inflicted on her.

Other permanent marks included things that weren't all so bad.

Just as Thanksgiving weekend rolled around and the leaves of the oaks surrounding the lookout had turned a deep orange, William and I sat on the grass at the edge of the tree line. The sun was sinking over Wandemore Valley, and our conversation had lasted for what felt like hours.

"No, that's the point. You're *supposed* to knock people out of the way," he said, going as far as demonstrating using a pretend lacrosse stick to nudge invisible players in front of him.

"Isn't that . . . violent?" I asked, laughing as he put a hand to his forehead in amusement. I leaned back, feeling the breeze blow my hair from my face. I hadn't worn lipstick in a long time or made myself uncomfortable with silk blouses and heels. I was me again—a different me, but still me.

"No, Chloe, it's so you can win."

Will's eyes crinkled with his smile, and his laughter subsided so he could lean forward and kiss me.

Of all the things that had come from the semester, having a *real* boyfriend was the last thing I'd expected. I'd wondered a lot about what Monica would have thought of everything, but I think she'd find this the most bizarre.

Chloe Whittaker falling for William Bishop.

ACKNOWLEDGMENTS

This book would not exist without some super encouraging and incredibly patient people in my life. To express my deep gratitude I'll start from the beginning, when this book was emerging from my mind and being born to the Wattpad community. Thank you to the many readers who have followed my writing journey so far and whose support ignited the fire manifesting this story. Thank you to Wattpad Studios, especially I-Yana Tucker for being a beacon of positivity, encouragement, and sense-making. And a huge thank you to the HarperCollins team, especially Catherine Wallace and Camille Kellogg, for putting so much time and expertise into me and my story, helping to truly work magic.

And of course, I must thank the people who were there unconditionally throughout the ups and down of creating *Clique Bait*, keeping me sane:

My family, especially my mother and grandmother, for gifting me their love for stories.

My close friends Emily, Adrian, and Amy for listening to me vent about plot points.

My honors group, Ashleigh, Liam, and Mia, for helping me hold together not only the book but my university education.

And lastly my unofficial photographer, Tom, who somehow has a never-ending pool of support for everything I do.